The
Hidden
Daughter

BOOKS BY SORAYA LANE

THE LOST DAUGHTERS

The Italian Daughter

The Cuban Daughter

The Royal Daughter

The Sapphire Daughter

The Paris Daughter

The Spanish Daughter

Soraya LANE

The Hidden Daughter

bookouture

Published by Bookouture in 2025

An imprint of Storyfire Ltd.
Carmelite House
50 Victoria Embankment
London EC4Y 0DZ

www.bookouture.com

The authorised representative in the EEA is Hachette Ireland
8 Castlecourt Centre
Dublin 15 D15 XTP3
Ireland
(email: info@hbgi.ie)

ISBN: 978-1-80550-071-1
eBook ISBN: 978-1-80550-070-4

PROLOGUE

THE MAJESTETISK HOTEL, SOGNEFJORD, NORWAY, 1950

Oskar stopped rowing the boat, his oars gliding through the crisp blue water one final time before he set them down. Amalie wriggled backwards and let her head fall to his chest. She listened to the steady beat of his heart, sighing when his arms came around her. She'd waited all day for this.

Amalie was at her happiest when it was just the two of them, surrounded by the beauty of the fjord, wrapped safely in Oskar's embrace. Usually she loved the silence; but today, the secret she'd been keeping pressed on her chest, an invisible weight that she couldn't hide any longer. All day she'd wrestled with whether to tell him or not, but now they were together again, she knew there was no keeping it from him. It was his news as much as hers. *I don't want to have secrets between us. I need him to know.*

'You're very quiet today,' Oskar said.

She tucked herself even closer to him, tears stinging her eyes when his lips pressed against her head. Oskar ran his fingers gently through her long hair as she fought for the right words, her secret tightening inside her.

'Amalie? What's wrong? Is it my family? Because I've made it abundantly clear that—'

Amalie took a deep breath before her words came out in a sudden gasp. 'Oskar, I'm pregnant.'

The words clung to the silence around them, echoing in Amalie's mind as she wished she could take them back, that she'd kept the secret to herself. But Oskar only held her tighter as she began to cry, tears slipping one after the other down her cheeks until she was powerless to stop them.

'Don't cry. Please don't cry,' he said, turning her so that she faced him, his eyes meeting hers as he gently smoothed his thumb across her cheeks, wiping away her tears. 'Everything will be all right, I promise.'

'But how can it be?' she whispered, searching his face. 'Your parents will never accept me, they've made that clear, and mine—'

'I love you, Amalie, and that's all that matters,' he whispered back, his lips meeting hers in a kiss so soft, so impossibly gentle, that it took her breath away.

When she finally pulled back, Oskar touched his forehead to hers.

'I promise I'll take care of you. We'll marry quickly, in autumn, before anyone can find out. There's nothing to be afraid of.'

Tears filled her eyes again, because as much as she believed in his earnestly spoken words, as much as she knew that he'd do anything to protect her, she was no fool. No matter how much they wanted to be together, no matter the dreams they'd shared, their future wasn't theirs alone. Not to mention they'd had a plan—they were supposed to wait until next summer, until he'd finished university, and he was free to choose his own path.

'Oskar, your parents will never let us marry. We're from different worlds, it could never—'

Her voice caught as his hands cupped her face, his eyes meeting hers.

'I would give up everything for you. I love you, Amalie, and no one will stop me from making you my wife, not even my parents.'

Amalie gazed back into the eyes of the man she loved, and hoped with all her heart that their love would be enough.

1

LONDON, PRESENT DAY

Charlotte loved this time of day. The kitchen was silent, every surface wiped down and gleaming, and as she so often did before beginning her work, she placed her hands on the stainless steel counter and gave herself a moment to take it all in. It was always first thing in the morning that she was able to catch her breath, close her eyes for a beat and prepare for the day ahead. But today was different. Today was her last day as executive chef at one of the trendiest hotels in Chelsea, and she wanted to savour every last minute; most especially the quiet before the space filled with other chefs and noise and the aroma of food.

She opened her eyes and took out her knives, placing them in front of her. There was no need for her to be there so early, but she wanted to leave one final, special new dish behind—a legacy of sorts—and her intention was to have it waiting for the other chefs and servers to enjoy when they arrived. Charlotte had always preferred to show her feelings through food, and she only hoped they could tell how much she loved them all from her final gesture.

Just as she was reaching for her apron, Charlotte's phone

buzzed in her back pocket. She smiled, knowing instinctively who it would be. There was only ever one person who would call her so early, before most people had even had their morning coffee.

'You should still be in bed,' Charlotte said, positioning the phone between her ear and shoulder.

'Ha! Says the girl who's already been for a run, showered and arrived at work,' said the slightly husky voice on the other end. 'Tell me I'm not wrong.'

Charlotte laughed. 'You're not wrong,' she said.

'Let me guess. You have your knives spread out on the counter in front of you, and you're staring at them thinking about what ingredients you need. And you probably only got five hours' sleep.'

Charlotte crossed the kitchen to get out the eggs, potatoes and beef that she needed, pulling open the door to the cool room. 'Are there hidden cameras in here that I don't know about?'

They both laughed this time, but Charlotte's laughter died in her throat when her grandma began to cough. It sounded worse than last time. Or maybe it was just her conscience telling her how long it had been since she saw her.

'Are you okay?'

'I'm fine,' her grandmother replied, clearing her throat. 'This is just what sixty years of smoking sounds like. It's nothing to worry about.'

'You could quit,' Charlotte said, knowing it was useless but saying it anyway. 'The lungs can recover remarkably quickly.'

'Quit? You'd deny an old lady her one last pleasure in life?'

Charlotte sighed and retrieved some of the other ingredients she needed, her ear still pressed to the phone. She didn't point out that her grandmother also drank vodka every night before bed and ate sugary desserts as if it were her last day on earth. Smoking was hardly her only pleasure, or her only vice.

'Grandma, is everything okay?' Charlotte asked. 'You're not calling to tell me—'

'Oh, I'm fine, it's nothing to worry about, but I do have a favour to ask.'

'A favour?' Her grandmother never usually asked her for anything. All she ever wanted was to hear her granddaughter's voice on the other end of the phone, and Charlotte had always been more than happy to oblige.

'I have a woman coming to drop something to your restaurant today. I was contacted by a lawyer who has something for me, and she wanted to hand-deliver it. Apparently, they've been trying to track me down for some time, and I asked them to just give whatever it is to you. I'm sure it's nothing important.'

Charlotte set down the butter and herbs she'd been carrying. She took her phone from under her ear and held it instead. 'What kind of something? Has something been left to you from an estate?'

'Your guess is as good as mine, but I thought it would be easier for her to just drop it to you, whatever it is. The woman's name is Mia, and I told her to come nice and early, before you get busy with lunch service. It all sounded a bit mysterious, but I'm sure it's nothing very interesting.'

'She didn't give you any details about what it is?'

'She said something about it being left for me when I was a child, and they had your great-grandmother's name, too. I'm almost certain it's nothing, but I was curious enough to want to see what it is, without incurring any postage costs to Norway, of course.' Her grandma coughed again. 'But if it's an inconvenience—'

'Not at all—anything for you,' Charlotte said, pausing for a minute before saying, 'I miss you.'

'Then come to visit! Who knows how long I have left?'

Charlotte nodded, even though her grandma couldn't see her. If only it were that easy.

'Your father would love to see you, too. I know you don't think so, but he misses you, Lotte. We all do.'

She cleared her throat, blinking away the tears that always seemed to come when they spoke about her father. 'Soon,' she said. 'I promise I'll come home soon, I've just been so busy, and—'

'I know, darling. I know,' her grandmother said. 'I'm going to let you get back to your morning, but promise you'll call me when you're finished for the day. I want to know what this parcel is all about.'

'I will. I love you.'

'I love you, too.'

Charlotte kept the phone to her ear for a moment, before finally slipping it back into her pocket. She hated how complicated things had become with her family, but she did what she always did to forget about her father—Charlotte picked up her knife and began to slice. Cooking had always been her escape; her way of clearing her mind and finding her peace with the world. And this morning was no different. She chopped herbs and whisked eggs with an efficiency that tended to intimidate the younger chefs she worked with, her senses coming to life as she pressed garlic and reached for a roasting dish. The kitchen was silent—there were no playlists or other chefs, no clang of plates or hum of patrons outside—and it was just the way Charlotte liked it. She craved the intimacy of being alone in the kitchen as much as she thrived on the busyness of service later in the day.

She prepared her sauce, placing her ingredients in the pot and stirring it as it slowly began to bubble on the stove. But the single tear that slipped down her cheek as she reached for the chopped herbs told her that perhaps she wasn't quite as good at making her feelings disappear as she'd thought.

One day she'd go home to Norway. One day she'd make

peace with her father. But that day wasn't today, and she wasn't even sure it was next month or next year, either.

Today, she just wanted to focus on creating brunch for the people who'd become like family to her, the other chefs who'd stood shoulder to shoulder with her this past year and followed her instructions with the dedication and care she'd demanded. Today, she wanted to enjoy her last day of standing in this kitchen.

She could think about her father and going home another time.

2

When one of the waiting staff called out that there was a woman asking to see her, Charlotte had forgotten all about her scheduled visitor. She nodded and finished plating up, taking a moment to appreciate the food spread out in front of her before wiping her hands clean.

The other chefs were due into the kitchen within minutes, and although she'd hoped to eat with them one last time, to gather round in the kitchen for one final meal before the first service of the day began, she knew her grandmother was counting on her.

She turned back at the last minute and took two of the plates, her stomach rumbling after so long cooking and not eating. She'd been up since before five, and so far she was running on coffee and little else.

With the two plates in hand, Charlotte walked backwards into the kitchen door so that it bumped open. The restaurant was still relatively quiet and completely empty of guests, and she gestured with her head to the staff who'd already arrived for their shift.

'Everyone, food's ready,' she called out. 'Plates are in the kitchen.'

'What is it today, chef?' one of the guys called out.

'I'm calling it the Cheeky Hash,' she said. 'Braised beef cheek, pressed potato and my special hollandaise. It's the perfect hangover cure.'

It was a breakfast she was certain would be a hit with the younger staff members in particular—they were always certain to have a headache on a Saturday morning and come to work bleary-eyed from the night before.

But before she could call out anything else, she saw a woman rise to stand at a far corner table. She was wearing jeans and a silk shirt, her long hair tied back in a simple ponytail and a coat slung over the chair behind her.

'You must be Mia,' Charlotte said. 'Sorry to keep you waiting. Any chance you're hungry?'

The woman had looked a little nervous, but at the mention of food she smiled. 'I actually haven't eaten this morning, but I don't want to impose.'

'You're not. It's my treat to everyone here for my final day, and I just happen to have cooked more than I needed to.' Charlotte set the plate in front of her. 'My grandmother tells me you're from a law firm. That something was left for her?' As she said the words, she wondered if it was strange for a lawyer to be working on a Saturday.

Mia shook her head as she sat down. 'I'm actually not, and it's rather a long story, but the lawyer who originally contacted your grandmother has been working for me, sorry, *with* me, to find the intended recipients for some items left behind many decades ago. I decided when I found them that I wanted to be the one to personally connect them with whomever they'd been left for.'

Charlotte frowned, suddenly wondering how legitimate this all was. She hoped her grandmother hadn't fallen for a scam.

She cleared her throat as she considered the woman sat before her. 'When you say items...'

'My aunt's name was Hope Berenson, and she ran a home for unmarried mothers and their babies. The women who gave birth there sometimes left behind a small box of special mementos for their child before they were placed for adoption, and only to be given to them when they turned twenty-one. I have one of those boxes with me, for your grandmother.'

Charlotte had been about to take her first mouthful of food, but she left her fork hovering as she lifted her gaze again to meet Mia's. 'I'm sorry, you're trying to tell me that my grandmother was adopted?' Charlotte shook her head. 'That's impossible, because my great-grandmother is still alive. If you'd seen them both, you'd know they were biologically related just from looking at them. It's just not possible.'

Mia's eyebrows pulled together, as if she was trying to figure something out. 'Well, here's the thing. We have no records for your grandmother of an adoption taking place, whereas with all the other women who had boxes left for them, there were meticulous records about their adoptions. It's why they were all claimed some time ago, but your grandmother's box was harder to connect with its namesake. Your great-grandmother was very hard to track down, as it happens, because it was her maiden name in the records, and she left no forwarding address. We had to hire a private investigator to find her.'

They sat in silence for a moment, and Charlotte took the chance to have a mouthful of food, trying to process what she was being told and placate her hunger at the same time.

'If my grandmother wasn't adopted, then why would you have a box for her?'

Mia looked as puzzled as Charlotte felt, but didn't say anything until after she'd reached into her bag and taken out a small wooden box. She placed it on the table between them, and Charlotte found she couldn't take her eyes off it.

'Since the other boxes were found, I discovered my aunt's diary, which helped me to better understand her work,' Mia said. 'I believe that your great-grandmother may have given birth at Hope's House, but then chose to leave with her baby. Or at least, that's what I've been able to piece together so far. For some reason, she doesn't appear to have proceeded with the adoption.'

Charlotte set down her fork and reached for the box. She hesitated before touching it, her hand hovering.

'May I?' Charlotte asked.

'Of course. To the best of my knowledge, it's never been opened, so I don't know if there's even anything inside, but I wanted your grandmother or someone close to her to be the one who opened it, just in case.'

Charlotte glanced at the handwritten tag with her grandmother's maiden name printed on it, running her fingers over the string that held the name tag and the box together. It was old and fraying at the edges, and it made her curious as to how long the box had been hidden, waiting for someone to claim it.

'Where exactly did you find it?' Charlotte asked as she lifted the box.

Mia had taken a mouthful of food now, and she held her hand up to cover her mouth as she spoke. 'This is really good,' she said. 'I mean, *really* good.'

Charlotte smiled. 'Thank you.'

'But to answer your question, I found a collection of these boxes beneath the floorboards in my aunt's office. The old house she lived and worked in was about to be pulled down, and I had one last chance to go in and look through her things, in case anything had been missed. I thought I was just going in to retrieve a rug and a couple of old lamps! I certainly had no idea there would be anything hidden, or quite what a journey it would take me on, trying to find each intended recipient.'

Charlotte turned the box over in her hands, still finding it hard to take her eyes from it. 'And there's nothing you want in return for this?'

The other woman's eyes widened. 'No, absolutely not. I don't want anything from you other than to return this box to its rightful owner and clear my conscience in the process. I couldn't stand to keep it, knowing how meaningful the items inside it might be.'

She was inclined to believe her. There was something about Mia that Charlotte was drawn to, a warmth perhaps, and as strange as it all was, she couldn't help but be curious.

'You mentioned that there was a collection of boxes. Did you return them all to the women they were left for?' Charlotte asked, setting the box down in front of her.

Mia's smile lit her entire face at the mention of the other boxes. 'Yes, the other six boxes were surprisingly easy to return. My aunt's lawyer invited the descendants of the six women to his offices, and we were able to reunite each box with the named recipient's family.' Mia's eyes met hers. 'I don't know if it was just by chance or if it was fate, but it's no exaggeration to say that those boxes changed the lives of the women who received them.'

Charlotte wasn't the type of person to believe in fate—she believed in hard work, sacrifice and determination—but she was still curious about the boxes. 'When you say their little boxes changed their lives...'

'I think you'll want to see what's inside, if the other boxes are anything to go by,' Mia said. 'You might be surprised what family secrets are waiting to be discovered.'

'Well, thank you for coming here today,' Charlotte said. 'I know my grandmother appreciated the personal delivery, as do I.'

'Please, take my phone number, just in case you want to talk about whatever you find inside,' Mia said. 'I've come to learn more about my aunt and the work she did over the past few years, since we first discovered these boxes, so please feel free to reach out.'

Charlotte took the card Mia held out with her number written on it and slipped it into her pocket.

'Thank you for brunch, it was delicious.'

Charlotte said goodbye and watched Mia go, the box still on the table where she'd left it. She glanced at the clock as she gathered up the two plates and turned back towards the kitchen, realising how much time had passed. Calling her grandma and finding out what was in that box would have to wait—she had lunch service ahead of her, and she wouldn't give up her last hours at Velluto for anything.

3

When Charlotte arrived home, she kicked off her shoes and placed her bag on the sofa, immediately rifling through it until she found the little box Mia had given her. She took it out and turned it over and around, unable to tear her eyes from it, before taking out her phone and calling her grandmother. It only rang twice before she answered.

'Curiosity is killing this old cat,' her grandmother said with a throaty laugh. 'Tell me what she gave you. Was it anything interesting? The deeds to a mansion, perhaps?'

Charlotte laughed, too, because she'd never been so curious as she was right now. She'd found it almost impossible not to think about the box through her shift, and even harder not to just go over and open it to see what was inside.

'I still don't know what it is, because I felt like it was yours to open,' she said. 'Grandma, I don't know how much you were told over the phone, but it appears that a little wooden box was left for you many years ago, decades ago, in fact. Mia told me that the other boxes she found were left by...'

Charlotte hesitated, but her grandmother was quick to urge her on. 'Left by who?'

She waited another beat, before finally saying, 'By their biological mothers. It seems that the house where the boxes were found was a home for unmarried mothers to have their babies. They were placed for adoption there, too, from what I can understand.'

'*Adoption?*' Her grandmother went quiet for a moment.

Charlotte grimaced, before repeating: 'Yes, that's what she said. For adoption. Although she was very quick to say that there were no adoption papers they could find in this case.'

'This house, it was in London?' her grandmother asked.

'Yes. She called it Hope's House.'

'Well, that's strange, because my mother always told me that she never went to London until she was much older, when they had to travel there for business.' She hesitated for a long while. 'I'm not sure what to make of it all.'

Charlotte didn't like that she was unsettling her grandmother, but she pressed on. They both had questions now, and she only hoped the tiny box provided some answers.

'Would you like me to open it? With you on the phone?'

Her grandmother didn't hesitate, and Charlotte could hear the eagerness in her tone and wished she'd been able to take it to her in person. 'Yes. Open it and tell me what's inside.'

Charlotte balanced her phone between her ear and shoulder, gently tugging at the old string. It sent fibres into the air as she used her nails to work on the tight knot. It was like being a child on Christmas Day.

'Grandma, whatever's in here, if there's anything at all, it doesn't mean that—'

'I'm not scared of what's inside, or of being adopted, if that's what this is all about. Whatever I find out about my past doesn't change anything about the life I've lived. But I just can't make sense of how this box has been hidden for so long, or why it's come to light now.'

Charlotte lifted the lid off the box and stared at the contents inside. She had no idea what she'd been expecting—perhaps a letter or a carefully folded birth certificate, but instead there was a very modest diamond ring twinkling back at her. She sat down and put the box beside her, taking out the ring with as much care as she would have lifted a tiny creature.

'Charlotte?'

Her grandmother's voice reminded her that she was waiting to find out what she was looking at.

'Grandma, there's a ring inside, perhaps an engagement ring by the looks of it,' Charlotte said, turning it to the light before trying to slip it on her finger. It was tiny, far too small for her ring finger, but she was able to slide it onto her little finger. She studied it, feeling as if she'd suddenly been given more questions than answers.

'A ring?' her grandmother asked, her voice much quieter than usual. 'Does it have any engravings on it, or any particular markings? Is there anything that links it to me or our family?'

Charlotte took it off her finger and turned it over and over again, peering at the ring. 'Nothing that I can see. But it has a very modest solitaire diamond set within the gold, and the band is very small.'

She put the ring back on her little finger and picked up the box again, her eyes widening as she saw something familiar.

'Is there anything else in there?'

'There's a piece of fabric, an emblem, of the coat of arms of Norway,' she said. Charlotte traced her thumb over the golden lion as it stared back at her from the red background. The emblem also bore a golden crown and an axe with a silver blade, and just seeing it gave her a pain in her heart as she longed for the country of her birth. 'And I think there's a photo at the bottom, too.'

Charlotte set aside the fabric and lifted out the carefully folded photo, frowning when she opened it and saw how damaged it was from the fold down the centre. But the two people in the image were almost perfectly preserved, and she gasped when she saw the woman.

'Lotte? What is it?'

She swallowed, not blinking as she stared at the faded photograph in her hand.

'Lotte?' her grandmother asked again. 'Tell me what you've found.'

Charlotte cleared her throat. 'Grandma, there's a photo of a very young woman and a man of a similar age. I could be wrong, but it looks like they're standing outside the hotel at the Sognefjord, the one you took us to when we were children.'

'Well, that's more than a coincidence,' her grandmother started.

'Grandma, the woman in the photograph, she looks...' Charlotte held it even closer to her face, hardly able to believe what she was looking at. 'She looks just like you, but I don't recognise the man.'

Charlotte turned the photo over, finding carefully printed words on the back as a shiver ran down her spine. If there had been any doubt as to her family's connection to this little box, the name staring back at her immediately put an end to them.

'The photo, it has your mother's name written on it. It says Amalie, 1950.'

Her grandmother was so quiet on the other end that Charlotte had to check she was still there. Everyone had always said that her grandmother was the spitting image of Charlotte's great-grandmother when she was younger, and although her own hair was lighter, more auburn like her mother's, Charlotte herself had inherited those same dark brown eyes.

'Grandma?'

'It certainly appears that the box has found its intended family,' she said. 'And you're certain it's the hotel at the fjord?'

Charlotte nodded, still staring at the photo. 'I'm certain. I know we only went there once, but I've never forgotten it.'

'Well, I think that's enough mystery for one night,' her grandmother said. 'You'll keep these things safe until we can figure out what they all mean?'

'Of course,' Charlotte said. 'I'm too intrigued not to take good care of them.'

They said goodbye, and when Charlotte ended the call, she picked up the box and carried it to her kitchen table. Then she poured herself a glass of wine and sat back to stare at the items from the box again, feeling overwhelmingly protective of young Amalie in the photo. She had a gnawing feeling in her stomach that Amalie might not be here for much longer, that they might not have long to find out what the clues meant. Because one thing was for sure: someone in her family had been lying about something in their past for this box to resurface so mysteriously all these years later.

Charlotte sipped the last of her wine and then tucked each of the clues back into their little box, placing them in the exact order she'd taken them out. Then she rose to go up to bed, flicking out the kitchen light, but having second thoughts, she picked the box up and took it with her, deciding to place it on her bedside table. For some reason, she wanted the box close to her, and she didn't know whether it was for safekeeping or because it had reminded her of how much she missed home, how much she wanted to see her grandmother and Amalie, too. Regardless, she liked glancing over and seeing it there as she changed into her pyjamas; it was oddly comforting having something related to her family nearby.

Why are you in that photo, Amalie? What secrets have you been hiding all these years?

And as she slipped beneath the covers, Charlotte had a feeling that no matter how tired she was from such a long day, those questions were going to run through her mind all night. As was the temptation to book a ticket to Norway in the morning just so she could hold her grandmother in her arms and inhale the sweet, flowery scent of her perfume.

The first thing Charlotte did when she woke up the next day was sit bolt upright, reaching for her phone to check the time, before realising that she hadn't slept in because she didn't have to get to work. She lay back down, checking her messages and the news on her phone, before stretching and heading into the kitchen to make a coffee. She took a hesitant sip and burnt her bottom lip as she sank into a chair, waiting for her emails to load on her phone. And then she almost sloshed the hot coffee all over herself when she saw the first unopened email.

She stared at it for a minute before opening it, forgetting all about her coffee as her eyes raced across the words.

Dear Charlotte,

You might remember meeting my wife and me when we dined at Velluto earlier this year. You mentioned your contract there ending soon, and I'd like to personally invite you to visit our exciting new hotel in Oslo. It just so happens that we're in need of an executive chef, with opening less than a month away now, and I have a feeling you might be exactly the right person for the job. I very much hope you can visit us this week or next, your schedule permitting, of course.

Regards,

Daniel Hatton, Executive Manager, Nordic Hotel Group

Charlotte reread the email to make sure she hadn't imag-ined it, thinking back to when she'd first met Daniel and he'd talked about his new restaurant. He'd mentioned to her then that he was opening a new hotel and was visiting the best hotels and restaurants in London for inspiration—it seems that she'd been interviewed for a position at the time without even knowing.

Her heart began to race and she reached for her coffee, forcing down another sip of the black, sugary drink before picking up her phone again. Offers like this didn't come along every day, she knew that, but she loved London—the city had been her home since she was fresh out of school and determined to make it as a chef. She'd trained at Le Cordon Bleu and proved to herself that she had what it took to succeed, that she wasn't crazy for wanting to make being a chef her career, and she'd never intended to leave. England felt like home to her in the same way Norway had when she'd been a child—it was where she was supposed to be.

But this? This was the opportunity of a lifetime, to be part of something from the very beginning, working for the most successful Scandinavian hotel chain in the world. She was no fool; she knew that they would have had an executive chef secured some time ago, and clearly that person had let them down or been fired. But she wasn't going to overthink the opportunity—someone else's loss, for whatever reason, could be her gain.

And it also meant that she could finally see her grandmother again, that she would have a reason to go home.

Charlotte stood and walked to her window, looking out over Chelsea and imagining what it would be like looking out from an apartment window in Oslo instead, trying to figure out if she was ready for it or not.

Call him. She knew in her heart whom she needed to talk to before she made a decision, and after pressing her forehead to the cool window for a long moment, she turned and went to retrieve her phone. She would never make a decision so big without consulting him, regardless of which way she was leaning.

It only took two rings for her brother to answer, although his voice sounded scratchy, as if he'd just woken up. She glanced at her watch and saw that it was only seven o'clock.

'Sorry it's so early,' she apologised.

'It's fine, I was on call anyway.'

'Are you free for breakfast? Or lunch?' Charlotte asked. 'I was thinking we could meet this morning.'

'If you can meet me at that café closest to the hospital in an hour, I'll be there.'

She breathed a sigh of relief. 'Thanks, Erik.'

'Is everything all right?'

Charlotte smiled just hearing his worried, big-brother tone. 'It will be. I'll see you soon.'

4

Charlotte hurried through the busy café when she saw Erik sitting at a table in the far corner. He stood and opened his arms, giving her a big, warm hug. They'd been through a lot together when they were younger, and no matter what they might have disagreed about as teenagers or adults, it would never break their close bond. She would have found being in London so much harder if he hadn't chosen to do his residency closer to her.

'To what do I owe the honour of breakfast?' he asked.

'Can't a girl just want to see her brother?'

'At short notice? I doubt it.' He laughed, sitting back a little when their coffees arrived. 'I took the liberty of ordering as soon as I got here. I'm still on call, so I might need to leave in a hurry.'

Charlotte took a deep breath, realising that they didn't have time for small talk until they'd covered the important things. She was used to it, though—he lived and breathed his job in the same way she did, which meant she had absolute respect for the hours he had to work and how committed he was.

'So, I've been offered a permanent executive chef position,' she said. 'Well, when I say offered, they want me to visit the hotel, I imagine work up a sample menu for their approval first, but essentially, I'm being considered for the role at a new restaurant in an exciting new hotel. It's going to be huge.'

Erik raised an eyebrow as he took a sip of coffee. 'Your contract has ended at Velluto?'

'It has. My last day was yesterday and I miss it already.'

'I feel like I'm missing something here,' he said. 'You're looking for a new opportunity, you've been offered one that sounds amazing, so what—'

'It's in Oslo.'

Erik set his cup down and folded his hands on the table. 'Ahh. And you want to know whether I think you should go back, or whether you should stay in London?'

She immediately felt tearful and hated how emotional she always became when she thought about going home. 'It's an amazing opportunity, I know it is, but—'

She watched as her brother ran a hand through his hair, and she recognised the exasperated look on his face. He'd never understood how her feud with their father had caused such a rift in their family, but then how could he? He was the golden child who'd done exactly as their father had wanted, and she was the one who'd defied him and turned her back on everything he wanted for her. Her father had never been one to mince his words, and he'd made it very clear how much she'd disappointed him.

'Lotte, I know I've said it before, but you can't avoid him forever. Would it be so bad to just put the past behind you? It would be easier than holding on to all that pain inside you.'

Charlotte reached for her coffee and took a long sip, before staring into it, taking her time before answering.

'I want him to be the one to say sorry,' she said. 'I know that makes me stubborn, but he's my father and it's time he realised that what I needed was his unconditional support back then, not his judgement. It's what I still need.'

Erik reached for her hand and clasped it in both of his. 'Sweetheart, you're one of the most acclaimed young chefs in London. You've succeeded in a way that I'm sure even you never imagined, so whatever Dad might have said to you back then, it means nothing now. You've done it, you proved him wrong. If he's not proud of you now, then he's the fool.'

'Says the son who followed the path that was set for him and is about to become a surgeon,' she said, frowning. 'All you've ever received is his adoration for following in his footsteps.'

He laughed. 'Hey, I can't help it if I'm an overachiever.'

She swatted at him, but he ducked and grabbed her hand again. That was what she loved most about him—his ability to make her smile when she felt low, to turn everything into a reason to laugh.

'Seriously, Lotte, this is a huge opportunity for you. And honestly? Imagine Grandma's face if you did go back.' He grinned. 'She'd be over the moon to see her favourite grandchild.'

They both laughed then. Charlotte had always strived to be their grandmother's favourite, especially in the wake of their mother disappearing and her father deciding to rule their household with an iron fist. It had been a difficult childhood in many ways, but their grandmother had wrapped her love around them with such ferocity that they'd both felt cherished, always, despite it all.

She sighed. 'You truly think I should go?'

'I truly think you should go. I mean, what's holding you back, other than Dad? You took London by storm, and now it's time for you to return home and make your name there. Or not. Going there for an interview doesn't mean you have to take it, it just means that you're open to the opportunity and to finding out more.' His smile was kind, as it always was. Erik had been the best big brother a girl could have hoped for, always encouraging her, always believing in her dreams. 'Besides, it doesn't matter what he thinks. *I'm* proud of you, Grandma's proud of you, and that's what matters. Don't let him control the decisions you make, not now.'

She nodded, quickly brushing away tears with her fingertips and wishing away her emotions.

Erik took out his phone from his pocket, turning the screen around to her after a few seconds. 'Let me book you a ticket. When do you want to go?'

Charlotte felt her chest constrict just seeing the landing page for Norwegian Air on his phone.

'I'm booking this flight whether you want me to or not, so either tell me what day or—'

'Tomorrow,' she said. 'Make it tomorrow.'

He grinned and tapped away, before setting his phone down. 'Done. The confirmation will be sent to your email.'

She groaned and reached for her coffee. 'Tell me I'm doing the right thing.'

'You're doing the right thing,' he repeated.

Charlotte shook her head, not convinced that she was but knowing that she'd always regret it if she didn't. It was an amazing opportunity, and perhaps it *was* time to forgive her father instead of holding on to the past.

The server arrived with their breakfast, to which Charlotte mouthed 'thank you' as her eggs Benedict with mushrooms was placed in front of her, and it was then that she remembered the box in her bag.

'Oh, there's something else I need to tell you,' she said, as her brother picked up his cutlery and began to eat with a speed that still managed to surprise her.

'Talk while I eat,' he said. 'If my pager goes off before I've finished this...'

Charlotte reached into her bag and took out the little box,

setting it between them and quickly filling her brother in on what had transpired the day before.

When Charlotte walked through arrivals at Oslo Airport the next day, she felt a familiar tightness in her chest that she usually experienced whenever she talked about her dad. But she quickly forgot her anxiety when a woman with her thick silver hair cut short, with chunky gold jewellery at her wrists and neck, strode towards her. Her grandmother was seventy-five, but she walked with the straight back of a woman half her age.

'Lotte!'

'Grandma.' Charlotte dropped her carry-on bag and opened her arms, enveloping her grandmother in a tight hug. They stood for what felt like forever, arms around each other as the other people who'd disembarked from her flight were forced to move around them. 'It's so good to see you.'

'I'd have told you to visit months ago if I'd thought it would work.'

Charlotte bent and retrieved her bag, slinging the other arm around her grandmother's shoulders. 'It's been too long, Grandma, it was time I came home.'

'Did your brother talk you into this, or was it the mystery of the box?'

She laughed and hugged her grandmother tighter to her side. 'Of course not, this was all me, and maybe just a little about the box.'

'You expect me to believe that you came all this way, after not coming home for eight years, just to see your old grandma?'

'That, and the fact that I was invited to visit the new hotel in the city. Have you heard about the new Nordic Hotel Group place down by the water? I believe it's almost complete.'

'Of course I've heard of it! It's all anyone in the city has been talking about,' she said. 'I've also heard about the restaurant. It seems no expense was spared on the head chef.'

'Well, apparently it wasn't enough for him to behave,' Charlotte said as they arrived at the luggage carousel. 'Because I hear the chef had an argument with the CEO of the hotel group, and he fired him just last week. But it's the CEO I'm meeting with, and he seems very reasonable, certainly someone I could work with.'

'You know,' her grandmother said, affectionately patting her hand, 'whatever brought you home, I'm just grateful to have you here. You get more and more beautiful every time I see you.'

Charlotte let go of her grandmother only to retrieve her suitcase, and then they walked side by side through the terminal to the parking area. It wasn't until they finally reached the car and were seated that her grandma turned to her, a sparkle in her eye as she held out her hand, palm up.

'Show me this box,' she said. 'When I told you the curiosity was killing me, I wasn't exaggerating.'

Charlotte reached into her handbag and took the box out. She'd carried it with her for fear of losing it—suddenly the little wooden box had seemed more important to her than even her chef's knives, which she'd packed carefully into her check-in luggage.

She watched her grandmother's face as she passed it to her, saw the way her eyes widened once it was in her hands. Charlotte had loosely tied the string again so that the experience was the same as when she'd first untied it, and her grandmother opened it so carefully, taking back the lid and finding the diamond ring just as she had only two days earlier.

'It's so small.'

'I know. I could only fit it on my little finger.'

Her grandmother's gasp when she unfolded the photo made Charlotte reach out to her, her hand on her shoulder as she saw the tears glisten in her eyes. When she looked up, Charlotte wasn't sure if she saw pain or hope in her expression, or maybe both.

'I thought this must have all been a misunderstanding, that you were getting carried away thinking you recognised the woman in the photo, but this?' She pointed to the young woman in the image. 'Even without her name being printed on the back of it, I'd have known it was her.'

'So, what do you think this all means?' Charlotte asked, as her grandmother held up the emblem and considered it, before putting it back in the box and studying the photograph again.

'I think that there's something in the past that's been kept hidden from me, and that at one point in time, my mother wanted me to find out what that secret was.'

Charlotte found herself nodding. 'But what would have made her change her mind? And if she's your biological mother, then what was she doing leaving clues for you at a house for unmarried mothers? None of it makes sense.'

Her grandmother passed the box back to her after carefully placing the ring back inside, before starting the car.

'There's only one person who can answer our questions, and that's my mother. Do you have anywhere to be today?'

Charlotte shook her head. 'No, I don't have my appointment at the hotel until tomorrow.'

'Good, because we're going to see Amalie now, before it's too late.'

Charlotte followed her grandmother into the reception area of the private hospice facility, before being guided to her great-grandmother, Amalie's, room. Although the interior had been created to look as light and airy as possible, it still sent a shiver down her spine being there—every room contained someone near the end of their life, and it was yet another reminder of how long she'd been away from home, how many years had passed and how much older her grandmother and great-grand-mother were.

'She's been sleeping most of the day, but I know she's always more lucid when she hears your voice,' the nurse said as she gestured for them to enter. 'I'll be in to check on her again soon, but I'm certain she'll be pleased to see you.'

Charlotte wasn't sure what she'd expected, but the room felt nothing at all like a hospital and very much like a personal bedroom within a home. The curtains were open to let the light in, there was a vase full of fresh flowers on the bedside table, and her grandmother's touch was all over the bed linen. It was white with intricate blue flowers printed on it, a cashmere blanket folded on the armchair that faced the bed, and the open shelves held books and more blankets, as well as a lamp that cast additional light through the room.

'It's beautiful in here,' Charlotte said. 'You've made it feel like her home.'

'She's such a proud woman. She hated the fuss of someone else doing all this for her, but I wanted to make it feel as comfortable as possible. It was the least I could do. Once you're this old, beautiful surroundings are all you have left.'

'I remember how much she loved reading,' Charlotte said, stepping forwards and reaching for the book beside the bed. She grinned. 'But *Bridgerton*?'

Now it was her grandmother laughing. 'I'm the one reading to her every evening, it's usually when she's her most alert, and she seems to enjoy it. I thought we could both do with a little romance.'

Her grandmother sat on the bed then, and Charlotte took the armchair, watching as her grandmother gently took Amalie's hand, stroking it as she spoke. It was hard seeing a woman who'd once been so vibrant, now so frail. Amalie's skin was paper-thin, her hair wispy and white around her face, her cheeks hollow. It was also scary for Charlotte because it reminded her that her own grandmother might reside in a place like this one day in the not-so-distant future.

'Mother, Charlotte's here with me. Can you hear me?'

Charlotte leaned forwards as Amalie's eyes fluttered open, as her grandmother offered her water and then carefully stroked her cheek as one might a very young child. She found herself having to glance away, tears pricking her eyes at the tender display between mother and daughter. When her own mother had left when she was ten, she'd asked her father over and over again how she could have just walked out on them like that. And now, it made those questions come back, made her ask all over again how a mother could ever just leave her child's life without warning, especially after everything they'd all been through.

'Charlotte, pass me the box, would you?'

She rose and passed it to her, watching as her grandmother placed it in Amalie's hand and closed her fingers around it.

'A little wooden box has been found,' her grandmother whispered. 'It has treasures inside, things that you left behind. And it had my name on the box. Did you leave these for me to find? Do you know anything about the little box?'

Amalie's eyes fluttered open, but unlike last time, this time they stayed open. They were clear and bright, and her grip visibly tightened on the box.

'Where... where did you find this?' she croaked.

Charlotte stood and reached for the glass of water, holding it for her to take a sip through the straw. Amalie cleared her throat once she'd had a drink, and her eyes widened as she lifted the box in her shaking hand.

'It was found at a place called Hope's House,' Charlotte said. 'In London. It had been hidden there beneath the floorboards.'

'I should never have left it there,' Amalie murmured, before turning her head on the pillow to look at Charlotte, her eyes widening and a panicked look crossing her face. 'Do you have my ring? Was the ring still hidden inside?'

Charlotte exchanged a quick glance with her grandmother as a shiver ran through her. 'Yes, the ring is still inside.' She hesitated before asking, 'Would you like me to put it on your finger?'

Amalie nodded, and Charlotte took the box and opened it. It was then she noticed how small Amalie's fingers were, and she slid it onto her ring finger as if it had been made for her. Which perhaps it had been. She glanced at her grandmother, who'd clearly thought the same thing.

'The photo?' Amalie asked.

Charlotte sat on the opposite edge of the bed to her grandmother, taking the photo and placing it in Amalie's hand. She helped her to close her fingers around it, watching as she lifted it, the recognition that passed over her face.

'Is this you in the photo?' Charlotte's grandmother asked. 'Amalie, is this you when you were a girl?'

Amalie nodded, her eyes filling with tears as she immediately traced her trembling finger over the image of the man. Charlotte could feel her pain, could sense that whoever was in this photo had once meant a great deal to her.

'He was so handsome,' Amalie whispered, clearing her throat and starting to speak a little louder. 'I'd never seen a man so handsome as my Oskar.'

'Oskar?' Charlotte and her grandmother both repeated at the same time. Part of her had wondered if it might have been her grandfather as a young man and they simply hadn't recognised him.

'I knew we'd never get married, but we were in love, and he was such a dreamer,' she said, wiping at her eyes with the backs of her fingers. 'I started to believe him when he said we'd be together forever.'

'Tell us who he was, Amalie,' Charlotte said. 'Who is this man in the photograph, and why did you hide this box all those years ago? What does it all mean?'

Amalie dropped the photo to her chest and stared at her ring, smiling, almost as if the memories were coming back to her just from looking at it. In that moment she looked younger somehow, as if thinking about the past had lifted the veil of age, taking her back to whatever day or month or year she was thinking of.

'We were so young, but looking back, none of it even seems real now. He was my first love, and I would have done anything for him back then.'

'He broke your heart?' Charlotte asked.

Amalie shook her head, wiping at her eyes again, and Charlotte wondered if it was the memory making her sad, or whether perhaps she couldn't quite grasp the memories she was trying to reach for.

'Tell us, Amalie. Please tell us your story, or what you can remember of it.'

You need to tell us now, Amalie, before it's too late.

'We agreed to keep it a secret, to never speak of what happened, to never tell anyone the truth. That box, I should have had it sent to me. I should never have left it there for so long.'

'Who agreed?' Charlotte's grandmother asked. 'What were you never to speak of, and who told you that you had to keep it a secret?'

'What happened with Oskar that summer,' Amalie murmured. 'I was supposed to forget it ever happened, and I tried, I tried so hard. But some things...'

Charlotte held her breath as she waited for her to continue, as Amalie's eyes filled with fresh tears and she turned her head to look out of the open window.

'It wasn't that we weren't happy, because we were, but I think we wanted to forget about him. In the end, it was like he'd never even existed.'

'What was supposed to be forgotten? Are you talking about this man in the photograph? About Oskar?'

Amalie nodded.

'Some things are just never meant to be forgotten.'

6

THE MAJESTETISK HOTEL, SOGNEFJORD,
NORWAY, 1950

Amalie knew that for as long as she lived, she'd never forget the moment she first saw Oskar. He was different to the other young men who worked at the hotel over the summer, although not in the way that some would have imagined. He was always going to be different, she supposed, in the fact that he wasn't one of them, but it wasn't just that he came from a different, much wealthier world. Oskar had a light burning inside of him, a warmth that felt as if it were pulling her towards him, and every time she glanced at him it was almost impossible to look away.

She'd heard the other maids talking about him when she'd arrived at the hotel, and her first glimpse had been when he'd been walking out of the kitchen, his apron thrown over his shoulder as he laughed and talked to the other young men finishing their shift. Then, she'd pressed herself against the wall and watched him, hoping he wouldn't notice her standing there. He was handsome, yes, but he was also magnetic in a way she'd never noticed in a young man before.

But it seemed that tonight, she hadn't got away with watching and not being seen. Her two friends had disappeared to talk to a group of young men they'd been making eyes at, but Amalie had been content to stay leaning against the pergola, taking little sips of her drink and watching the party from afar. Until she saw that the man she'd been admiring had noticed her and was suddenly heading her way, and she immediately wished she had the company of friends around her to make the encounter less awkward. Part of her wanted to turn and flee, too nervous to speak to him, but the other part of her knew to keep her feet planted to the spot. She'd been hoping to meet him for days, eager to find out if he was as charming as he was handsome, and it seemed her wish was about to come true, whether she was ready for it or not.

'I don't think we've met before,' he said, his eyes burning brightly into hers as he held out a hand. 'I'm Oskar.'

Amalie liked that he didn't give his last name, and she wondered if that was because he expected her to know it already, or if it were a simpler reason, and he in fact didn't care for her to know who he was. His easy, friendly demeanour made her think it was the latter.

'Amalie,' she said, placing her palm against his as butterflies danced in her stomach.

He held her hand just a little too long, squeezing it gently before letting go, but his eyes never left hers. 'Are you having a good night? Anyone would think you're hiding from the fun over here.'

She blushed and glanced away, not sure what to make of the attention. Why would he choose her to come and speak to, when there were so many other young women for him to talk to? Young women who would be more articulate and worldly than her; who were surely more beautiful and had more to offer.

'I am,' Amalie finally said. 'I think it's wonderful that we're having a party for everyone to get to know one another, but I prefer watching from afar sometimes. It's less intimidating than being in the middle of it all.'

He held out his arm, and Amalie hesitated, taken aback by the unexpected gesture.

'I understand, but perhaps it's not so scary if you're with someone. Join me?'

She couldn't. Amalie glanced at his arm then just as quickly shook her head. She opened her mouth to answer, but he just smiled, sparing her the embarrassment of turning him down.

'I can see that I've been too forward,' he said, his smile still warm and not appearing offended in the least. 'Could I at least bring you a drink? Then I promise to leave you alone.'

Amalie grinned, catching her bottom lip beneath her teeth as she tried to stop it. He was certainly charming. 'A drink would be lovely, thank you.'

She had no experience with men, and certainly none as handsome and confident as Oskar, but she could say yes to a drink. All she had to do was stand and wait, after all, and it would give her time to watch him.

'I'll be right back.'

Oskar disappeared with a wink, and she found herself standing there, her cheeks on fire from the attention, watching as he moved through the crowd. It was then that her friends reappeared, their cheeks as flushed as hers, but from dancing.

'Was that who I think it was?' Anna asked.

'*Oskar* was talking to you?' Nora gasped.

'He, I...' She cleared her throat, still lost for words. 'He's gone to get me a drink.'

They both gasped, forgetting all about the young men they'd been dancing with as they craned their necks looking for Oskar. It took all of Amalie's restraint not to do the same, and she was thankful that they both fell silent when he did, finally, return.

'Ladies,' he said, glancing at her friends before passing her a glass of champagne.

'Thank you,' she whispered as their fingers brushed, as she looked up and found his eyes trained on hers.

'You're welcome,' he said, leaning in a little closer before speaking again. 'It was nice meeting you, Amalie.'

He turned, his eyes catching hers one last time, before he disappeared back into the crowd.

'Amalie!' Anna hissed.

She giggled and took a sip of her champagne as her friends peppered her with questions that they didn't give her time to answer. The bubbles tickled her throat as she stared into the crowd. *I'll be braver if I meet him again. Next time, if he offers his arm, I'm going to say yes.*

But not tonight. Tonight, she was going to enjoy her glass of bubbles and keep thinking what it had felt like as he brushed his skin against hers, even if it had just been his hand. And she knew that no matter how tired she was, there was no chance she'd be able to go to sleep, and it had nothing to do with the champagne.

7

The next time Amalie saw Oskar, he was having a cigarette with some of the other kitchen staff as she was returning from her lunch break. He offered her a warm smile and held her gaze until she disappeared into the hotel, but when she'd glanced back out of the window, she could see that he was still looking at her. Her cheeks had flooded with heat, and her stomach had flipped the same way it had at the party, even though she'd tried her very best not to think about him. But every night when she crawled into bed, she'd close her eyes and see his face; remember the way his fingers had touched hers and the way he'd looked at her.

Her friends kept asking her if she'd seen him, teasing that they'd have him for themselves if she wasn't interested, but Amalie had just shrugged each time, pretending that her heart didn't leap every time she passed the kitchen, hoping to catch sight of him. And then one day, almost a week after their first meeting, she was asked to take a plate of food up to the room of an important guest. Amalie ran her hands over her skirt, cursing her uniform and wishing she was wearing anything else, before taking a deep breath and walking into the kitchen.

The kitchen was a lively place, with pans clattering and raised voices, but it was one of the younger men who cleared his throat when he saw her.

'I'm, ahh, here to collect a steak for room...'

'Amalie!'

She forgot entirely what room she was supposed to be collecting for when Oskar appeared, a kitchen towel thrown over his shoulder as he strode towards her.

'Oskar, get back to your station!' an older chef barked.

He rolled his eyes and she laughed, his smile making her heart thud all the way to her toes.

'Are you coming tonight? To the party?'

She resisted the urge to wring her hands, folding them in front of her instead. 'Ahh, maybe.'

'Please come,' he said, glancing over his shoulder as his name was called again. 'I'd love to see you.'

She hesitated.

'Maybe tonight we can have a drink together,' he said. 'You'd make my day if you said yes.'

'All right,' she said, forcing herself to accept, to be brave enough. She'd promised herself, after all. 'I'll come.'

'You will?' His eyes widened as his name was yelled this time, and he started walking backwards, as someone else passed her the tray she'd been waiting for.

'I will,' she said, receiving a final grin from Oskar before he disappeared again.

The chef who passed her the tray gave her a wink, but she ignored him. There was only one man in this kitchen she had eyes for.

I'm meeting him tonight. I'm actually going to see him again. And this time if he offers me his arm, I'm going to take it.

It felt like déjà vu to Amalie, as she stood on the fringes of the party. Only this time, she was the one looking for Oskar. She sipped her lemonade and glanced around, smoothing one hand down her dress as she wondered whether she'd made a big mistake or not in coming. Her friends had left to dance some time ago, and she had a sinking feeling inside that Oskar had decided not to come after all.

She set down her drink and wrapped her arms around herself, scanning the crowd one last time.

'Amalie!' Oskar called at the same moment she turned to walk away.

She looked over her shoulder, relief thundering through her body as she saw him standing there, his cheeks flushed and his hair messy, as if he'd just hurried straight from work.

'I thought you weren't coming,' she said, as he stepped closer.

He bent over, making her laugh as he caught his breath. 'I've run all the way from the kitchen. I'm so sorry, I couldn't get away earlier.'

'It's fine. I—'

Oskar's grin warmed her as he shook his head and stood up straight. 'It's not fine. I wouldn't have kept you waiting if I could have helped it.'

She stood, staring back at him, not sure what to say, but knowing that she very much liked the way he was smiling at her.

'May I introduce you to everyone?' he asked, holding out his arm. 'I have a feeling you're too shy to move away from this spot otherwise.'

She went to slip her hand through his arm, but something stopped her. 'You're not doing this because you feel sorry for me, are you? Because I'm perfectly happy standing here on—'

'No,' he said, placing his hand over hers and guiding it through his arm as his eyes met Amalie's again. 'I'm asking you because you're the most beautiful girl here, and I want you tucked by my side before all of the other men here form a line and ask you to dance.'

She blushed furiously, her cheeks on fire as his lips turned up into a sweet smile. But no matter how embarrassed she was, Amalie never let go of his arm as he indeed whisked her around the lawn, past hanging lanterns and a table full of champagne and soft drinks, to a group of men slightly older than her who she soon learnt all worked in the kitchen in various roles, some of whom she recognised from earlier in the day. Oskar might be different to them, but he had a way of immediately putting everyone, including her, at ease.

Amalie sipped champagne until her head was light and laughed so hard her cheeks hurt, but it was when Oskar took her hand in his and tugged her gently away from the noise of the crowd that her heart began to race. She was loving every moment in his company, but she wasn't sure about being completely alone with him yet.

'I'm not so certain—'

'Trust me, Amalie,' he said softly, his fingers interlaced with hers as he lifted them and placed a warm kiss to her skin. 'We can sit over here by the water, close enough that the party is within earshot. And it's the middle of summer, so it won't get dark, everyone can still see us.'

Amalie had never been alone with a man before, and as much as her heart was telling her to go with him, she was nervous. But Oskar seemed to sense that she was about to pull away from him, and so he let go of her hand, their fingertips brushing as he took a step away. He took off his jacket and settled it around her shoulders with so much care that she wondered if it was silly to be so cautious, before putting a small distance between them again. She'd waited all week to see him, and now that she was with him, it was like she was trying to talk herself out of it.

'How about I sit down over there, and you just come as close as you feel comfortable?' he suggested, pushing his hands into his pockets and strolling a few steps away.

The sky reflected off the water despite the late hour, and as stunning as the fjord was during the day, somehow it was even more magical at night. Without the party in the background, it would have been silent, and it wasn't the first time she thought how different the air was here at the fjord. It was clear and crisp, almost as if it were untouched by other parts of the world, and the light was magical enough to take her breath away.

Amalie followed Oskar but sat a small distance away, snuggling into his jacket. She hated to think how cold he must be, but there was something reassuring about inhaling his cologne and warming herself with his clothes.

'Is it true that your family own this entire hotel?' she asked.

Oskar chuckled. 'All I wanted was to come here as an unknown, without anyone knowing my family name. But everyone seemed to know who I was before I even arrived.'

'Why *are* you here?' Amalie asked. It was something she'd heard a few of the others musing about, why a young man from such a wealthy family would want to spend his summer working long hours in the kitchen. 'Did your family want you to work for the summer? To know what it was like to have a job?'

'I come here each summer because I love it. This place, being in the kitchen, it lights a fire within me,' Oskar said. 'When I'm here, it's as if I'm finally where I'm supposed to be, although I know that makes no sense at all. I couldn't stand lying about all summer doing nothing when I could be here.'

Amalie nodded, even though she didn't really understand. She couldn't imagine working so hard if she didn't need to— she'd gladly have a summer lazing about by herself without having to work until her back ached and her hands felt raw.

'I've wanted to be a chef since I was a boy, and this is the only time I get to be close to that dream,' he said. 'My future was written for me before I was old enough to walk, but for now, until I finish my studies, my summers are mine to do with as I wish.'

'How many summers do you have left?' she asked, shyly.

'Two, including this one.' He sounded sad. 'So I'm going to make the most of every minute.'

She stole a glance at him and bit her bottom lip when he caught her looking. But Oskar didn't say anything, he just lay back on the grass and stared up at the sky, reaching out a hand. Amalie did the same, positioning herself so that she was staring at the sky above, eventually feeling brave enough to extend her arm towards his and wiggle her fingers as far as she could reach them.

Their fingertips touched, only just, but it was enough to make her heart race all over again.

'Amalie!' one of her friends, another maid, called out from behind them. 'Amalie, where are you? It's time to go!'

She sat up, reaching for the jacket to give it back to him, but Oskar shook his head.

'Keep it,' he said, standing and offering her a hand to help her to her feet.

Amalie stared up into his eyes, wishing they'd had longer together, that the night wasn't about to end. But she wouldn't stay out alone with him, not if everyone else was slowly starting to leave. She was drawn to him in a way she'd never experienced before, but she still knew to be cautious.

'When can I see you again?' he asked.

Oskar bent, his face inches from hers before he leaned in and brushed a kiss to her cheek.

'Amalie!'

She turned at the call, realising that Oskar still had her hand when she went to move away.

'Sunday night,' he said. 'If you want to see me again, meet me here after your shift ends.'

Amalie touched her fingers to her cheek as she ran, lifting her skirt as she fled back towards the party. And although she hadn't given him an answer, she knew without a shadow of a doubt that she was going to see him again.

Sunday night couldn't come soon enough.

8

PRESENT DAY

Charlotte glanced at her grandmother as she pulled out into the traffic. It had been a long day, and she felt more confused than ever. At the very least it had stopped her from worrying about her father, but now her mind was spinning with information.

'I can't stop thinking about the way her face lit up,' Charlotte said. 'When she spoke about Oskar, it was as if she were a young girl again, don't you think? I've never seen her like that.'

Her grandmother glanced back at her as she stopped for a traffic light. 'I thought the same. It was as if she reverted to a younger version of herself while she was talking about the past, but I think that's what makes older people happy, thinking about their younger years. Maybe it's one of those memories that's stayed with her, while others have been forgotten. Or perhaps he was her great true love, and she's kept him hidden all this time.'

'But if that's true, then who is this Oskar? And why haven't we heard about him before? How has she kept him secret her entire life until now?'

'Honestly, I don't know what to think. Part of me wonders if she's confused, but then the look in her eyes...' Her grandma sighed. 'Maybe I just don't want to imagine a reality where my father wasn't the love of her life. It's hard to hear, even without him being here.'

'For what's it worth, I don't think she's confused,' Charlotte said. She'd always been honest and up front with her grandmother, and even though it might be difficult to face, she had to say it. 'She was so lucid and emotional, and it seemed to be a memory that hasn't left her even after all these years. What I don't understand is why it had to stay hidden, or who she was referring to when she said it was supposed to stay a secret. Who would have asked that of her? Oskar?'

'But if this Oskar was her great love, then what does that say about my father?' Charlotte's grandmother asked. 'If the date on the photo is correct, then she married my father the year after she met this Oskar, and she became pregnant with me immediately, which means...'

Charlotte heard the sadness in her grandmother's voice. It wasn't an easy thing to find out a secret about a parent; she knew that first hand.

'Right now, it doesn't mean anything. It's just a memory being shared,' Charlotte said, patting her grandmother's hand. 'Other than to say that Amalie might have had two great loves, it doesn't mean she wasn't in love with her husband. We don't know that. Perhaps Oskar was just a summer fling, after all?'

But as she shifted slightly to stare out of the window, Charlotte was wondering herself just what other secrets Amalie was hiding, about the life she'd had before she was married, about secrets that had been kept now for decades. And she also found herself impatient to go back the following day to hear more of Amalie's story. The nurse had told them not to push too hard for answers, to remember how tired Amalie would be after talking for so long; but Charlotte had a feeling her great-grandmother wanted to keep talking, and with her health deteriorating so quickly, they didn't have long to find out everything they could about the mysterious Oskar. Or how Amalie's connection to him had led her to leave behind a mysterious box of secrets.

'Did you see her face when she held that little box?' Charlotte realised they were outside her grandmother's house already.

'I did. It was as if someone had breathed life back into her lungs,' Charlotte replied. 'That's what I thought, too.'

Charlotte's only regret about the afternoon was that they'd had to leave the box behind at the respite hospital, rather than taking it home with them. Amalie's fingers had tightened around it, and even in sleep her grip had been firm, which meant that neither of them had had the heart to prise it from her hand. They'd also left the ring on her finger, not wanting to upset her by trying to take it off.

'I think we should go back tomorrow afternoon,' her grandmother said, as they both reached into the back seat for the groceries they'd bought on the way home. 'I have this horrible feeling that she might lose consciousness before we hear the whole story, and that I might have to spend the rest of my days wrestling with it, trying to figure it all out.'

'Then we will. After my meeting, we'll both go back and see if she can't tell us the rest of her story. I have a sense she'll be ready to tell it the moment we walk in the door.'

'You're feeling okay about your interview tomorrow?' her grandmother asked. 'Is there anything I can do?'

Charlotte grinned. 'Let me cook for you tonight. It's the best way for me to settle my nerves.'

Her grandmother met her around the front of the car, looping her arm through hers and standing on tiptoes to press a kiss to her cheek. 'I'll take every meal and every moment with you, Lotte. It's so good to have you home.'

Charlotte clasped her grandmother's hand, keeping her

close and touching her head to hers. *I'm happy I'm home, too, Grandma.*

It had been too long, and no matter what happened with the job interview or what they discovered from Amalie, Charlotte knew that she could never leave it so long again. It would break her heart to think that something could have happened to her grandmother and she might never have seen her again. Seeing Amalie had made her understand just how quickly a loved one could deteriorate.

This is home. No matter how hard it is, no matter what's happened in the past, this is home and always will be.

By the time of Charlotte's late morning appointment, she'd already run through her old neighbourhood, showered, made breakfast for her grandmother and had time to walk part of the city. As much as she'd have loved to sleep in, rising early and making the most of her morning was as much a part of her as cooking was. It also meant that she'd had plenty of time to prepare.

The hotel was magnificent, and Charlotte couldn't help but appreciate the modern architecture. In London, she'd loved the history of the buildings and admired it all, but this was contemporary design at its finest, built close to the water and somehow looking as if it had always been there. It managed to blend modern with classic, and she could only imagine how stunning it would look lit up at night, and how popular it would become with tourists visiting the city.

She approached the door, noticing the closed sign but pushing it open anyway. Daniel had told her to come straight in and that someone would take her to the restaurant, and once she was inside, she could see that it was a hive of activity, with furniture being moved and people coming and going. There was even an enormous chandelier-style light being hung in the foyer, with someone down below calling out instructions.

'It would be so exciting to be part of something so new and vibrant,' she whispered to herself.

'I'm sorry?'

Charlotte jumped when a man with a British accent spoke, laughing at herself and shaking her head. 'It's me who's sorry, I was talking to myself. I'm told it's the first sign of madness.'

The man standing beside Charlotte was tall, almost half a head taller than her, and he had thick, dark brown hair and eyes just a few shades lighter. He was dressed in jeans and a white T-shirt, with worn boots, and he had a jacket slung over his arm, and it occurred to her that he was very casually dressed for an employee. Although on second thoughts, he might have just been there looking for someone, the same as her. She wasn't sure.

'May I give you directions?' he asked. 'The hotel is still closed to the general public, but you have that look about you as if you're trying to find someone.'

So she'd been right about him working here. 'I'm looking for Daniel,' she said. 'He said one of the hotel staff members would show me where to go, so thank you.'

'Happy to be of service,' he replied, giving her a half-smile that was hard to read, before pointing to the far corner. 'Daniel is straight through there, in the restaurant. Just be careful, there's a lot happening today with all the finishing touches taking place.'

'Thank you,' she replied.

Charlotte began walking again, glancing over her shoulder at the handsome man who'd helped her and wondering who he was. She guessed he could be a manager or even one of the concierges. But she didn't have long to wonder, because the moment she stepped into the restaurant, Daniel was on his feet and coming over to greet her.

'Charlotte! Thank you so much for agreeing to meet with me.'

She returned the air kiss to her cheek and clasped his hand in return. 'I'd forgotten how much I missed it here, so I think it's me who has to thank *you*. There's nothing quite like coming home.'

'Well, whatever the reason, I'm happy to have you here in Oslo. I know you'd be perfect as our executive chef, and although you weren't involved in the design of the kitchen or restaurant, you would have full creative control over the menu if you were to accept our offer. I have complete trust in your ability to deliver the very best in modern cuisine for our guests.'

'There's already an offer?' she asked, her lips twisting into a smile as she sat where Daniel gestured. 'I was under the impression that this was just a conversation, but you appear to have jumped straight in at the deep end.'

'I can have an offer in writing by the end of the day if you're interested,' he said. 'As far as I'm concerned, there's no one better suited to the job. My wife and I loved what you did at Velluto when we visited London, and if you can bring the same creative flair to our restaurant, you'd make me a very happy man. You're exactly the person I need here, and to be honest, your experience and culinary skills speak for themselves.'

'You don't have any questions for me?' She'd been expecting a more rigorous conversation, not to be offered the job on arrival!

'One,' he said with a grin. 'What do you think of the hotel? I want your honest opinion.'

'I love it,' she replied. 'It's one of the most stunning hotels I've ever set foot in.'

'Exactly the answer I was hoping for. I've built a few hotels in my lifetime, but this one is special,' Daniel said, leaning forwards and resting one arm on the table between them. 'Which is why I need the very best people working for me, because a beautiful building means nothing without the right people at the helm, creating an atmosphere like no other.'

She listened, waiting for what he was going to say next.

'I'm proposing that we agree to a three-month term. You design our menu, I get to announce the news of such a successful young chef returning home, and at the end of the term you're free to walk away if you don't like it here. I don't want to force you to stay if you want to move on.'

'Three months?' she repeated.

'You will be well remunerated, and my hope is that once you're here, you won't want to leave.'

Charlotte sat back in her chair and surveyed the dining room around her, catching a glimpse of the kitchen when she turned her head left as she thought over his offer. It was all still very much a blank canvas, and she wanted to see the kitchen space for herself before she indicated whether she might take the position, especially when she hadn't been expecting to be offered the role so quickly. But there was a feeling building inside of her, a pull to her heritage combined with the excitement of a new project, that was all pointing towards this being the right career move for her, especially with the short initial term he'd offered. What did she have to lose by saying yes? She could just amicably move on after thirteen weeks if she wanted to return to London.

When she turned back to Daniel, she saw that the hotel staff member who'd helped her earlier had walked in. She cleared her throat, trying to indicate to him that there was someone there listening to their conversation. But Daniel's reaction to the man's interruption wasn't what she'd expected.

'Harrison! Come and join us,' Daniel said, waving his hand towards the vacant seat beside Charlotte. 'I'd love you to meet Charlotte, who might just be our first executive chef here at Nordic Hotel Oslo. Charlotte, this is Harrison. I'm so pleased you're able to meet each other today.'

Charlotte opened her mouth, but the mystery man spoke before she could, as if sensing her confusion and wanting to put her at ease.

'We actually met by accident a short time ago,' he said, holding out his hand. Charlotte reciprocated, feeling the slight roughness of callouses on his fingers when his palm clasped hers and wondering what he did to get them. 'It was only fleeting though, so we didn't have the chance to introduce ourselves properly.'

'I, ahh, I'm sorry, I don't—' She stumbled over her words.

'Harrison is the lead architect on this project, so anything you don't like about the design? You blame him.' Daniel laughed. 'It's no exaggeration to say he's my right-hand man, and I'm fortunate enough to have him here in Oslo until the opening, overseeing everything.'

'You're the architect?' Charlotte asked, still trying to catch up on the conversation. 'I...' She stopped talking, deciding not to confess that she'd thought him the underdressed concierge or manager. How wrong she'd been.

'Guilty as charged,' Harrison said, and the kind smile he gave her made her wonder if he could tell what she was thinking—that he knew the presumption she'd made about him earlier. 'Please don't let me interrupt, though, I was only coming through to—'

'You're never interrupting, Harrison, it's great to have you here. You know, I have a feeling you two would get along great. I actually have to get to another meeting, but after you've looked at the kitchen, Charlotte, perhaps Harrison could give you a tour of the rest of the hotel? I'd love you to really see everything we're trying to create here, and I hope that after you've taken it all in, we might be able to talk more about you accepting my offer.'

She found herself nodding to Daniel, and discovering that it was quite hard to look away from the handsome architect sitting across from her, his legs casually crossed at the ankle as he smiled back at her.

'I'll just take myself for that look at the kitchen first,' Charlotte said, clearing her throat and rising, 'then I'll be ready for the grand tour.'

Daniel stood, which made Harrison stand as well, and she suddenly felt as if she was living in a different generation where all the men at a table stood whenever a lady did. It almost made her laugh, although out of respect for both of them, she managed to keep a straight face. She appreciated the chivalry.

'Shall I have that offer prepared?' Daniel asked, holding her gaze across the table.

'If you have it prepared, I'll look over it and come back to you,' she said, not wanting to be pressured into saying yes, but also not wanting to miss the opportunity. It was obvious that he was a man well used to hearing *yes* when he asked a question. 'And thank you for inviting me here to see this place, it's nothing short of exquisite.'

'You know I like you, Charlotte, and I want to give you time to think this through, but if you don't accept, I'm going to have to start searching for someone else straightaway,' Daniel said, taking his phone from his pocket when it started to ring. 'Shall we set Friday close of business as our deadline to make this happen?'

'Agreed,' she said. Friday worked—it gave her enough time to properly consider the offer and have her lawyer read it through, but not too much time to overthink things. 'I'll come back to you before then with my answer.'

He took the call then, so she gave him a wave goodbye, which he returned, then took herself into the kitchen without looking over at Harrison. She needed a moment to centre herself, and just like she always did when she was feeling rattled, she placed her hands on the cool stainless steel of the counter, closed her eyes and slowly inhaled. Even when she'd been a child, when thinking about her mum had over-whelmed her, it was going into the kitchen and preparing something that grounded her and helped her move past the panic.

'It's quite something, isn't it?'

Her eyes popped open at the sound of the smooth, deep British voice behind her.

'It is,' Charlotte said, looking around and admiring the huge workspace, with its gleaming brand-new surfaces and appli-ances. Shiny pots and pans were placed in the spaces below, and she found herself walking the length of the kitchen, her fingers trailing the handles and then across the counter. *Now this is a kitchen I could work in. It's everything I've ever wished for—a perfect, custom-built space just waiting for me to make my mark, to show the world what I've accomplished.*

'Daniel's been talking about you all morning, telling me you're the only chef he wants. I was with him the day you replied saying you'd visit, and I don't think I've ever seen him smile like that.'

Charlotte laughed. 'Just because I came to see him, doesn't mean I'm going to say yes.'

Harrison gestured for her to follow him. 'Then come with me and let's see if I can impress you with the rest of the place. He'll never forgive me if I don't talk you into staying.'

He had a long, relaxed gait and she fell into step beside him as they crossed through the restaurant and out into the lobby. The enormous light fitting was still being hung, and he lightly placed a hand to her back to guide her past it and out of the fall zone.

'Do you have a say in everything, including the lighting?' she asked. 'I've never actually thought about all the little details that have to be considered, and who the person making the deci-sions is.'

Harrison's smile was easy, and she wondered if he was the

same as her—more comfortable talking about work than anything else.

'I've liaised closely with Daniel's interior designer on this project, but the short answer is yes. When I start a project, it's about considering every angle, the way the light will filter into the building, the atmosphere my design will create. I'm always involved, from the moment the actual design begins until the day the building is completed.'

'I have a feeling you love what you do,' she said. 'Am I right?'

'I do. Design is my life, I live and breathe it, much the way I imagine you live and breathe food.'

'It takes a workaholic to know one, hey?'

Harrison laughed, but his face became more serious as he gestured around them. 'When guests step into the hotel, I want them to feel two things. First, that it's somewhere special, making them pause to look around and drink in their surroundings, and second, that it feels like a place they could stay for a long time. It has to feel magical, but at the same time almost like it could be their home away from home. I want to balance cutting-edge design with a sense of comfort.'

'That's quite the design brief.'

Harrison grinned. 'Tell me about it. I feel like I've barely slept this past year, especially now that we're almost at the end.'

'Is it more nerve-racking coming up with the initial design, or imagining people walking through the completed project?'

'Definitely the latter. My anxiety starts to rise from the day construction starts,' he said, as they began to walk again. 'You?'

'The menu creation is when I'm at my happiest, but watching someone eat my food is by far the scariest part of my job,' she said. 'I mean, I'm always confident with my flavours, and I'm much more so now than I was earlier in my career, but there's always that moment of hoping others can understand what I've tried to create.'

'Who would have thought that a chef and an architect would have so much in common?'

Harrison caught her eye, and she couldn't help but smile. He certainly wasn't wrong. Over the next thirty minutes, they toured the first few floors of the hotel, and by the time they came back down in the lift to the lobby, she'd gone from impressed to absolutely in awe of his design.

'You deserve every accolade,' she said as they strolled slowly across the polished tiles to the door. 'It's absolutely stunning. I don't think I've ever been in a hotel like it.'

Harrison held open the door for her, his expression telling her that he most definitely wasn't comfortable with the praise. 'Thank you. I'm relieved you like it.'

'You don't know of the closest place to get a coffee, do you?' Charlotte asked, glancing back at him before stepping through. 'It's been a long day already, and I think I'll have to break my rule of not drinking caffeine in the afternoon.'

'It just so happens I do,' he said. 'Come with me, I'll take you there.'

'I don't want to be an imposition, you could just point me—'

'Not a chance. I have back-to-back meetings all afternoon, and trust me when I say I could use the fresh air *and* the caffeine.'

They walked down the street, sunshine making it seem warmer than it was, until they reached a small café that hadn't been there the last time Charlotte was in the city. And after they'd ordered, they stood near the counter and waited, making small talk, until their names were called. Charlotte almost wished they hadn't ordered takeout cups so they could have stretched out their time together longer.

'Well, I'd better head back to the hotel,' Harrison said, turning to her as they stood on the footpath, ready to go their separate ways. 'But it was a lovely surprise meeting you today,

Charlotte. I'd be lying if I didn't say that I hope you take the job. Daniel's right, I have a feeling you'd be perfect for it.'

'Did he plan this? For you to show me around, impress me with the hotel, and then convince me to say yes to him? I'm starting to feel like this was a set-up.'

'I promise you, it wasn't planned, but if it helped to get you across the line...'

He smiled and took a sip of his coffee, and she suddenly had an idea.

'Harrison, may I cook for you?' Charlotte asked. 'If I'm going to seriously consider this offer, I need someone who's not my grandmother to taste my new recipes and provide honest feedback before I make my decision on Friday. I want to work in the kitchen first.'

'I don't know if I'm qualified to—'

'You're the type of clientele who'll be staying here, not to mention you're the visionary for this entire hotel. You're the perfect test subject.'

Harrison's eyes met hers, and she suddenly wasn't sure whether she was asking him from a professional connection, or because she just didn't want their time together to end. Not that she'd ever admit to the latter.

'What do you say?'

'Well, when you put it like that...' He laughed. 'Yes. Daniel would kill me if I said no, and I'm also incredibly curious to see what you have planned.'

Charlotte grinned. 'See you at the hotel kitchen tomorrow then? Early evening? Pending Daniel's approval to use the space, of course.'

'I'll be there.' He went to turn, one hand casually pushed into his jeans pocket, before looking back at her. 'It was really nice to meet you, Charlotte.'

His smile made her heart flutter a little, but before she had time to respond, he was walking away and she was left standing in the street, staring up at the incredible hotel he'd designed and wondering what she'd been thinking, offering to cook for him.

Just admit you wanted to see him again.

She took a sip of coffee and lifted her face to the sun, feeling happier and more content than she had in a long time. Perhaps coming home wasn't the worst thing in the world.

Perhaps this is where I'm supposed to be; I was just too stubborn to see what was right in front of me.

Or maybe it was something different. Maybe she was simply ready to show her home city what she'd learnt, to give back to the place that had still been her home even when she'd tried to pretend that it wasn't.

And even though she had no intention of telling Daniel until she'd had time to think about it, Charlotte already knew the decision she was going to make.

9

THE MAJESTETISK HOTEL, SOGNEFJORD, NORWAY, 1950

When Amalie stepped outside, Oskar was already waiting for her. She had a moment before he saw her, and she was able to drink in the sight of him—the way he stood with his hands in his pockets, staring out at the fjord, his back to her and the hotel. There was something about him that made her want to know more, a way he made her feel when she was with him, and she'd be lying to say she'd thought of anything other than him all day. She'd hurried through her work making beds and cleaning rooms, not hearing her name being called and missing half of what the other girls had said to her, because she couldn't stop thinking about meeting him.

And now here he was.

Amalie cleared her throat as she stepped out onto the grass, smiling shyly when he turned. But she needn't have been shy or nervous that he didn't want to see her, because Oskar returned her small smile with a wide one, his eyes lighting up. It wasn't like they hadn't seen each other, either. They'd been catching stolen moments all week, even if it had only been an hour to sit together after their shift ended, or for him to walk her the long way back to her room, but tonight was the first time they'd planned to spend longer together. It was why her heart was racing and her stomach was full of knots.

'I wasn't sure if you'd come,' he said, walking towards her.

He kissed her cheek and she breathed in the scent of him, her stomach dancing at the closeness of him to her body.

'I was worried you wouldn't be here.'

His laugh was easy. 'Yet I came early just in case you finished ahead of schedule. When have I ever not been waiting for you when I promised to?'

He had her there. He'd been as reliable as clockwork, always waiting for her when he said he would be.

Oskar began to walk then, and she followed beside him, not touching but close enough that their elbows might bump, and every time he glanced at her she felt a now familiar warmth spread through her body. He was like no other boy she'd ever met before, and it both excited and terrified her.

'Tell me how you came to work here,' he said. 'I want to know everything about you.'

'I'm not all that exciting,' she said. 'I'm sure the other young women you usually meet are far more interesting.'

He shook his head and stepped in front of her, his eyes meeting hers as she stopped before him. 'I wish you could see yourself how I see you,' Oskar said, his voice low. 'I knew from the moment I first saw you that you were special.'

Amalie glanced away, embarrassed but also flattered, and when Oskar took her hand in his, she let him. If she'd been at home, if there was any chance of her parents hearing about her date or her sister seeing her, she'd never have let him touch her so openly. But it was summer and she was far from home, and for the very first time she no longer wanted to follow the strict rules that were usually set for her. She wanted to have fun and enjoy being herself.

'Come with me, I have something to show you.'

She followed him to a spot on the grass, the farthest point

from the hotel and the closest to the water, where a small basket had been placed alongside a folded blanket.

'You brought these?' she asked, looking between him and the basket.

Oskar shrugged. 'I rushed down after my shift ended. I thought you might be hungry.'

Her stomach gave a little growl in response that made them both laugh, and he let go of her hand to throw the blanket out across the lawn. He sat on the edge of it and beckoned for her to join him and she did, tucking her legs to one side and shyly glancing at him again.

'How about I prepare our food, and you tell me about your family. Where are you from? Do you have any siblings?'

Amalie could see from the way he was looking at her that he truly wanted to know about her, and she decided to indulge him, even though she couldn't see what would be interesting to a man like him about her comparatively simple life.

'I have a sister, Hilde, she's older than me, and I've lived my whole life near Sandvika with my parents,' she said, watching as he opened the basket and placed a plate between them. 'Hilde worked here for three summers before she was married, and it's because of her that I got this job.'

Oskar took out freshly baked bread, smoked salmon, cheese and some cold meats.

'I wasn't sure what you'd like, so I packed an assortment of things,' he said. 'But tell me more. What was your childhood like? What are your dreams?'

She laughed. 'My dreams? I don't know if I have any. I know what's expected of me, that I am to work to help my family, and then marry as best I can, but—'

'You must have dreams,' Oskar said earnestly, as if it wasn't possible that anyone could live without them. 'No one can take the things we dream of away from us, no matter how impossible they might be to achieve.'

Amalie sighed, suddenly sad as the weight of his words settled over her. 'I did have dreams, when I was a girl. I wanted to ride horses and live in a big house, to stay in the types of beautiful hotels that the women in my family clean rooms in. But that was a long time ago.'

'You don't dream of those things anymore?' Oskar asked.

She smiled, wondering if he was naive or simply a man so used to dreaming and knowing that those dreams could come true, that he couldn't understand what her life was truly like.

'I suppose I grew up and realised that that's all they were. Dreams, and nothing more.'

Oskar took her hand and held it tightly, staring into her eyes. 'How old are you, Amalie?'

'Nineteen,' she whispered, her words catching now that he was touching her again.

'You're too young to give up on your dreams,' he said. 'You speak as if you're an old maid, not a beautiful young woman with your entire life ahead of you. Please, keep those dreams alive.'

Amalie laughed, but he pressed his palm to her face and looked deeply into her eyes.

'Promise me you won't give up on them, Amalie. We only have one life, and we have to live it in the best way we can.'

His eyes were wide and serious, and she bravely reached out her hand and placed it to his chest, feeling the way his heart was racing, sensing that he was burning with a determination and passion that was like a fire inside of him.

'Tell me your dreams,' she said, bravely. 'Perhaps they will be contagious and help me find mine again.'

Oskar's smile lit his face, and she immediately relaxed when he began to speak, far more comfortable listening to him than being the centre of attention and having to talk about herself. She was also grateful for the chance to help herself to some of the food he'd brought, realising just how hungry she was from working all day without more than a ten-minute break.

'I want to be a chef,' he said. 'I want to work side by side with the best chefs in Norway. I want to spend my days perfecting the most beautiful dishes, instead of studying at university.'

She nodded, swallowing her mouthful of salmon. 'What are you studying?'

'Finance and business,' he said. 'My father wants me to take over his business one day. He wants me to start working for him the day after I graduate.'

Amalie didn't pretend not to know who his family were. They owned the sprawling hotel behind her and others that were renowned for being the most exclusive in the country—Oskar was heir to a substantial fortune. She'd heard some of the other staff talking about how wealthy he was.

'They know you want to be a chef?' she asked.

Oskar grimaced. 'Oh, they know. Their compromise was letting me work here in the kitchen over the summer, as if I'd quickly tire of it if I spent long enough doing it.' He sighed and stretched out on the blanket, propped up on one elbow. 'They like the idea of me learning from the ground up, working in the hotels and understanding the business from all sides, until I graduate. Then they want me in an office for the rest of my life, to take over the company one day, to follow what *their* dreams are for me.'

'And if you defied them? When you left university?' she asked. 'If you made the decision for yourself and told them that you have a different life planned to the one they imagine?'

Oskar's face crumpled. 'I would be ostracised from the family, and they would make sure that I wasn't employed at any hotel or kitchen in the country. I know because we've already argued about it.'

Amalie swallowed, feeling as if the salmon was suddenly

stuck in her throat. The way he'd said those words, the pain held in them, told her that what he was saying was no exaggeration. 'Your family truly holds that much power?' she asked.

He nodded. 'They do.'

'And you believe they would exile you from the family like that? You don't think it's a threat and nothing more?'

Oskar's laugh was shallow. 'No, Amalie, it's no threat. Once you meet my parents, you will understand.'

Amalie didn't tell him that she didn't ever want to meet his parents, that she disliked them already just from hearing how they held such power over their beautiful son and his destiny, but it did make her realise why he was interested in her dreams. Because it sounded as if his dreams might be as far-fetched as hers, after all.

She lay down beside him, the plate of food the only thing separating them, and reached for his hand, threading her fingers through his.

'Tell me why you want to be a chef,' she murmured. 'Tell me all your dreams, Oskar. They're safe with me, I won't tell a soul. I promise.'

Oskar's smile was sweet, his eyes softening as he blinked back at her, and when he pushed up slightly and leaned forward, bridging the gap between them, she let him kiss her.

And the way he gently whispered a kiss to her lips was even sweeter than his smile.

10

No one had ever bought Amalie flowers before, and they had certainly never taken her by the hand and led her down to a waiting boat on the clear blue water of the fjord. The boys she'd met at home were as romantic as a lump of wood, and they certainly wouldn't have been so thoughtful. So, when Oskar met her after work the next week, presenting her with a pretty bouquet of flowers that she quickly took back to her quarters, and then helped her into a little wooden rowing boat that he had waiting by the edge of the water, she wondered what she could have possibly done to deserve such a fuss. If he'd wanted to make her feel special, then he'd succeeded.

'Where are we going?' she asked, holding on to the sides of the boat to steady it as Oskar hopped in, hoping it wouldn't rock from side to side or even worse, sink.

'We're going to row for as long as my arms will take us, then enjoy the scenery in the middle of nowhere.'

It sounded like heaven to Amalie, and as he pulled the oars back and forth through the water, she told him every-thing that had happened that day; the rooms she'd had to clean and the gossip from the other maids, as he rowed and listened. It wasn't until she paused for breath that he set the oars down.

'Listen,' he said.

And she did, but there was nothing. 'I can't hear anything.'

'Exactly,' he replied. 'The silence is so loud it's almost ringing in our ears, don't you think? It's as if you can actually hear the sound of nothingness.'

Amalie moved carefully across to Oskar, settling her body against his so that her back was to his front, realising that she was happiest when she was in his arms. Her head fell back against his chest as she stared at their surroundings. It was as if they were the only two people in the world.

The fjord was nothing short of breathtaking. The water around them was the most vivid of deep blues, the sky above was clear, and it was as if they were surrounded by sleeping giants covered in green. She'd never seen a landscape like it, or perhaps she simply hadn't been looking before. It was almost as if the scenery around them had been created by an artist's brush; a romantic background that made Norway one of the most beautiful countries in the world. She knew that's why so many people came to the hotel—it was renowned for its position and magnificent scenery—but she'd always been too busy working to really see it with her own eyes. Until now.

'When I come here, it makes me think that anything is possible,' he whispered against her hair. 'That my dreams are mine, that no one can tell me what my life will become. That's why I wanted to bring you here with me.'

She tilted her head back, staring up at his face. Being here made her believe that anything was possible, too. That she and Oskar could have a life together, that they weren't destined to break each other's hearts at the end of summer when their time together was over.

But instead of saying anything back to him, Amalie lay contentedly in his arms, breathing in the pure, fresh air and basking in the feeling of his warm body pressed into hers. If someone had asked her even a week ago whether she would let a man place his hands on her or trail kisses along her skin, she'd have laughed and told them not to be ridiculous, yet here she was with Oskar, feeling as if she'd known him forever, yearning for the touch of his skin against hers.

'Sometimes when I'm here, lost in my own thoughts, I think I could run away and leave it all behind,' he said. 'I think I could even give up being a chef if it meant I could just live my life away from my family, to create a life for myself rather than the one they want to give me.'

'You don't mean that, Oskar,' she said. 'Your family is your family, it's the one thing in life we can't do anything to change. Whatever happens, they'll still love you.'

'I don't know if it's love, but my mother...'

Amalie waited for him to speak again, sensing that what he was about to tell her was going to break her heart. 'Your mother what?'

'My mother would rather me be dead than a failure,' he said. 'She has an image to protect, it's all she's ever cared about, and she wants her two sons to follow the path she's so clearly laid out for us. I don't think all families are as kind and caring as yours.'

Tears filled Amalie's eyes. 'Don't say that! No mother would ever wish her son dead.' Oskar didn't talk about his family again, strumming his fingers across her arm instead and pressing his lips into her hair as she nestled into him. It made her wonder how such a horrible, cold-sounding woman could have created such a kind, warm-hearted son.

'Tell me what your family would do, if you shared your dreams with them?' he asked, taking her by surprise.

'My family?' Amalie laughed. 'Well, my father would tell me not to be a fool, that it does no good to dream things that will never come true. He believes in being happy with who you are, and wanting things that aren't out of reach. My mother would tell me to put my time into finding a nice husband, and letting his dreams become my own. I don't think she believes that a woman should have independent thoughts or dreams, because she's likely never had any of her own. But it's not because they're cruel. They just don't want me to be disappointed, I suppose.'

Amalie's cheeks heated and she knew she was blushing, because he'd taken her hand in his when she'd mentioned *husband*. She didn't dare let herself dream that someone like Oskar could ever be the man she'd spend the rest of her life with.

'I'd like to meet your family,' he said. 'I think they sound much nicer than mine.'

Amalie didn't tell him that she'd like that, too, because she couldn't imagine Oskar ever coming to her family's modest home, or sitting with her father at the dinner table as they ate a simple bowl of her mother's fish and potatoes. Not that he'd likely complain; she could already tell his manners were impeccable and he seemed so at ease with anyone, regardless of who they were. She'd seen that first hand at the party the very first time they'd met. But she still doubted it would ever happen.

'We're from different worlds,' she whispered. 'You must see that?'

'And yet here we are, together,' he whispered back, as the boat rocked gently from side to side, a cooler breeze blowing across the water. 'Just you and me on the fjord.'

Amalie pushed all thoughts of how different they were from her, deciding instead to enjoy every second of being with Oskar. Even if it wasn't to be, even if she did end up with a broken heart, she hoped it would be worth it. Because she couldn't have turned away from him if she'd tried.

· · ·

After an hour or so on the water, Oskar gently helped Amalie to her seat, picked up the oars again and began to row, taking them back to where they'd started. They never spoke, but it was a comfortable silence, as if they'd known each other forever and were happy to just be by each other's side.

When they finally slid back to shore, Oskar jumped out and pulled the boat in, his trousers rolled up at the ankles, reaching for her hand once he'd secured the boat. He lifted her and she laughed, her head against his chest as he swung her around and threatened to drop her into the water.

'No!' she cried. 'Oskar, put me down!'

He laughed and carefully set her on her feet, taking her hand and leading her across the grass. Everything suddenly appeared to be cast in a reddish-yellow light, and she'd just thought it when Oskar spoke.

'The midnight sun,' he said, still holding her hands as he spun her around in a circle. 'Isn't it spectacular?'

She tilted her head back, face raised to the sky. The Sogne-fjord was the most beautiful place on earth, of that she was certain—where else in the world would the light be so magical, as if everything had been brushed with a burnt orange hue, the moon never taking over from the sun during the peak of summer? When they finally stopped spinning and she stood tall, still holding on to Oskar for balance, he drew her in close, his mouth hovering over hers as if to make certain she wanted him to kiss her. She closed the distance between them, her lips parting as she breathed him in, their hands still linked as their mouths brushed back and forth against the other.

Oskar was the one to break their kiss, his fingers stroking her hair back from her face, his eyes alight with mischief.

'I think we should go for a swim,' he said.

Amalie laughed as she shook her head. 'It's far too cold for me, and I don't have anything to swim in.' She was no prude, but she certainly wasn't going naked. Perhaps if she'd been with her sister and there had been little chance of anyone at all seeing them she might have, but not here and not in front of Oskar.

'We can strip down to our undergarments,' he said, as a grin took over his face. 'What do you say?'

'I say...' Amalie's voice died in her throat as Oskar quickly began to strip down. Within seconds his shirt and shoes were off, and then his trousers, and she was left blushing furiously as he ran down to the water's edge in his underpants.

'Come on! What are you waiting for?' he called back. 'I won't even look, I'll turn my back, just come into the water. Please!'

Amalie looked after him, watching as he splashed into the water, making it look far more inviting than she imagined it actually was, before hurriedly taking her own clothes off, her arms folded over her brassiere as she ran. She may as well have been completely naked, she felt so bare, and when he turned around she squealed.

'Oskar! No looking!' she cried. 'You promised!'

But he ignored her completely, splashing her as she squealed even more at the cold water against her warm skin, then grabbing her hands and tugging her into the deeper water with him, his eyes never leaving hers. She was terrified of what might be lurking beneath and she wasn't a strong swimmer, but Oskar seemed to sense her fear and kept her close, immediately less playful and more protective.

'Don't let me go,' she said, clutching his arm. 'I'm not used to deep water.'

'Trust me, Amalie. You're safe out here with me—I've been swimming my whole life.'

Oskar lifted her then, his hand beneath her as he pushed her up, floated her across the surface of the water, her hair fanning out around her as she slowly relaxed and began to trust him. Her body and the back of her head were completely submerged as she spread her legs and arms wide, realising that she was getting the hang of it.

'Close your eyes and relax, just breathe and push your chest to the surface, try to balance your body,' he said. 'I've got you.'

But Amalie couldn't close her eyes, she didn't want to. She wanted to stare at the sky and admire the midnight sun, to see everything, to remember everything. When she went to sleep at night, she wanted to close her eyes and see this—this was what she wanted to remember every night for the rest of her life when she lay in bed. This was the memory she wanted to return to when she needed something to lift her spirits.

'I think I've fallen in love with you.'

Oskar's whispered words wrapped around her, and even though she knew they were too young to fall in love so fast, that adults would tell them they didn't yet know what love was, she knew in her heart that she felt the same.

Amalie's words stuck in her throat then as he carefully let go of her and floated beside her, hand in hand as they drifted together on the water, as if they had the entire fjord to themselves. Oskar was like no one she'd ever met in her life before, and she doubted she'd ever, for as long as she lived, meet another man who came even close to him.

11

Later that night, sitting on the bank and wrapped in the blanket Oskar had brought, still shivering just a little from their long swim in the fjord, Amalie stretched out like a cat in a puddle of sunshine.

'I couldn't have planned a more magical night if I'd tried,' Oskar said. 'I only wish I'd thought to bring food with us this time.'

She brushed her fingertips over his leg, which was still bare, and she felt goose pimples ripple across his skin.

'What do you think of me cooking for you tomorrow night?' he asked. 'I'll make us dinner and we can eat in the restaurant after everyone else goes.'

She laughed. 'But the staff aren't allowed to dine there. What if someone sees me?'

'Hmm,' he murmured. 'No, you're right, I couldn't be seen with a maid there, imagine what the paying patrons might say.'

She swatted at him, but he deftly caught her hand. 'You know what I mean. I don't want to get either of us in trouble.'

'Meet me in the kitchen tomorrow night, after closing,' he

said. 'I'll have it all planned, but please, just let me cook for you. I want you to try something I've been working on lately, hoping to perfect. No one will reprimand you, not if you're with me.'

'You can cook for me whenever you want, Oskar,' she said, truthfully. 'I'll sneak out to see you every night for the rest of summer if I have to.'

'Tomorrow night, then. And every night after that.'

She closed her eyes for a moment, knowing that when she opened them, he'd still be staring down at her.

'Whatever happens, I'll never forget you, Oskar,' she whispered as she gazed up at him, her head on his lap as he stroked her hair. 'These have been the best days of my life.'

He bent and kissed her, his lips warm and hungry against hers. 'I love you, Amalie.'

Tears filled her eyes. It was almost the middle of summer— their time together had flown past, and now she couldn't imagine not seeing him every day, not being with him at the end of each shift; not feeling his arms around her or his fingertips brushing against her skin.

I love you, too, Oskar. So much that sometimes I can barely breathe at the thought of losing you.

'Stay here the night with me?' he asked.

The way his fingers tugged so gently through her hair, his lips finding hers again before she could even answer, made her melt into him. Right now, she would have said yes to anything.

I need to go back to my room. I can't stay out all night. What will the other girls say?

'It will just be us, the fjord and the midnight sun,' he whispered against her lips. 'We don't have to do anything you don't want to. I just want to lie here with you in my arms and never let go.'

And just like that, Amalie found herself nodding, powerless to say no to the boy she'd fallen head over heels in love with, and knowing that if he asked her to, she'd walk to the end of the earth, give up everything, just to be with him.

Amalie didn't remember falling asleep, but when they woke in the morning the amber light of the sun was still casting a pretty, soft glow around them. She tugged the blanket up around her, shivering from the early morning air even though she was nestled against Oskar.

'I've dreamed of waking up beside you,' he said, leaning over and kissing her on the mouth.

Amalie tucked in closer to him, his arm around her shoulders as they watched the beauty of the morning unfold around them. The lush forest covered the land to each side, the water a dark blanket stretching out in front of them, and Amalie knew that she'd never witness anything so beautiful in her life as what she was looking at right now.

But despite it all, despite the happiness blossoming inside of her, she still had a little worry that wouldn't go away, that had begun to play on her mind the night before even though she'd done her best to banish it.

'Oskar, may I ask you something, and will you promise to answer honestly?' she asked.

He gave her shoulders a squeeze and pressed a kiss to the top of her head. 'Anything. I have nothing to hide from you.'

Amalie cleared her throat. She hadn't wanted to say anything, but everything seemed so perfect, and she didn't want to be lulled into a false sense of what they were, of who she was to Oskar. He'd told her that he loved her, but her older sister had always warned her how easily men could say words to get what they wanted from a woman. She might be in love, but she didn't want to be a fool in love.

'I overheard some of the maids talking about us yesterday.

They were whispering about how I was your fun for the summer, and that I'd be left broken-hearted once you left. That you'd done this last time you were here.' Amalie took a deep breath and it shuddered from her lungs as she looked up at him, wanting to see the expression on his face. 'Will I ever see you again, after this? Or is this just a summer fling for you, something you do with a pretty maid you find every year?'

She hoped she could keep the look on his face in her memory for the rest of her life, because the way his eyes softened, the way he stared back at her, told her everything she needed to know. Amalie could tell that she'd hurt him just by asking.

'This is real, Amalie,' he said, holding her hand. 'I've never felt this way about anyone before, and I'm not leaving here at the end of summer without you. Whatever they've said is because they're jealous of what we have, nothing more.'

She smiled, even though her eyes had filled with tears. 'We come from different worlds, Oskar. Even if we wanted to stay together, even if—'

'Shhh,' he murmured, wrapping his arms even tighter around her. 'We will find a way. I promise you, Amalie, we will find a way to be together.'

She closed her eyes, even though they were supposed to be taking in the view, feeling him against her, wanting to remember forever what it felt like to be in his arms. Only she wasn't sure what was worse—knowing this was only for the summer, or that they both wanted to be together and couldn't.

Within minutes, she'd have to rush back to her quarters and get ready for work, but for now, she wanted to soak up every second of being in Oskar's embrace, of feeling his breath against her cheek; the soft thud of his heart as she turned her head against his chest.

It was the strangest feeling, but it was as if her heart was expanding and growing like a flower under Oskar's tender love and care, at the same time as it was slowly starting to break in anticipation of what was to come.

'Tonight,' he said. 'We'll be together again tonight, and every night after that if I can help it.'

12

PRESENT DAY

Charlotte hadn't been so nervous about her menu in a long time. Not when she'd first been put forward for the role at her previous restaurant, Velluto, for the year-long contract as executive chef, or her very first head chef job at a top London eatery. Creating food for Harrison felt like a much more intimate affair, despite the fact that he was essentially a stranger.

But he's a very handsome stranger who has Daniel's ear, and one who could put an end to this opportunity with one phone call.

And the strange thing was, she suddenly *wanted* this job. From the moment she'd set foot in the hotel, she'd felt that it was the right place for her, as if it were her chance to come full circle. She'd last been in Oslo as a young woman with a dream and little else, and now she was an accomplished chef with something to prove. The timing couldn't have been better.

Charlotte finished plating up, smiling when she heard a tap on the door to the kitchen. She looked up and found Harrison standing there, a bottle of wine in hand and a hard-to-read expression on his face.

'Is it strange that I brought wine?' he asked. 'I didn't want to turn up empty-handed, but I'm also well aware it's not a dinner party.'

'Wine is perfect, and just what I need after three hours in the kitchen,' she said. 'If you want to find two glasses, I'll have a quick tidy up.'

'It's oddly peaceful in here,' he said, as she continued to work and he wandered around opening cupboard doors. 'I think I could get used to having an entire restaurant to myself.'

'I could say the same about the kitchen,' she said. 'Daniel was worried about me being here alone, but he has a security guard patrolling and honestly, I kind of like how peaceful it is. Kitchens are usually high-stress, chaotic places at this time of night, but for creating something new? The quiet has been nice.'

'Why do I think you usually love the fast pace?' he asked, grinning as he held up two glasses triumphantly and walked them over to her.

Charlotte was the one grinning now. 'Guilty as charged, I've always loved it. But I also love being alone when I'm creating new menus like this. The solitude lets me just focus on what I'm doing, but the busy team atmosphere is like nothing else at a good restaurant.'

'These are all new dishes you've created?' he asked. 'They smell amazing.'

'Tonight, I'm trying out a selection of entrées for you,' she said, happily receiving the wine he offered her. She wiped her hands on the towel beside her and took off her apron, folding it and placing it on the counter. 'Two of them are similar to other dishes I've made before, but the others are new flavours inspired by coming home. It's been a while since I've had access to such fresh, beautiful seafood, and I really wanted to pay homage to the produce we have available here.'

She surveyed each plate and moved them closer to Harrison, who was frowning at the bottle of wine.

'Now I'm thinking about it, I should have asked the chef which wine was most appropriate. Is Pinot Noir suitable for what we're eating? I won't be offended if you tell me to put it away.'

'I'm sure it will be perfect,' Charlotte said, holding up her glass. 'To being in Oslo.'

Harrison held his glass up high in reply. 'To being in Oslo,' he repeated. 'A place that I never considered travelling to before, yet one I find I'm falling more and more in love with each day. And it would be remiss not to toast the hotel's *potential* new chef.'

'Well, let's see about that, but I'm really pleased you're enjoying it here so much. I loved London for so many reasons, but I still think Oslo is one of the most beautiful cities in the world. Has anyone given you a proper tour? Taken you to see any of the fjords or the lovely little villages?'

Harrison shook his head, looking guilty. 'I've seen nothing more than the city, although I have found myself walking down to the water often, watching the boats go out, and just last week I went for a walk to see the Royal Palace. It's always fascinated me that it's so close to the city.'

'The most beautiful thing about this city is that it's surrounded by nature. The forest is almost at our fingertips, or at least that's how it always felt when I was sitting in class at school and staring out the window, waiting for the day to end. You'll have to let me show you around, if I don't scare you away with my food tonight, that is.'

They both took another sip of wine. 'It would be nice to be shown around by a local, so I might just take you up on that.'

Charlotte was surprised how comfortable she felt being alone with Harrison, especially given how many times she'd questioned why on earth she'd offered to cook for him so soon. 'You know, I thought we'd just stand here and do a tasting, but shall we sit? I feel like I've been on my feet for hours. It'd be nice to relax for a bit.'

'Excellent idea. I'll carry the wine.'

Charlotte ferried the first two plates through to the dining area, glancing at Harrison as he deftly put down the two glasses and the bottle he was carrying.

'I'll bring the rest, you just—'

Unbeknown to Charlotte, he was right behind her, and when she spun round she almost went head-first into him. But she appreciated the help, and within seconds they were sitting with six plates between them—a private dining feast for two.

'I was thinking,' she said, as she gestured towards the plate he was to try from first, 'that I could suggest a chef's table in the kitchen if I take the job. There's enough space, and it would be a special experience for a couple or even a group of four each night. What do you think?'

'Would they order, or would the chef choose their meal?' he asked.

'Hmm, I think the chef would choose. Perhaps a tasting plate so they get to try a selection of dishes, or whatever's the special that night. I'd like to make it a unique experience.'

She watched as Harrison took a forkful of cod, her eyes fixed on his face as he chewed then swallowed. Her favourite part of her job wasn't tasting her own food, it was observing others and seeing their reaction. It told her everything she needed to know about whether to keep something on a menu or return to the drawing board.

'Thoughts?'

'Exquisite,' he said, and she could tell from the way his eyes widened and his brows lifted that he'd enjoyed it. 'It was an explosion of flavour. I think Daniel was right about you being the best in the business.'

'Please, have some more,' she said, cradling her glass of wine and watching as he ate half of it before sliding the plate over to her. Seeing him enjoy her food was just what she'd needed.

'If everything else is as good as this...'

Charlotte had learnt to accept praise, and she happily took his. If he hadn't liked it, she would have seen it written all over his face, but she could tell he meant it. She tasted it herself as he moved on to the next dish of clams, pleased with the flavour and happy she'd made detailed notes about how she'd achieved such depth to the sauce.

'So, tell me why you left Oslo in the first place,' he said. 'Had you always wanted to live in London?'

She finished her mouthful, looking up and wishing she'd been quicker to turn the conversation around to him. Talking about herself was not something she did often or was comfortable with.

'I have what you might call a complicated relationship with my father,' she said, collecting her thoughts as she swapped the plates around to put the clams in front of him. 'I haven't seen him in years, actually, and it's the main reason I don't come home often.'

'Family can be complicated at the best of times,' he said. 'I get it.'

'My mum left when we were young, just walked out on us and started a whole new life, and my dad changed overnight. First, he grieved her, and so did we because it was almost as if she'd died when she left us, but then it was as if someone had flicked a switch, and he stopped being the easy-going father we'd grown up with and became hyperfocused on us achieving to the highest level at school and mapping out our futures for us.'

'By *us* you mean—'

'My brother and me. My father wanted, no *expected*, us to become surgeons just like him,' she said, remembering the way he'd yelled at her when her science grades hadn't matched his expectations, or how he'd reacted when she'd dared to share her own dreams with him. 'Thankfully my brother lived up to my father's dreams, but when I decided to forge ahead with my own plans, the only way was to leave home and do it on my own.'

'As soon as you left school?'

She watched as Harrison ate another clam, deciding that she may as well tell him the truth. She had nothing to hide; she'd just always kept most of her story about how she'd ended up training in London to herself.

'I left home at eighteen, with some money my grandma had saved for me, and I've barely returned until now. I came back once for a funeral, and again for a wedding, where I chose not to see him.' Charlotte took a deep breath and slowly let it go. 'Sometimes I feel sorry for him, because of what happened with my mum, but then I remind myself that he was a father to two kids, and he chose to treat us that way. When I didn't want to follow the path he'd determined for me, he made me feel as if I was no better than the wife who'd walked out on him.'

She paused to try one of the clams herself, loving the flavour of the white wine and garlic she'd cooked them in. Charlotte made a mental note to include a slice of fresh rye bread or toasted wholegrain loaf with this dish if she served it on a menu —it would be a shame not to have something to soak up the juices with. And it was then she realised that this was the first conversation she'd ever had with anyone where she'd been able to talk about her family issues without feeling emotional. Perhaps it was because he was a stranger, but Harrison was proving very easy to talk to.

'Have you seen him since you returned?' Harrison asked.

She shook her head. 'I haven't. I will, but it's been so long that I'm not quite sure how to go about it, so I thought I'd bide my time a little bit.'

Harrison set down his fork, and she found herself studying

how handsome his face was. 'I know I don't know anything about what your childhood was like or how it was becoming estranged from your father, but if I can give you one piece of advice, it's to go and see him while you still can,' Harrison said, his eyes locked on hers as they stared at each other across the table. 'You never know when the choice might be taken from you.'

He cleared his throat and glanced away, and she took a small sip of wine to give him a moment, feeling as if they were talking about more than just her father. But she didn't want to ask, and he didn't offer more.

'I will go and see him,' she said. 'Because you're right—if something happened to him and we hadn't reconciled, I'd never forgive myself. Besides, there's a family mystery I need to tell him about.'

'Well, that sounds rather interesting.'

She laughed and took another sip of wine, enjoying how relaxed she was with him. It should have felt ridiculous and strange being the only two people seated in a room designed for over a hundred, but somehow it felt like one of the more inti-mate dinners she'd had in a long time. And she knew that if she did take the job, she'd never forget her first experience of cooking in the kitchen and enjoying the evening with him. She'd always be able to glance out and remember what a nice night they'd had together, and that somehow he'd seemed to understand her complicated family relationships.

'Trust me when I say that it's a long story,' she said.

He sat back and folded his hands behind his head. 'It just so happens I have all night, especially with all this delicious food on board.'

So, Charlotte told him about the box—how it had been discovered and what was inside—watching as his eyebrows pulled together in disbelief when she got to the part about all the others being left for babies who'd been placed for adoption.

She'd barely paused for breath, finding that she wanted to share it all with him despite barely knowing the man.

'Do you have the box with you?' he asked.

'Unfortunately, I don't. I left it with my great-grandmother, Amalie. Honestly, I think I would have had to prise it from her fingers if I'd wanted to take it. Just looking at it seemed to take her back in time, maybe to a happier place.'

'What's your gut feeling about it all?' Harrison asked, leaning across the table to take the bottle of Pinot Noir and pour a little more into each of their glasses. 'Why do you think it was left? What do you think the secret is about?'

She shrugged, cradling her glass in her hand as she considered his question. She'd gone round and round it so many times in her mind, trying to figure out why Amalie would have left it, but she'd still come up with nothing. Her only conclusion had been that a secret adoption had indeed taken place; but if that wasn't the case, then she had nothing.

'Honestly? I don't know. I think that this is bigger than just my great-grandmother keeping a secret. It feels as if it's something that's been kept from our entire family. But then again, maybe I'm being dramatic.'

'Maybe not. Times were different then, secrets were kept that we wouldn't have to keep now,' Harrison said. 'How did she react when you asked her? Did she seem upset by it all? Could it be that your great-grandmother had another child? Another daughter who isn't your grandmother?'

'She seemed, I don't know, almost happy to see the photo. It was as if she came to life again the moment she saw him and said his name, so perhaps you're right about something being hidden just simply because of the times. But honestly, I don't think she could have had another baby, given my grandmother's birth date. The timeline just doesn't add up.'

'Perhaps a secret she didn't want to keep then?' Harrison asked. 'Something related to the birth but not what you've thought of so far? Or a secret that someone else forced her to keep for them?'

'But if Oskar is her secret, and then she married my great-grandfather, then who was Oskar? Was he her great love, and she's had to keep him hidden all this time for fear of hurting anyone's feelings? And if he was her one true love, then why didn't she marry him? What reason could there have been for them to be parted? It honestly doesn't make sense.'

Harrison shrugged. 'Maybe. But then maybe a person can have two great loves? It doesn't mean that she loved her husband any less, so perhaps he simply came before your great-grandfather, and they weren't to be.'

'You truly think so?' Charlotte asked. 'I mean, it's not that I don't believe a person can fall in love twice, but within such a short space of time it just seems...'

'I think none of us knows what love and loss will do to us until we experience it ourselves.'

Charlotte sighed, noticing the way Harrison looked away again, as if he wasn't comfortable talking about relationships, his voice husky. It was the same when he'd told her to be sure to see her father again before it was too late. But she didn't feel that she knew him well enough to ask about his own relationships.

'Anyway,' she said, 'I might discover more in the morning. We're going back to see Amalie, and hopefully she'll have another lucid moment and be able to share some more of her story with us. I'm only grateful that she's still here to tell us what she can, because if this box had surfaced in a few years' time, it might have all remained a mystery forever, and we'd never have known anything about it.'

'Well, on that note, I think I might call it a night.' Harrison looked at the plates around them. 'Actually, I've just realised that despite being in a restaurant, there's no one to take these plates.'

'It's fine, I can—'

'Not a chance,' he said, clearing their plates and cutlery and leaving Charlotte to collect the wineglasses as he walked back to the kitchen. 'We'll get it done quickly if we do it together.'

She set the glasses she was carrying down on the counter and stood back as he filled the large sink in the kitchen with soapy water and began to wash, surprised by how at ease he was. The one and only serious boyfriend she'd had would never have rolled up his sleeves and got to work like this—whether she'd cooked for him or not—whereas she had a feeling that no matter how much she'd protested, Harrison wouldn't have walked away.

'You don't seem to mind the clean-up,' she said, adding pots and pans to the dirty pile to his right. 'It's nice to see.'

'My sisters made sure that I always did my share of the chores growing up,' he said, 'and we always had this unwritten rule that the chef never had to clean up. If you were on cooking, you got to do whatever you wanted once everyone was fed.'

'Ahh, someone who knows my entire life philosophy.' Charlotte laughed. 'My brother used to believe it was the only reason I cooked, so that he had to be on dishes through all his teenage years. But then he was the golden child, so it did him good to have to do something he didn't want to.'

She bumped her shoulder into Harrison's without meaning to, but she found that she liked standing close to him and didn't move away. There was a calm energy about him, a feeling that he would be almost impossible to fluster, and she also found that she didn't particularly want the night to end. He was easy to be around, and she would have liked to have found out more about him. She realised that all she'd done was talk about herself all night, albeit because he'd asked, but still, she'd have liked to end the evening feeling as if she knew him a little better.

'I'm sorry you had to hear about my family dramas,' she

said. 'It's something I usually avoid talking about at all costs, and yet I told you almost everything in one night.'

'It's fine, I liked learning more about you. It explains a lot, actually. Why you've achieved so much at such a young age, and where the fire inside you comes from.'

'Next time, I promise to let you do all the talking and I'll try out some of my new mains on you. If you're game, that is.'

'I actually haven't had such a nice evening in a very long time, so thank you,' Harrison said, as he let the water out of the sink and she put the last dish away. 'And yes, I wouldn't miss it. You tell me when, and I'll be here.'

Harrison moved closer to her then, and Charlotte placed one hand on the counter to steady herself. She looked up into his eyes, wondering for a fleeting moment if he was about to kiss her, but instead he took her hand and squeezed it gently before collecting his coat, catching her eye one last time before turning away. The wine had clearly gone straight to her head if she'd thought he was going to do anything more—their night together had been lovely, but it certainly hadn't been a date.

'Goodnight, Charlotte. Thank you for the most wonderful culinary experience.'

'You're very welcome,' she replied. 'Thank *you* for letting me experiment on you.'

She clasped her hands together, watching him go. And when he turned at the door and glanced back at her, she had a feeling that there were so many more layers to the man she'd just spent the evening with.

Usually that would make her want to run. She didn't have time for men in general, let alone ones she couldn't figure out on the first date, which was of course not what this had been, but Harrison was different. Harrison was the kind of man who made her want to find out more, and it had been a very, very long time since a man had made her feel that way.

If one ever had.

Realising that she had no way of contacting him without going through Daniel, Charlotte quickly dashed after Harrison, running out into the empty foyer and calling to him.

'Harrison.' Her voice wasn't loud, but it still echoed through the vast space as if she'd shouted it.

He stopped walking and turned, one hand pushed casually into the pocket of his jeans.

'I was thinking I could show you around tomorrow, since there's so much you haven't seen. If you still want that tour, that is?'

Charlotte knew she would never forget the smile that lit his face, the way his chocolate-brown eyes seemed to soften. 'I'd like that. But could we say the day after tomorrow?'

'Sure. After lunch? Early afternoon?'

'I have meetings until two, but I can meet you in the lobby straight after.'

'I'll be here.'

And this time when he left, she knew she hadn't been imagining the spark between them, and she also knew that it would be impossible to sleep, because the idea of showing him around, just the two of them, was even more daunting than devising a bold new menu for the biggest, newest hotel in Oslo.

13

THE MAJESTETISK HOTEL, SOGNEFJORD, NORWAY, 1950

The days were racing past, and Amalie couldn't stop counting the weeks they had left together. The summer had become a blur of work and time spent with Oskar, and even though she knew her friends missed her, she wanted to spend every spare minute she had with him. Whenever he finished a shift, no matter how late, she was waiting for him, sitting on the low wall outside the hotel as she stared at the water, knowing he would always bring something delicious for her to try. And then they'd walk or go out in the little rowing boat he'd commandeered, or lie on the grass and stare at the sky. Sometimes they talked, sometimes they just lay there in silence, content in each other's company, fingertips touching as they stretched out their arms. Other times Oskar would wrap her in his embrace and they would kiss until they were breathless, their bodies intertwined, making her wonder how she could ever live a day without seeing him.

Tonight though, it seemed that Oskar had other plans, and she could tell from the mischievous look on his face that he was up to something. He had a spring in his step and the corners of his mouth were tilted up into a smile.

'How was your night?' she asked, grinning when he passed her a small plate with a slice of *bløtkake* on it. She loved his layered cream cake, and she took the dessert fork he gave her and quickly ate her first mouthful, closing her eyes as it dissolved in her mouth. It was divine, as was everything he brought for her.

'Do you want a piece?' she asked, offering him the fork back.

'No. I just want to watch you as you eat it.'

'This is truly the best cake I've ever had, and I'm not just saying that because I love you.'

He leaned in and kissed her forehead, his lips soft against her skin. 'Good, because I've made a decision.'

She stopped eating and looked up, hearing how serious he was.

'I want to be a dessert or pastry chef,' he said, and she could tell from the contented look on his face how pleased he was with his decision. 'I am at my happiest when I'm making something sweet in the kitchen. I love the artistry of it and the ingredients, and I love watching you eat what I've created. I want to make desserts and cakes and pastries for the rest of my life, with you by my side.'

Amalie set down her plate and put her arms around his neck, drawing Oskar in for a kiss. 'I'm so proud of you.' She didn't ask how he was going to do this or what he would tell his parents, because she preferred their little bubble of pretending it was just the two of them, and that whatever they dreamed of or talked about existed only between them. She didn't know whether this was even something he could make happen, but if he thought he could, then she would support him.

When their lips parted, he smiled down at her, his gaze warm and kind. 'Finish that cake and then let's walk down to the water's edge.'

She didn't need to be told twice, eating her dessert and laughing as he recounted tales of the grumpy old chef he worked under, and how the man's face had turned beetroot red when he'd tasted the truffle sauce and found it to be so salty it could make his moustache stand on end. When she was finally finished, Oskar stepped forwards and brushed his thumb against the edge of her mouth, wiping away a little bit of cream. The way his eyes fixed on hers made her feel as if he had a window straight to her heart.

'Come with me,' he said, holding out his hand. 'I've waited all night for this.'

Amalie placed her palm against his and expected Oskar to lead her away from the hotel, but instead he pulled her close once they reached the little courtyard adjacent to where she'd been sitting.

'Listen carefully,' he whispered.

She did, and she heard it straightaway. There was the faintest sound of music coming from the hotel, and Amalie smiled against his shoulder as he looped his other hand around her waist. Usually they basked in the silence of the fjord when they took the little boat out, but tonight, it was music.

'There's an event in the dining hall tonight,' he said, as he held her out and twirled her, making her laugh. 'When I realised we'd never danced before, I knew it was our chance.'

Oskar pulled her in close again after the spin and she placed her head to his chest, listening to the steady beat of his heart as they moved slowly from side to side. She could barely even hear the music now, but she swayed in time with his body, loving the way his arm encircled her. She'd only ever danced with boys at her town's dances, and she'd always been careful to keep her distance, not wanting to even accidentally bump her body into theirs.

She imagined that Oskar had grown up going to balls or watching his parents dance, that he'd lived a life so different to hers, which made her wonder what their life might be like if they found a way to stay together.

'When we're married, we're going to dance like this every night,' he murmured against her ear. 'Just you and me, in the middle of our house. When we have children, they'll have to watch me dance with you every night after dinner.'

She tilted her head back and looked up at him, wanting to believe him but also knowing how much it was going to break her heart to have these memories, if the summer was all they had together. 'Stop teasing me,' she said. 'You're going to go back to university and forget all about your summer romance.'

'Never,' he said, stopping her from saying anything by covering her mouth with his.

'Oskar!'

The call was so sharp and unexpected in the almost silent night air, that it cut straight through them and made Amalie leap back in surprise. Oskar stared down at her for a fleeting second, his eyes filling with what she could only imagine was disbelief before looking over his shoulder.

'It's my mother.' His words were barely audible, but she heard them. 'What is she doing here?'

Amalie closed her eyes, taking a breath before slowly turning to follow his gaze. His mother was exactly as she'd imagined she might look, with her blonde hair brushed off her face and piled high, diamonds glittering at her neck and dressed in clothes that, even from where she stood, reminded Amalie just how different Oskar's family, his *life*, was to hers. Amalie felt like a poor church mouse in comparison, and she hated that this woman had seen her kissing her son so passionately. If she'd known there was even a chance of them being seen by a member of his family, she'd never have so much as held Oskar's hand.

'Oskar! Come inside, your father is waiting.'

Amalie was surprised when Oskar took her hand, and when she tried to pull away, he held firm.

'Oskar, you don't need—'

'I'm not leaving you out here as if she's caught me doing something wrong,' he said. 'Amalie, it's time for you to meet my mother. The timing isn't perfect, but it doesn't matter.'

I don't want to. I know how she's going to look at me, what she's going to think of me. I don't want to feel her loathing.

'Oskar, it's fine. You don't have to,' she said.

He surprised her by lifting her hand and pressing a kiss to it, all while his mother's gaze rested on them from afar. 'I do, and I am. We have nothing to hide.'

It was a mistake, she knew it was, but Amalie didn't have the heart to tell Oskar no. Not to mention that part of her wanted to see if she was wrong. *Maybe his mother won't be so bad, after all? Maybe I've over-imagined her reaction.*

'Oskar, what are you doing out at this time of night? Surely you have better things to do than—'

'Mother, it's good to see you,' he interrupted, leaning in to kiss his mother's cheek and embrace her. 'You should have sent word that you were coming.'

Amalie found herself studying the woman's face for any likeness to Oskar, and finding none. She also knew what she'd been about to say, or close enough to it.

'Your father wanted to visit, and I wanted to make certain my youngest son was behaving himself.' His mother gave her a pointed look, and Amalie's cheeks flooded with heat. 'I don't know why you insist on working here when you could be enjoying the summer with us, or just staying here as a guest, although you've clearly found a way to entertain yourself.'

'Mother, I'd like to introduce you to Amalie,' Oskar said, taking a step back so that he was standing beside her, as if he hadn't even heard her words.

His mother gave her son a long, steady look, as if to question why he was making her say hello, before fixing her gaze on Amalie.

Amalie knew then that her fears had come true. She'd never

felt as small in all her life as she felt in front of Oskar's mother in that moment. She'd come from a nice family, surrounded by hard-working people who loved their children and strived to do what they could for them. But when she stood in front of Oskar's mother, it was the first time she'd understood how insignificant she was. That she would never, ever be enough for this woman's son.

'It's lovely to meet you,' Amalie said, forcing the words out.

His mother didn't even bother to acknowledge her. It was as if Amalie hadn't even spoken.

'Oskar, come and join your father and me for a late supper. The kitchen has reopened for us.'

'Mother, this is Amalie,' Oskar said again, his voice louder this time. 'We've spent the summer together so far, and I've been looking forward to introducing you to her.'

His mother raised an eyebrow and gave Amalie a fleeting glance that consisted of looking her up and down, before audibly sighing. Tears pricked at Amalie's eyes, and she wished that she'd just stayed in her little bubble with Oskar, that she hadn't had to meet this awful woman who made her feel as if she wasn't even worthy of speaking to.

'Come along, Oskar,' she said. 'I don't want to keep your father waiting all night; it was a long drive to get here.'

Amalie could sense Oskar's hesitation this time, and she wondered how many times he'd actually stood up to his mother before. But she couldn't help but be proud of him when he didn't move, even when his mother turned away. It was obvious that she was well used to her son obeying her.

'I actually already have plans with Amalie, but if you'd allow her to join us...'

His mother did a half-turn, her eyes boring into Oskar's as if she were trying to set him alight. But instead of giving in to her, he held out his hand and took Amalie's. Amalie was proud of him, but she knew that, somehow, she'd be blamed for this, as if she'd made him behave in this way.

'Oskar, it's late, and I'm so very tired,' Amalie forced herself to say, avoiding his eyes when his searched hers. She wasn't going to let his mother see her behaving in anything other than a respectful way. 'Please, go and enjoy the evening with your parents. We can see each other tomorrow.'

He didn't move, and she wished he would because her eyes were filling with tears now and she didn't know how long she could hold back the sob that was building inside of her.

'Are you—'

'I'm certain. Thank you for the *bløtkake*, it was delicious.'

Oskar stepped nearer to her, embracing her and kissing her cheek, his lips gently skimming across her skin. When he squeezed her hand, it was all she could do not to burst into tears right there in front of his mother, who was still waiting for him, hovering as if she wanted to forcibly snatch her son away from her.

'I'll see you tomorrow,' he whispered. 'I'm sorry.'

She nodded and watched him go, and she knew that she would never, ever forget the look of disdain his mother gave her when she glanced back at Amalie over her shoulder. Oskar might love her, but his mother couldn't even stand to breathe the same air as her, and she'd conveyed exactly what she thought of her in one long, cold stare.

Later that night, when Amalie was curled up in her bed, tossing and turning and unable to sleep, there was a light knock at her door. She startled, thinking she was imagining it, but as she lay there listening to her roommate snoring, it happened again. There was someone knocking.

'Amalie,' came an urgent whisper. 'Open the door.'

She quickly rose, smoothing her hands down her nightgown

to check that she was decent, before tiptoeing across the floor-boards and opening the door as quietly as she could.

'Oskar! What are you doing here? If we're caught—'

Oskar's mouth met hers, stealing her words with his kisses, his hand cupped to the back of her head. When they came up for air, he took her hand. Clearly he wasn't concerned about being caught.

'My mother is awful and I hate the way she treated you tonight,' he said. 'But I'm not going to let her ruin this. I love you, Amalie, and that's the last and only time I'll let my mother ignore you like that.'

Amalie hesitated, glancing back at her sleeping roommate and knowing that she should stay. Her job was too important to her, and if Oskar's parents laid a complaint and had her fired, her own parents would be furious with her. But the idea of saying goodnight to him and crawling back into bed, of letting his mother win and drive a wedge between them, didn't appeal to her.

'Where are we going?' she asked.

'You'll see,' he said.

So Amalie closed the door as silently as she could, knowing that she would follow Oskar anywhere. All he ever had to do was ask.

They walked quietly, hand in hand but barely making a noise, until they reached the service door at the end of the hallway and made their way outside. But it wasn't until they reached the edge of the water that they finally spoke.

Now that it was nearing the end of summer, the midnight sun wasn't as bright, the light more muted than it had been when they'd first begun spending the evenings together, but it wasn't any less magical.

'I believe I owe you a dance,' Oskar said, holding out his other hand to her.

'But we don't have any music,' she said, giggling as he lifted his hand and spun her in a little circle.

'We don't need music. We only need each other.'

She felt silly to start with, but once they started swaying, it was if they had their own beat, and they stayed like that for what felt like hours, dancing beneath the burnt orange sky, swaying back and forth.

Oskar cradled her against him as she held him close, and when they finally slowed, she tilted her chin to look up at him and their eyes met.

'Your mother is never going to accept me. Did you see the way she looked at me?' she said. 'It doesn't matter what you say or what you want, I'm not the type of girl she wants for you, and I never will be.'

He shook his head, leaning in and kissing her. 'I told my mother you were my girlfriend,' he said. 'I told her that this wasn't just a summer romance, that you meant the world to me and that she'd have to accept you.'

She felt her eyebrows shoot up in surprise. 'You did?'

Oskar nodded. 'I did. I also told her that she was rude and that I expected her to show you the respect you deserve.'

Amalie didn't ask any more questions. Whatever his mother's response had been, she didn't need to know, because what mattered was how Oskar had spoken about her. If he was prepared to stand up for her, to demand his mother respect her, then maybe they did have a fighting chance.

'But I don't want to talk about my mother, Amalie.'

She swallowed, her eyes still on his. 'What do you want to talk about?'

'I want to know if you'll wait for me,' he said. 'I promised my parents that I'd finish my degree, and I'm not going back on my word, but that means leaving you until then. Will you wait until next summer for us to start our life together? I know it's a lot to ask, but I want to finish my studies.'

Her breath shuddered from her lungs. 'Yes, Oskar. I'll wait for you as long as I have to, of course I will.' And she would. For Oskar, she would wait forever.

'I'll have my own money then, and we'll be able to move wherever we want, to have a family of our own,' he said, lifting her hand and kissing her knuckles. 'My parents will come round, I know they will, and until then, it's just you and me.'

She beamed back at him. It was a life she'd been imagining for weeks, him as a pastry chef with his own restaurant, her with a bonny baby who looked just like his father on her hip. All these years she'd dreaded marriage and having to find a suitable man, having to leave her family home and follow the path her sister had already taken, but Oskar had changed everything. All this time she'd never imagined a love match; had hoped to simply find a man who would be kind to her and their children. But now there was Oskar.

'I think we should have a swim to celebrate,' he said, whisking her off her feet and into his arms before she had time to protest, and running to the shore and straight into the water.

Within seconds her white nightgown was soaked through, her hair dripping over her shoulders and down her back, but Amalie couldn't have cared less.

She never remembered being so happy, so *carefree*, in all her life.

Oskar was everything to her. This summer, she'd fallen in love with a boy, and now she couldn't imagine not seeing his face every day. He made her feel happy and loved, warm and content, and even floating in the cold water of the fjord, there was nowhere else she would rather be.

14

PRESENT DAY

Amalie had begun to cry, her hand pressed to her heart as she started to whisper Oskar's name over and over again, and Charlotte found it hard to witness without becoming emotional herself. She'd recounted so much this time, but the joy in telling her story had seemed to fade, her voice cracking as she'd talked about meeting Oskar's family. Charlotte couldn't imagine what it must have felt like to be belittled like that, to truly feel as if you weren't good enough to even breathe the same air as the people whose company you were in. But it meant little to them when they still had no clue who Oskar was and where he fitted into their family story.

'Charlotte, why don't you go and find a nurse? I think we might need something to help calm her down,' her grandmother said.

Charlotte walked quickly into the hall and stopped the first nurse she saw, pointing her towards Amalie's room, but she didn't follow her. Instead, Charlotte leaned against the wall, tipping her head back and taking a moment to close her eyes and process everything Amalie had told them.

No matter what they might have thought, she knew in her

heart that Amalie was telling the story of the greatest love of her life, and she wasn't sure she was ready for what was to come next. Her heart was already breaking for Amalie, and she could see that the more she talked about Oskar, the more painful Amalie seemed to find it. She knew her grandmother was finding it hard to sit there and listen to a part of her own mother's life that she'd never known anything about.

Charlotte didn't know if it was being with the two women or the emotions of it all—perhaps both—but since arriving to see Amalie all she'd been able to think of was something Harrison had said to her about visiting her father before it was too late.

She took a deep breath and pushed off from the wall, taking her phone out of her pocket and staring down at it. Charlotte looked up her father's number, something she hadn't done in years now, and decided to send him a message.

I'm in Oslo and thought it would be nice to meet. Could I come by the house and see you, or we could have lunch? Charlotte

She pressed send before she could change her mind, staring at the screen and immediately seeing little bubbles appear, indicating that he was typing back. But as quickly as they appeared, the bubbles disappeared, and she pushed her phone back into her pocket, telling herself she wouldn't stand around and stare at it, waiting for him. She'd sent the message, she'd reached out, and now it was up to him. She would look at her phone again later.

Charlotte forced her feet to take her back in the direction of Amalie's room, knowing that her grandmother would be wondering where she was, when her phone pinged in her pocket. And, of course, despite her best intentions, she quickly looked to see if it was him.

Lovely to hear from you. Come round tonight if you're free? I'll organise dinner for us.

She took a deep breath. Whether she was ready or not, it was time to see her father again.

When Charlotte arrived on her father's doorstep with a bottle of wine in hand, she felt more like she was going to a dinner party at an acquaintance's house than visiting her family home. She was almost surprised he still lived here and hadn't sold it to buy something smaller, and she realised then that she hadn't even thought to ask him or her grandmother whether he'd moved or not. She just presumed he was still here, or they would have told her otherwise, and she hoped she was right when she lifted her hand to knock.

When the door opened, she stood almost frozen, but he immediately closed the space between them and gave her a hug. It was a little awkward, but she returned it, grateful that he'd been so quick to embrace her.

'Charlotte! It's so good to see you.'

'You, too, Dad,' she murmured into his shoulder, as he slowly released her.

'What brings you back to Oslo?' he asked as he ushered her inside and took her coat.

'A job, actually,' she said. 'Have you seen the new hotel in the city? Down by the water?'

'I certainly have; everyone's talking about it. Stunning architecture, if you ask me.'

Charlotte smiled. She hoped she remembered to tell Harrison that when she saw him next.

'You're here for an interview, or have you already got the job?'

'I've received an offer, but I'm still thinking it over,' she said, glancing around and seeing that much had stayed the same. But things had changed, too. The photos of her and her brother were still placed everywhere, but the sofas and the dining table were new.

A wave of nostalgia hit her as she thought about their old dining table; the little scuff marks on it from when she and her brother hadn't been careful enough; the nights they'd spent eating family dinners. She still had memories of her mum sitting there, entertaining them with stories about what had happened that day and making them all laugh, her father bringing dinner to the table and wondering what was so funny. But that was before.

'So you're still enjoying your cooking?' he asked, taking the wine from her and walking into the kitchen.

Charlotte took a deep breath, forcing herself to stay calm. *Cooking.* He'd always referred to what she did as cooking, as if she pottered away in her kitchen at home. But she was not going to argue with him, not tonight.

'I've actually been offered the role of executive chef at the new hotel,' she said, following him and watching as he poured two glasses of wine. 'It's a pretty big deal.'

When he passed her a glass, his eyes met hers, and she saw something there that she hadn't seen in a very long time.

'I've followed your career, Lotte. I know how successful you've been in London.'

Her eyes widened. 'You have? I presumed that you didn't even know what I was doing. You always refer to it as just *cooking,* so...' She took a sip of her wine.

'I'm impressed with what you've done, and your brother is always regaling me with tales of how wonderful you are. I'm sorry if I didn't use the correct terminology, or it implied I wasn't proud, because it certainly wasn't my intention.'

He couldn't have surprised her more if he'd tried, and a glimmer of hope lit within her.

'That means a lot, more than you can imagine. Thanks, Dad.' Tears prickled her eyes but she blinked them away.

She took a sip and wandered with glass in hand to the table. 'I like what you've done with the place. It's nice.'

'I actually have a lady friend, and she's helped me choose some new things. I never did have much of a flair for interiors.'

Charlotte wasn't surprised he'd met someone, or that she didn't know. 'Well, I'm happy you've met someone. Life's too short to be alone.' She regretted her choice of words the moment they came out of her mouth. 'I'm sorry, that came out wrong, I meant—'

'Your mother left a long time ago, Charlotte. You have nothing to apologise for.'

But that was the problem. She always felt as if she did have something to apologise for. For her mother leaving, for not studying medicine, for leaving Norway, for choosing to return for her mother's funeral. Somehow, it always ended up being her fault, or at least it felt that way.

'You know, I wanted to see you because it's been too long,' she said. 'I couldn't stop thinking that if I didn't see you now...'

'That I might die, and you'd have missed your chance?' her father asked with a laugh.

She sighed, although she did appreciate that he could find the humour in it. From the moment she'd walked in the door, she'd noticed how much older her father seemed. 'If I'm honest, yes, but also there's so much unsaid between us. I suppose my hope is that we don't go another ten years without seeing each other after this.'

He held up his glass of wine, leaning forwards to clink it gently against hers. 'Now that's something to drink to. How about we agree to start afresh? For all the things I should have said or said in error, I wholeheartedly apologise. I love you, Lotte, and I'm just grateful to see you again.'

Charlotte nodded and clinked her glass back, taking another sip, pleased that she'd brought such a nice bottle with her.

'May I ask you something, though?' she said, hoping she wouldn't regret it. 'Because if I don't, I feel like it will always be unresolved between us.'

'Of course.'

'Why could you not accept my decision to become a chef? Was it truly such a terrible choice of career?' she asked. 'Your reaction felt akin to me announcing I wanted to become an adult entertainer or a circus performer.'

'Charlotte, if I'm honest, it had nothing to do with you wanting to be a chef.'

She sat back and listened. It was a question she'd wanted to ask him for so long, one she'd turned over and over in her mind, and she wanted to hear him out. To truly listen to him rather than bristle at whatever came out of his mouth next.

'When your mother left, I suppose it felt as if the only way of keeping you and your brother close was to take charge of everything that happened after that point. I thought that if you both just followed the path I'd set for you, if I could just have you do what I planned, that I would have some semblance of control over our lives, to stop anything else painful from happening to our family. That I wouldn't lose you, too.'

His words washed over her, and she closed her eyes for a beat as they sank in. 'It truly had nothing to do with me being a chef? It wouldn't have mattered if I wanted to be a lawyer or an architect?'

'I'm embarrassed to admit it, but it's true,' he said. 'I've spent years questioning myself, wishing I'd handled things differently, but you were a young woman determined to forge your own way in the world, and that scared me.' Her father shook his head, sadness bracketing his face. 'My greatest fear was losing you, and yet look what I managed to do.'

'Why didn't you reach out? Why has it taken me coming

home for you to tell me all this?' she asked, trying to stay calm even as her temper flared. 'We've missed out on years, Dad. All this time we could have had a relationship, and even when I came home for Mum's funeral...'

The silence stretched between them. 'I couldn't understand why you came,' he said. 'After what she did to us, the way she broke up our family, the pain she caused, the way she left us. I couldn't come to terms with how you forgave her.'

'Dad, you should have just asked me, because I *never* forgave her. I hated her for what she did to us, but she was still my mother. Who would I have been if I didn't come back? If I didn't attend her funeral? I was worried I wouldn't be able to live with myself if I didn't, and I didn't want to take that chance.'

Her father stood then, and she pretended she didn't notice the way his voice had choked up or the tears she'd seen shining in his eyes. 'I think we might need the rest of the bottle,' he said, gruffly. 'For a man not used to talking about his emotions, this is turning into quite the evening.'

Charlotte laughed despite it all, and then so did he, and when he returned with the bottle she stood and gave him a hug. It was awkward and more of a pat on the back, neither of them really knowing what to do, but it still felt like a step in the right direction. She decided not to confront her dad about the years after her mother had left, about how she still felt as if she'd lost the father she'd loved then, too; that conversation could wait for another day. Bringing it up now wasn't going to change anything, but trying to enjoy his company might change everything.

'Should we catch up on the last few years?' her father asked her. 'I hear a little from your grandmother about where you are and what you're doing, but it'd be nice to hear it from you.'

Charlotte settled into her chair, her eye landing on a photo of her with her brother from their teenage years, his arm protectively around her. *He would love seeing me here, knowing that I'd finally come back to the house.*

She turned to her dad, and this time, her smile came easily. 'Where should I start?'

The next afternoon, as Charlotte waited in the lobby of the hotel for Harrison, she felt lighter somehow, and she knew that her reconciliation with her father was the reason. There were parts of their evening that had felt uncomfortable, but there were also parts that had felt more than nice, so she was chalking it up as a win. And her grandmother's face when she'd told her the news over coffee that morning had made it all worth it.

'There she is.'

Harrison's voice made her turn, and the moment she saw him walking towards her, she realised how much she'd been looking forward to seeing him. He was dressed in what appeared to be a similar outfit to the other day—perhaps his uniform—of dark jeans, a black T-shirt this time and slightly scuffed boots, but this time he also had a coat over his shoulders.

'Where are you taking me?' he asked.

Charlotte stepped forwards and kissed his cheek, inhaling the faint citrus scent of his cologne.

'We're exploring as much as we can in the time we have,' she said. 'First, we're going to have a quick lunch, and then we're driving to Tønsberg. It's Norway's oldest town, and you'll be able to admire the views on the way as we drive south.'

'Will I finally be seeing a fjord?' he asked.

'You will,' she said. 'I promise that you'll enjoy the scenery, too.'

They fell into step side by side, with Harrison only breaking their stride when he opened the main heavy glass door for her.

'So tell me, have you thought any more about Daniel's offer?'

She laughed. 'I thought you'd at least wait until we'd ordered lunch before asking.'

'If I'm honest, Daniel found out I was meeting you, and he's expecting me to pass on some insider knowledge.'

'Well, in that case, you can tell him that his offer was very generous, and that I sent it to my lawyer,' she said. 'I'm tempted by it, truly I am, but I need another day to think it over. If the offer was in London, I'd have said yes already, but there's more than just the restaurant to consider here.'

Harrison nodded, and she could tell he understood.

'But, and it's a big but,' she said, glancing over at him. 'I followed your advice and went to see my father.'

'And?'

'It was the best thing I could have done, and I have you to thank,' Charlotte told him. 'I'd become so consumed by the past when it came to reconciling, but it was worth it. So, thank you.'

'You're very welcome.'

She pointed to her rental car across the street and when they were both seated, she turned to him. 'So, what did you do yesterday while I was consumed by family matters? Were you in meetings all day?'

'Ahh, not as such. I actually had some personal matters to attend to.'

'All okay?' she asked, frowning at the look on his face. He suddenly looked as if all the colour had drained from his cheeks, and she hoped that he was feeling all right.

'It will be, and exploring today is just what I need to take my mind off things.'

'Then let's go,' she said, pulling out into the traffic, not about to make him uncomfortable by asking further questions. 'My favourite little café isn't far from here, and then once we've eaten we can head farther afield.'

'Tell me, how's it going with your great-grandmother? Have you discovered any more family secrets?' Harrison asked.

'I think we have more questions than answers, but she's still talking, so that's what matters.' Charlotte quickly looked over at him and found that he was watching her, which made her grip the steering wheel and focus her eyes on the road. She hadn't thought about being in such a small space with him, or about keeping the conversation going for the 100 kilometres or so it would take them to get to their destination. 'Are you close to your family?'

'Yes,' he said, without hesitation. 'We're very close, but my sisters are busy raising families, so it tends to be a very hectic gathering when we all get together.'

'They haven't been tempted to visit you here?'

'No, but I actually have friends arriving tomorrow, Luke and Louisa,' he said. 'They fly in tomorrow afternoon.'

Charlotte couldn't resist the urge to glance at him again. 'How long are they here for?'

'Just a few days for our annual get-together. I'm looking forward to seeing them.'

'Why don't you let me cook for you all while they're here? Unless you already have plans, that is?' Charlotte asked. 'I want to work in the kitchen one more time, to try out the mains I'm planning. When I accept...' She stopped talking, realising her error one word too late.

'You're going to accept the position?'

Charlotte groaned. 'I didn't mean that to slip out, but I am seriously considering it, especially given the shorter initial term. And if I do, I want to have a sample menu to show Daniel. I want him to know how much thought I've put into this, and I want to hit the ground running when it comes to recruiting the very best chefs to work with me. I'm even thinking of doing a special tasting for some influential locals, to show them what they can expect when visiting the hotel.'

'You've put a lot of thought into this already,' Harrison said. 'I'm impressed.'

'Well, just don't tell Daniel yet, because I still have to think about it and see what my lawyer says about the contract. But invite your friends, spend time sampling the food and giving me feedback, and if it goes well, fingers crossed I'll be able to accept.'

Harrison's eyes met hers once she'd pulled into the car park near the café.

'Deal,' he said. 'But be warned, my friends can be a lot. And they drink wine like it's their last night on earth.'

'I promise I can handle them,' she said, feeling a familiar warmth between them, which diffused as soon as Harrison opened his door. It was almost as if the moment he felt it, he quickly put distance between them, although she was certain she was just imagining it.

'Okay, a quick bite to eat and a coffee to go, then we're on the road again.'

15

'You know, I don't think I realised how much I needed this,' Harrison said as they stretched their legs and began to stroll. 'This project has taken everything out of me.'

'I know the feeling,' Charlotte said. 'This is the very first time I've finished one job and not had another to dive straight into. I'm not used to building in downtime.'

'Which means that if you take the position at the hotel...'

'That I won't be breaking with tradition,' she finished for him. 'A few days' break is more than I've had before, though, so I wouldn't be complaining.'

'Not what I was thinking, but sure. I'm not the right person to talk you down off that ledge, trust me.'

'Do you know much about the Vikings?' Charlotte asked, looking out at the water as they walked. She'd always loved staring out at the horizon as a girl and imagining what it must have been like, seeing the Viking ships as they sailed home, or perhaps as they left, the mist in the air as the hull disappeared from sight.

'Other than from what I've seen in TV shows, not really,' he replied.

'In the harbour there, you can see a replica of the Viking Oseberg ship. The original is displayed in the Slottsfjell Museum,' she told him. 'The history here is very special, something I've always held dear to my heart, anyway.'

'Speaking of history, have you mentioned what your great-grandmother has told you to your father? Could he shed any light on it at all?'

'Perhaps. But I feel like we're only just finding our way with each other, so I didn't really talk to him about it,' she said. 'It's actually my grandmother who I think could hold at least some of the answers to our questions, though. She's had me up in the attic taking down old photo albums and boxes of old clothes and mementos, almost as if she's convinced that she'll find something in storage that will give us the answers we need.'

'What do you think?'

She stared out at the horizon again and, before she could think about it, gave Harrison her most honest answer. 'I think we're on the cusp of discovering something in our family's past that has the power to divide us, just when I'm finally finding my footing with my father again.'

'Could it not draw you all closer together? Maybe it's not as sinister as you think it might be.'

Charlotte shrugged and pointed ahead. 'I hope you're right. But enough about my family dramas—it's time to start exploring. It's not a very big town, but there's still lots to see.'

They fell into step again and Charlotte felt as if she was seeing everything through fresh eyes with Harrison. It helped that it had been so long since she'd been there as well—a walk down memory lane at the same time as feeling new.

'You know, my mum used to bring us here,' Charlotte told him. 'My father worked long hours at times, so my mum was always taking us on little day trips. The only place I remember my father coming with us was to the hotel at Sognefjord.'

'Sognefjord?' Harrison repeated.

'It's the place Amalie keeps talking about when she disappears into the past,' Charlotte told him. 'It's strange that the one place she keeps revisiting in her mind is the one I keep visiting, too. For me, it was the last time I remember my family being happy, that I can see my mum smiling in my mind and my dad laughing as we splashed him with water. It's the best and only proper holiday we ever had. That I've *ever* really had.'

Harrison stopped walking, and she recognised the look on his face, because she'd seen it so many times before. It was pity. The same look everyone had given her after her mother had disappeared.

'I'm sorry, I—'

'Don't,' she said, holding up her hand. 'It was a very long time ago and I don't want anyone, least of all you, feeling—'

'Pity for you?'

Her eyebrows shot up. 'How did you know?'

'Trust me when I say that I know the look well, and that's not what I was going to say, or what I was feeling towards you.' Harrison's voice was gentle without being patronising. 'I was just going to say that I'm sorry it's the only nice memory you have, but maybe it's better than having no good memories at all. It took me a long time to really understand that, but a friend made me see that any happy memory should be a positive, not a negative.'

He was right. Boy, was he right. She wouldn't have given up that one lovely memory for anything, even though she had cried over it night after night when her mother had gone.

'Do you see down there? They're working on another replica ship. Shall we go down and take a look?'

'Lead the way,' Harrison said. 'I'm all yours.'

Charlotte grinned and placed her hand to his back to guide him, surprised when he stiffened beneath her touch. But when he glanced back over his shoulder at her and smiled, she wondered if she'd imagined it again, because he certainly looked relaxed now.

'Harrison, when did you say your friends were arriving?'

'Tomorrow afternoon.'

'I think I'm going to have to come up with a list of all the touristy things you need to do with them,' Charlotte said, looping her hand through his arm without thinking, tugging him along with her. 'I'm not letting you leave Norway without seeing the sights. A couple of Viking ships are definitely not enough.'

Harrison cleared his throat, and when he glanced down at her, she felt that familiar flicker between them. But as soon as his gaze dipped and landed on her mouth, her lips parted, he pulled away, and she was left wondering all over again why the gorgeous, presumably single man beside her was running so hot and cold.

16

THE MAJESTETISK HOTEL, SOGNEFJORD, NORWAY, 1950

Amalie had butterflies in her stomach as she walked beside Oskar. He was holding her hand, which was the only thing stopping her from running in the opposite direction. She couldn't stop thinking about the last time she'd met his mother, and although she'd begged Oskar not to bring her this time, he'd insisted. He didn't want to hide her, and although Amalie loved him for that, she wasn't convinced that it was even worth trying when it came to his parents.

'Just keep smiling,' Oskar whispered as they neared the table. 'You deserve to be here—don't let them make you feel that you don't, no matter what is said.'

But her smile had already begun to falter when she saw that the table was only set for three. She hesitated, trying to pull away from Oskar, but his grip on her hand was firm.

'Everything will be fine,' Oskar murmured, leaning in slightly so that his words were only for her. 'All you have to do is trust me.'

His father rose when they approached the table, and a little something inside of Amalie flickered with recognition. He was an older version of Oskar, albeit one with flecks of grey peppered through the sides of his otherwise dark hair.

'Father, I'd like you to meet Amalie,' Oskar said, shaking his father's hand before gesturing to her.

His father at least gave her the courtesy of a smile. 'Pleased to meet you, Amalie,' he said. 'Unfortunately, this is a family dinner, but perhaps—'

She glanced at his mother as Oskar interrupted.

'I booked the table for four this evening,' Oskar said, before waving out to one of the waiters. 'We'll need another place set, when you have a moment.'

Amalie watched as Oskar faced his father, his stature defiant but his demeanour friendly. 'It's very important to me that Amalie joins us.'

His father cleared his throat, but as if on second thoughts, nodded. 'Of course. Please excuse me, Amalie, I expected to discuss family matters tonight and wasn't aware you'd be joining us.'

A lie, she was certain, but she smiled politely and took the seat that Oskar pulled out for her. He sat beside her, his hand comfortingly on her knee as he spoke to his mother.

'Amalie and I met soon after I arrived here,' Oskar said. 'I thought I'd have to bring her home to meet you both, but I'm pleased it was able to happen sooner.'

His mother finally looked at her, and Amalie felt like a spotlight was shining on her. 'Amalie, it isn't that we didn't expect our son to have a summer fling while he was here—it's best for young men to get these things out of their system while they're young and carefree, after all. I just didn't expect to have to meet the object of his lust.'

Amalie froze, her eyes widening as she realised what this woman had just said to her. She may as well have slapped her, she was so shocked.

'Don't you *dare* speak to her like that again,' Oskar said, his voice rising. 'Amalie deserves your respect.'

His mother raised an eyebrow and smiled, shaking her head as if the entire situation was somehow amusing to her.

'And what, precisely, will you do if your mother doesn't heed your words?' Oskar's father asked, taking a sip of an amber-coloured drink that Amalie presumed was whisky. She wasn't much of a drinker, but she almost wished for a whisky of her own. 'It sounded very much like a threat, son, if I'm not mistaken.'

Oskar was silent then, and Amalie spoke, filling the ominous silence between them all. 'If my presence makes you uncomfortable, I'll go,' she said, lifting her gaze and looking first at his father, then his mother. 'I love your son very much, and I respect you as his parents, so please, if—'

'Enough!' Oskar muttered, taking her hand again. 'I have spent the most magical summer with Amalie, and all I wanted was for you to show her a little respect for one night. Is that too much to ask? Because all my life you've told me to show gratitude and respect, to behave politely and understand my place in the world, and yet you, Mother, you're behaving like a petulant child.'

His mother looked as if she'd sucked a lemon, her face sour as she stared at her son. But it was his father who settled everything, his gaze never wavering.

'Oskar, you're right,' he said. 'Amalie, I owe you an apology. A friend of Oskar's is a friend of ours. Let me order you both a drink and then we can look over the menu.'

His mother was still silent, but something inside Amalie softened. It wasn't acceptance, but it was something, and if she could win over his father then she might just have a chance.

'Sir, I'd like to commend you on your hotel,' she said. 'It's the most beautiful I've ever seen, and the guests here are always commenting on what a wonderful stay they've had.'

His smile seemed genuine, but all he gave her was a nod, before going back to studying the menu.

'Oskar has gathered quite the name for himself in the kitchen,' she continued, undeterred. 'His desserts really are something.'

'I'm pleased he's enjoying this last summer here,' his father said. 'Next summer he'll be interning at my office, so he'll have to find a wife to cook for him. There'll be no time for being in a kitchen once he's a businessman.'

Amalie held her tongue and looked down at her plate, feeling the anger radiating from Oskar beside her. Her heart broke for him.

'I've already told the kitchen staff that I'll be back next summer. Father, this is my—'

'Passion?' His father laughed. 'Son, this is a *hobby*. Men like us don't spend our lives toiling away in a kitchen.'

'I told you we shouldn't have indulged him like this.' His mother finally spoke, finishing her drink and staring at Amalie. 'He should have worked for you all summer instead of—'

'Enough,' Oskar said, quietly but with enough force to stop them both. Everyone at the table had turned to face him. 'We can discuss all this later. I suggest that I order for us all, and that we change the subject to something less heated for the sake of not causing a scene.'

His father nodded, but the look his mother gave Amalie told her that nothing would ever change the woman's opinion of her. When she glanced over at Oskar, she could sense that he was still hopeful, and his hand on her knee beneath the table reminded her that he cared enough for her to bring her to dinner, to at least try when it came to his family.

Even if she did think that there was nothing his mother wouldn't do to keep them apart.

Their entrées arrived soon enough, but Amalie found that her stomach clenched the moment she smelt the *stekt* fish in front of her. *It's only nerves, you'll be fine*, she told herself. But the moment she had a small mouthful she knew it wasn't sitting right with her.

'Please excuse me,' she said, placing her napkin on the table and forcing herself to walk as sedately as possible.

She could usually eat anything, and fish had always been one of her favourites, but his family had clearly done more than twist her stomach into knots, and when she reached the restroom she only just made it to the stall before being violently unwell.

Amalie had kept her distance from Oskar since dinner, and thankfully the hotel had been so busy she'd been fully occupied with work, but once his family left, they finally had time to be together without being under his mother's watchful eye. Oskar stopped rowing the boat, his oars gliding through the crisp blue water one final time before he set them down, and Amalie wriggled backwards and let her head fall to his chest. She listened to the steady beat of his heart, sighing when his arms came around her. She'd waited all day for this.

Amalie was at her happiest when it was just the two of them, surrounded by the beauty of the fjord, wrapped safely in Oskar's embrace. Usually she loved the silence; but today, the secret she'd been keeping pressed on her chest, an invisible weight that she couldn't keep hidden any longer. All day she'd wrestled with whether to tell him or not, but now they were together again, she knew there was no keeping it from him. It was his news as much as hers. *I don't want to have secrets between us. I need him to know.*

'You're very quiet today,' Oskar said.

She tucked herself even closer to him, tears stinging her eyes when his lips pressed against her head. Oskar ran his fingers gently through her long hair as she fought for the right words, as her secret tightened inside of her.

'Amalie? What's wrong? Is it my family, because I've made it abundantly clear that—'

Amalie took a deep breath, before her words came out in a sudden gasp. 'Oskar, I'm pregnant.'

The words clung to the silence around them, echoing in Amalie's mind as she wished she could take them back, that she'd kept the secret to herself a little longer. But Oskar only held her tighter as she began to cry, tears slipping one after the other down her cheeks until she was powerless to stop them.

'Don't cry. Please don't cry,' he said, turning her so that she faced him, his eyes meeting hers as he gently smoothed his thumb across her cheek, wiping away her tears. 'Everything will be all right, I promise.'

'But how can it be?' she whispered, searching his face. 'Your parents will never accept me, they've made that clear, and mine—'

'I love you, Amalie, and that's all that matters,' he whispered back, his lips meeting hers in a kiss so soft, so impossibly gentle, that it took her breath away.

When she finally pulled back, Oskar touched his forehead to hers.

'I promise I'll take care of you. We'll marry quickly, in autumn, before anyone can find out. There's nothing to be afraid of.'

Tears filled her eyes again, because as much as she believed his earnestly spoken words, as much as she knew that he'd do anything to protect her, she was no fool. No matter how much they wanted to be together, no matter the dreams they'd shared, their future wasn't theirs alone. Not to mention they'd had a plan: they were supposed to wait until next summer, until he'd finished university, and he was free to choose his own path.

'Oskar, your parents will never let us marry. We're from different worlds, it could never—'

Her voice caught as his hands cupped her face, as his eyes met hers.

'I would give up everything for you. I love you, Amalie, and no one will stop me from making you my wife, not even my parents. Will you marry me?'

Amalie gazed back into the eyes of the man she loved, and hoped with all her heart that it would be enough. If they were to marry, he'd have to give up so much, leave behind the life he'd always known to walk his own path, if his family didn't accept her or the baby. Once they were married, there was little his parents could do, but they could certainly cut him off financially.

'Amalie,' he said. 'Will you marry me?'

'Yes,' she whispered back. 'Yes, Oskar, I will marry you.'

'We're going to be parents,' he whispered, his palm covering her stomach, which was still flat and taut, not showing any signs of the life growing inside of her. 'You'll be the most beautiful mother, I can already see you cradling our baby in your arms.'

Oskar kissed her, his hand stroking her hair as his lips tenderly met hers, the boat rocking gently from side to side beneath them.

Maybe dreams do come true.

'There's nothing to be scared of, Amalie. It's just you and me against the world.'

17

PRESENT DAY

For someone who'd dreaded coming home, Charlotte had to confess that nothing about being back had played out as she'd expected. Harrison had been a very pleasant distraction, and despite wondering if she was crazy offering to entertain his friends, it had proved to be a good decision. They were as fun and easy-going as he'd promised, although he hadn't exaggerated about their wine consumption.

'Something smells amazing,' Harrison said.

She glanced up to see that he'd come over to join her. Charlotte had asked Daniel if she could move a table into the kitchen to see how it might work, and her chef's table idea had immediately come to life.

'I was going to try out a few main dishes on you all, but I decided to do a full chef's evening experience instead, to see how the timing might work if my idea comes to fruition.'

'Well, I'm loving the idea so far. It's nice to be enjoying this hotel rather than worrying about it.'

Harrison seemed more relaxed tonight, which she imagined had a lot to do with having his friends close.

'Go and enjoy seeing them, I'm sure they've missed you.'

Harrison was watching her, and she looked up, her hands hovering over the plate. 'You're making me nervous. Go, sit, enjoy,' she said.

Harrison did as he was told, and soon she was carrying the first course over to the table, placing a selection of plates in the centre. She'd worked all day in the kitchen, and there was nothing quite like seeing all her hard work rewarded.

'These are all made to share, so please taste a little of every-thing, and don't forget to be honest with me. I'm not lying when I say that I genuinely want your feedback.'

'Charlotte, this is amazing! Harrison wasn't joking when he said he'd met the best chef in Norway,' his friend Louisa said. 'I love the salmon.'

'Please, can't you sit with us?' Luke asked, gesturing for her to take the empty chair between him and Harrison.

'I'll sit once I have the main courses served,' she said, watching them all for a moment and swelling with pride as she listened to their comments after tasting each dish. 'There's a lot more to go before I can relax.'

She'd always been that way—little tastes of each course to make sure she was happy with flavours, but there was never any relaxing until she was finished for the night, not even a quick bite if she was starving hungry. Charlotte liked to give her abso-lute attention to what she was doing, and usually it wasn't until afterwards that she'd realise how thoroughly she'd neglected herself.

She listened to their laughter, hearing Luke tease Harrison about something, and it reminded her of how isolated she'd become lately. She'd been so focused on her career that her life had become work, and other than seeing her brother most week-ends for a drink or dinner, she barely even had a social life outside of the kitchen.

Charlotte tossed the kitchen towel over her shoulder and turned her attention back to the food she'd already prepared that was in front of her. She had a leg of lamb in the oven, a side of salmon still to cook and sides to finish assembling, and as she listened to them raving about her dishes, a sense of calm settled over her. But it also made her wonder about something Amalie had said, about her Oskar and his passion for cooking, about what he'd been prepared to give up in order to follow his heart. And she couldn't help but see the similarities in her own life and wonder if there was somehow a connection.

She'd been prepared to turn her back on everything to follow her dreams, and when she went over everything Amalie had shared, Charlotte found herself still trying to grasp how this Oskar fitted into their lives, and why she felt so oddly connected to him. She knew it was probably the fact that he dreamed of becoming a chef, just like her, but still, there was something about their story that she felt a deep connection with.

Her grandmother had gone deathly pale after their last session with Amalie, the pregnancy news coming as a shock to both her and her grandmother. But Amalie had become agitated when they'd asked if she was certain she wasn't misremembering things, and the nurses had had to come and settle her, even suggesting that whatever they were coming to talk to her about every day was beginning to upset her more and more.

'You look lost in thought.'

Charlotte turned, narrowly avoiding burning her hand when she misjudged the handle she reached out for. She secured the towel more carefully around it and took the salmon off the heat before acknowledging Harrison—that was a rookie mistake, and she'd have been furious if she'd seriously burnt her hand.

'I was actually just thinking about Amalie. I saw her again this morning.'

'Any more answers about how everything ties together?'

She shook her head, not taking her eyes off what she was doing as she plated the salmon and dressed it, wiping the edge of the plate and passing it to Harrison only once she was certain it looked perfect.

'I'm honestly starting to wonder if we shouldn't just let sleeping dogs lie,' she said, waving him away with the plate. 'She said something along the lines of how some things aren't supposed to stay secret when I first showed her the box, but that might not be the case. I'm happy I came back, but part of me wonders whether we shouldn't have just ignored the clues and pretended they didn't exist, given how she's reacted to it all.'

Charlotte watched as Harrison placed the plate on the table then turned back to her, but she waved him away again as soon as he came back.

'Sit, eat! I'll finish up here and come and join you shortly.'

Harrison hesitated, as if he didn't want to eat without her.

'I'm the chef, I'm not supposed to be at the table,' she said. 'But I promise I'll join you soon. I'm looking forward to an end-of-service glass of wine.'

He seemed to accept her reply and rejoined his friends, and she realised that she *was* actually looking forward to sitting down with a glass of wine, trying some of her own food and just enjoying the company of others.

When she finally joined them some time later, Charlotte was delighted to see that they'd barely left a bite of food, and she happily let Harrison fill her glass. She'd kept aside a plate for herself, and she began eating while listening to the friends talk, happy to be the observer rather than the centre of attention. But that changed the minute she finished eating. Louisa turned to Charlotte as she dabbed the corners of her mouth with a napkin.

'So, I want to know how you two met,' Louisa asked. 'From what Harrison's told us, you're almost a fully fledged Londoner.'

'Ha, well, I suppose you could say that. London has a way

of making you fall in love, and I do see it as my home now, or at least I did until very recently.' She grinned. 'I love my family, but I've found it can be good to have some distance.'

'I think that's why Harrison came here,' Luke said. 'He was running away from his family, and by family, I mean us.'

'We've known each other since—'

'Okay, enough talking about us,' Harrison said, interrupting Louisa and giving her a sharp look that Charlotte couldn't decipher. 'How about we talk about what sights you're going to see while you're here? I'm sure our host has plenty of recommendations.'

Charlotte took another sip of her wine, looking between them and seeing that there was definitely some tension linked to whatever Louisa had been about to say.

'Well, I would recommend the MUNCH museum to see the Edvard Munch art exhibition, and the Viking Ship Museum, too. It's hard to explain what it's like to see a ship from the 9th century until you've actually stood there and looked at it with your own eyes,' Charlotte said. 'You could book a cruise on the Oslo fjord, and I have some great walks I could recommend, if you feel like being active.'

'All of the above, except perhaps the walking,' Louisa said with a conspiratorial grin. 'Harrison, you'll be our tour guide? Please tell us you'll be joining us on our adventures?'

'Ahh, I'll think about it,' he said, before excusing himself to go to the restroom, calling back over his shoulder, 'Although you're talking about the guy who's been here for months and has barely seen any sights!'

Charlotte watched Harrison walk away and found she couldn't stop smiling. He'd been unfailingly good company, and she didn't know what it was, but she felt different when she was with him. The fact that he seemed to love her food helped, but it was more than that—she'd been alone for such a long time, so focused on work—but he was making her wonder what it would be like to have someone special in her life. Although there was that little matter of him putting distance between them every time they got close, which told her that she was either way off the mark in thinking he was attracted to her, or that there was something else holding him back. Or maybe she'd just forgotten how to flirt and was somehow getting it all wrong.

She turned to the couple seated at the table across from her, and she rose to retrieve the bottle of wine she'd left on the kitchen counter, seeing that they both needed another top-up. The night had been a wonderful success, and seeing the way they'd all reacted to her menu had helped her to make her decision. She was going to say yes to Daniel about the job. Perhaps she was always going to accept, but this was the first time she hadn't sought her brother's approval before making a big decision, and it felt good.

'You know, we didn't expect him to be in such good spirits today,' Louisa said as Charlotte joined them at the table. 'It's nice to see him happy again.'

'Lou,' Luke said, shaking his head.

'I can imagine it's been very stressful for him, but hopefully once the hotel opens...' Charlotte stopped talking. There was something about the look they were both giving her that told her she was wrong, that they knew something she didn't. 'Why are you looking at me like that? What have I missed?'

'That's not,' Luke started, before clearing his throat and looking to his wife. 'It's not our place, Lou. Just leave it.'

'He hasn't told you?' Louisa asked, seeming to ignore her husband.

Charlotte's brow furrowed as she looked between the couple seated across from her. 'Told me what?'

They exchanged looks, which only made her feel even more unsettled than she already was. What exactly did they expect him to have told her?

'If you're trying to make me feel confused, you're doing a great job, because I truly don't know what you're talking about.'

'Charlotte,' Louisa said, gently, as if she was the bearer of bad news. 'Harrison's wife, Elly, passed away two years ago. The day before yesterday was the anniversary of her death. It's why we're here.'

She finally understood the true meaning of wishing the ground would open up and swallow her. A line of sweat beaded across Charlotte's upper lip and her entire body felt clammy as she digested the news. *This was the reason for the annual trip? This is the personal matter he was referring to from the day before?* So, it hadn't been her flirting that had been off, it was the fact that he was a widower. 'I'm sorry—he, Harrison,' she cleared her throat, trying to straighten it all out in her mind. 'He had a *wife?*'

Charlotte wished her voice didn't sound quite so high-pitched, but the surprise news seemed to have stolen her usual deeper tone. Why wouldn't he have told her? Why would he have kept something like that a secret from her when she'd told him so much about her own family? He'd encouraged her to open up, but she could see now that he'd barely told her anything, that she knew scarcely anything about him personally.

'Elly was my best friend,' Louisa said, her voice cracking slightly as she took a big breath. 'I was bridesmaid at their wedding, and we promised Elly before she died that we'd never let Harrison be alone on the anniversary of her death, that we'd do anything to make sure we were all together, especially for his sake.'

'This year is easier than last year,' said Luke. We were surprised to see how well he's doing, and we wondered...'

'No,' Charlotte said, firmly, realising what he was hinting at. 'We're colleagues, acquaintances, whatever you want to call it, but there's nothing romantic, we're not...' She stopped talking.

Why was everything always so complicated? 'We've been getting to know each other, that's all.'

'If you were,' Louisa said carefully, as if she was trying to coax a small child to do something they didn't want to do, 'it would make us happy. Don't think it wouldn't, because I'm telling the truth when I say that all we want is to see Harrison's smile come back. If you're the person who does that, then we'll love you for it.'

Charlotte let Luke pour her a little more wine and she took a grateful sip, trying to process what they'd just told her.

'What happened?' Charlotte asked, realising that everything suddenly made sense now. The way he'd encouraged her to see her father, the hesitation for anything to happen between them, the way his expression always changed when they'd talked about loss or family. It had been there; she just hadn't taken the time to piece it all together. 'May I ask how she died?'

'Elly had brain cancer,' Louisa said. 'They thought she'd beaten it, but when it came back, she only had a few months, and then she was gone. She chose not to have any more surgery, but to just live for the moment and enjoy what little time she had left.'

'We'd all been friends since we were first dating. There was no Luke and Louisa without Harrison and Elly, so we go back a long way,' Luke told her. 'We think he took this job to get away from London and all the memories there. It's been great seeing him immersed in a project, and I think the change has been good for him. Honestly, when he told us he had plans for us tonight, we couldn't believe it.'

'Right,' Charlotte said, feeling completely out of her depth, not to mention extremely uncomfortable. Her hands were still clammy and she had the most overwhelming feeling that she was going to be sick. 'Well, I'm pleased you're here for him. It shows what good friends he has.'

When she looked up and saw that Harrison was headed

back towards them, she rose, not wanting to be sitting there when he came back. She'd single-handedly inserted herself into their annual anniversary get-together by inviting them for dinner, not having any idea what a special occasion it was, and now she had no idea how she was even going to look at him without bursting into tears. *He had a wife.* Here she'd been, dreaming of a summer fling with the man, and he was grieving his wife and probably wishing she'd stop flirting with him and leave him the hell alone.

'Don't walk away,' Louisa said, catching her around the wrist and holding her there. 'It should have been Harrison telling you, not me, but for what it's worth, this is the first time I've seen him happy in a long time. If I was to guess, I'd say that he didn't tell you, or maybe anyone here, about what he'd been through, because it gave him the chance of a fresh start. Everyone back home knows what happened and it all got too much for him. He particularly hated the looks of pity everyone gave him.'

So that's why he'd understood why I didn't like that look. He was used to being on the receiving end of it himself.

Charlotte hesitated, her heart sinking when she saw the big smile Harrison gave her as he walked towards them. *He doesn't know I know, and he doesn't need to know.* Louisa was right, it should have been him telling her, and she respected him enough not to ruin the evening. She took a deep breath, refusing to run away even though she wanted to.

'Please,' Louisa said, 'just, just give him a chance to tell you himself. He will have had his reasons for keeping it a secret, but I know he won't keep it from you forever.'

Charlotte met her gaze, knowing she was right but finding it hard to stay seated anyway.

'Maybe he just didn't want to be the guy whose wife died, for once,' Louisa whispered. 'Please, let him be that man, at least for tonight.'

Charlotte quickly turned and dabbed at her eyes, not wanting him to see her tears.

Harrison sat down. 'So, what did I miss? And also, how is that entire bottle of wine gone? That's our third one!'

Louisa looked at Charlotte, and she forced a smile, not able to resist a glance at Harrison's ring finger, wondering if she'd missed a mark where his wedding band had once sat and knowing immediately how silly that was. She quickly lifted her gaze.

'I was, er, just telling these two that I've decided to take the job,' Charlotte lied, hoping her voice didn't sound forced. 'I love it here. Being back, this kitchen, the hotel.' She sighed, hating that she was feeling so emotional. She brushed another tear from the corner of her eye before it could escape, only this time she didn't have to hide it, because she knew he'd presume that it was related to the job. 'You know, if I could tell the little girl in me that she would be standing in a kitchen like this one day, that she would have creative control of designing a menu from scratch as executive chef? I don't think she'd believe me. Part of me still doesn't.'

Charlotte hoped that her emotions were disguised behind her words, and Harrison certainly didn't seem to think that anything was amiss as he held up his glass.

'To the new executive chef of Nordic Hotel Oslo,' he said.

The others toasted her as Charlotte took a sip of her drink and then excused herself, intending on bringing out the dessert that she'd forgotten about. She'd been so eager to get to the table, not to mention that desserts weren't her forte; but still, she didn't want them to leave without a little something sweet to finish the evening with.

'Hey,' came a voice from behind, followed by a warm hand on her shoulder. 'Is everything all right? I know this must feel like a big decision for you.'

She nodded and cleared her throat. 'Of course. I just, it's a lot. I'm sorry about my little emotional outburst.' Charlotte didn't want to turn around and she most definitely didn't want to look at him, but instead of keeping his usual distance between them, Harrison caught her hand.

'You deserve this, Charlotte. If you're doubting yourself, don't,' he said, his fingers squeezing gently against hers. 'I know how I felt when I was offered this project. It would have been so easy to tell myself I couldn't do it, but it's become the highlight of my career, and I know you'll feel the same way about this job. Sometimes things just happen, opportunities present themselves, just when we need them.'

She forced another smile, but in truth all she could think about was the way he was touching her, especially in the light of what she now knew.

'May I play sous chef and help you with dessert?' he asked, his eyebrows waggling and making her laugh. She hadn't seen this playful side of him before, and she liked it, although part of her wondered if it was the two bottles of wine he and his friends had consumed.

'It's just a very simple Kvæfjord cake,' she said. 'Have you had one before?'

Harrison shook his head. 'I can't say I have, but then I've been woefully inept at learning your language while I'm here, so I may well have eaten it without recalling the name.'

'It's what you would call a sponge cake, with meringue, vanilla cream and almonds,' she said. 'We call it the world's best cake, and it was seeing my great-grandmother that reminded me of it. When I was very young, Amalie used to make it on special occasions for us. My brother and I always asked for it on our birthdays, and I'll never forget when my mother left, Amalie turned up with this cake.' Charlotte turned around and took the lid off the cake stand so Harrison could see it. 'She came every Sunday with one after that, and even though my father told her to stop, she kept doing it for years, almost as if it was her way of showing us how much she loved us.'

'Is that where you get your love of cooking from?' he asked.

Charlotte laughed as she took a knife and cut the first slice of cake. 'Most definitely not. I think she spent her entire life perfecting her cake, but she had very little interest in cooking meals. We always joked that she hated being in the kitchen, which was unusual for a woman of her generation, and I have to confess that my first hire will be a pastry or dessert chef.'

Harrison reached over and swiped the first slice, immediately sliding his fork in and tasting it.

'This is great,' he said, his eyes widening as he went back for another mouthful. 'I don't think you're giving yourself enough credit.'

She laughed and dished up three more plates. 'This is the kind of cake I'd serve at home to dinner party guests. I'm not sure it's refined enough to serve here, although perhaps it could be available for room service, in case guests want a taste of home.'

When Harrison looked up from his plate, she noticed that he had a dash of cream caught in the corner of his mouth. She set down the two plates she was about to carry over to his friends and reached out, carefully catching it on the tip of her finger.

Harrison's eyes met hers then, and she found it hard to breathe as her hand hovered, not wanting to pull away from him just yet. But this time it was her, not him, who turned away.

He had a wife. The words echoed through her mind, impossible to ignore.

Had not *has*, she told herself. He *had* a wife.

'Come on,' she said, taking two plates and indicating for him to carry the other. 'Let's go and have dessert.'

'Charlotte,' Harrison said, his hand falling over her forearm and almost making her drop the plates. 'I was thinking, have you ever thought about going to the hotel Amalie talks to you about? The one at Sognefjord?'

'Have I?' she repeated. 'Well, I mean, yes, because I recall it from my childhood and would like to see it again, but—'

'It's come to my attention that I'll be a national embarrassment if I don't see the sights before I go home, and I promised Luke and Louisa that I'd show them around. Any chance you want to play tour guide again?'

Charlotte swallowed. Hard. His hand against her skin, his eyes on hers, the shake of her hand as she tried to keep hold of the plates... If only his friends hadn't told her, she wouldn't be feeling as if she were betraying someone who wasn't even there.

'Tell Daniel you can start next week,' he said. 'It's been a long time since I had a vacation, and I could really do with a few days away. If I'm not being presumptuous?'

She should have told him she'd think about it. She should have told him that there were reasons she didn't want to go back there. But instead, Charlotte found herself nodding.

'Sure,' she replied. 'I'd love that.'

18

THE MAJESTETISK HOTEL, SOGNEFJORD, NORWAY, 1950

Amalie's heart ached as Oskar held her hand in both of his, pressing kisses to her knuckles. She'd been preparing for this day, but still, it didn't make it any easier.

'This is only for a few weeks,' he said.

'I know,' she whispered, leaning into him so that their foreheads were touching. They were standing by the water, their favourite place to be, but summer was coming to an end, which meant that the wind blowing off the fjord was cooler now, making the little hairs on her arms stand on end. Or perhaps it had nothing to do with the weather at all.

'When you finish here, you make your way to my home in Oslo,' he said. 'I'll be waiting for you.'

She nodded. They'd gone through every detail of their plan and his address was in her pocket, but it was still comforting hearing him say it again.

'Everything will be all right, Amalie, I promise you,' he said. 'We're going to be our own family, and no one can stand in our way, do you hear me? It doesn't matter what anyone says.' Oskar placed a hand on her stomach, still flat, not showing any hint that their baby was already growing there. 'I think it'll be a little boy, as strong as an ox. Our own little Viking,' he teased.

'Or a girl, with dark brown eyes just like her father,' she said, already imagining a daughter. From the day she'd found out she was expecting, she'd felt in her heart that she was carrying a girl.

His smile warmed her heart.

'What if they don't approve though, Oskar?' Amalie asked. 'What then? What if they never accept me?'

'Then we go to see my brother, Alexander,' Oskar said. 'He'll help us, I know he will, and he'll love you just as much as I do.'

Amalie wasn't convinced about that, but she didn't voice her concerns to Oskar. She'd already imagined that his older brother would be like his parents—cold and unimpressed by her lineage—but if he was anything like Oskar, then maybe he would be different.

'Come here,' he murmured, drawing her into his arms. Oskar held her close, kissing the top of her head and then cupping her face in his hands so that he could kiss her lips. His mouth was warm and familiar after an entire summer of being wrapped in each other's arms.

'I have something for you before I go,' Oskar whispered against her lips, gently pulling away from her.

She caught her breath as he reached into his pocket, and when he took out a velvet ring box she gasped, her hands covering her mouth.

'Oskar,' she began, looking from him to the box and back again.

He dropped to one knee and took her hand, and she began to cry as he gazed up at her. 'I know I've already asked you, but I have a ring this time, and I want you to know that even without the baby, I would have asked for your hand. Amalie, will you marry me?'

When he opened the ring box, the diamond inside was only modest, but it was more than she'd ever imagined a ring could be. It sat on a shiny gold band, and as he moved it, the small diamond caught the light and glinted brilliantly.

'It's beautiful,' she said, holding out her hand and letting him slide it onto her finger. 'And it fits like a glove.'

He grinned up at her, and it was then she realised that she hadn't given him an answer. 'Yes, Oskar, I will marry you, a thousand times over. With or without a ring.'

He stood and kissed her again, and she held out her hand to stare at her diamond, loving the way it twinkled as she moved it. Her mother and sister only had plain gold bands, not engagement rings, and she couldn't imagine how excited they'd be for her when they saw it.

'Tell me again what you're going to do,' he asked, gathering her into his arms and holding her against his chest, his chin resting on her head.

'I'm going to go home to my family after I finish here, and tell my father that you've asked for my hand,' she said. 'I'll share our secret with my mother, if I feel that she's open to it, and then I'll make my way to you in Oslo.'

'You have the money I gave you?' he asked. 'It's somewhere safe?'

'Sewn into my coat,' she said. 'I'll be fine, Oskar. I'm well used to looking after myself.'

'But you're not just looking after yourself now, Amalie.'

There was a call from the hotel, and she felt Oskar's body stiffen. It was time for him to go.

'I'll see you soon,' he murmured, lifting her hand to his lips again and holding it there, before finally letting go and turning to walk away.

'Oskar,' she said, calling after him.

She committed the image of him to memory; his soulful

dark eyes, the way his slightly too long hair moved in the breeze, the hint of a smile on his face when he looked at her.

'I love you,' Amalie said.

He pressed a kiss to his fingertips and then blew against them. 'I love you, too.'

And just like that, she was left standing with the fjord behind her, their most special place in the world, as the man she loved walked away from her, headed home to his family.

She only hoped that he was right about them coming to accept her, because if they didn't...

Amalie placed a hand to her stomach. *Heaven help us.*

19

THREE WEEKS LATER

Amalie had written to Oskar to tell him the day she'd be arriving, but she was still nervous as she stepped through the gate onto his family's estate. He'd told her about where they lived and described it to her in some detail, but she hadn't imagined quite how grand it would be, or how she'd feel standing at the bottom of the steps staring up at his house. She wiped her palms against her skirt, but they felt damp again almost immediately, and she adjusted her blouse to give her something to do as she stood there.

Oskar had told her they had money, but this was more than money. This was wealth on a level she'd never imagined, and it at least made sense to her now why his parents had been so cruel. Oskar wasn't just a boy intended to work in the family business; he was a young man on the cusp of inheriting a fortune.

But Amalie needn't have worried, because the moment she placed her foot on the first step, the enormous front door was flung open and Oskar was running down to her.

'Amalie!' he called.

Any doubts she'd had about whether he'd still want to see

her disappeared. The joy written all over his face was only surpassed by her own excitement, as she flung her arms around him. He cupped her face and stared down at her, his eyes searching hers before giving her a quick kiss.

'I was worried you might change your mind,' he said, taking her hand and grinning up at her, the diamond still sparkling where he'd placed it all those weeks earlier.

'Me? Change my mind?' Amalie laughed, before glancing at her stomach. 'Never.'

'Let's go inside,' he said, keeping hold of her hand as they walked up the steps together and into the house.

'They know I'm coming?'

He stopped and turned to face her. 'They know I'm expecting a visitor, and that I need to speak to them. I didn't want to give them any reason not to say yes.'

Amalie nodded, a familiar knot forming in her stomach. It was the same one that had been there at the awkward dinner she'd shared with his family at the hotel.

'How did your family react?' Oskar asked, his voice hushed as he led her down the hallway.

Amalie tried not to stare, but the paintings alone were impossible not to notice. She'd never seen anything like it—it was even more sumptuous than the Majestetisk Hotel, and she'd thought that was the epitome of luxury. 'They were happy for us,' she replied, keeping her voice low. 'But my mother guessed about the situation before I told her. She suggested we marry quickly, and visit them afterwards so that they can celebrate our news rather than have anyone ask questions.'

Oskar paused in front of a closed door, turning to her once more and gently brushing a tendril of hair from her face. 'Then marry quickly we shall,' he said. 'But first, let's get this out of the way, and don't let them make you feel less than you are for so much as a second, do you hear me? We are marrying whether they consent to our union or not.'

Amalie nodded, bravely tilting her chin and facing the door, her hand safely held in Oskar's. She had worries she wouldn't voice, like how they were going to get by financially if his family cut him off, or where they might live, but she intended to keep those thoughts to herself for as long as she could. Oskar was prepared to give up everything for her, and she needed to let him figure it all out.

He pushed open the door and held it for her, and Amalie had a few seconds to survey the room before his family saw her. It was enough for her to feel his mother's fury at having to see her again—in her eyes, Amalie could sense a storm brewing.

'Mother, Father, you remember Amalie?' Oskar said, still holding her hand as they stood before them. 'Amalie, this is my brother, Alexander.'

His family were seated at the dining table, but their meal lay untouched before them. It had clearly just been served. There were two other places set—a place for her this time— although maybe it was only because they'd been told a friend of Oskar's was joining them and not her specifically.

His brother stood as Oskar's parents sat in silence. He was taller than Oskar and wore a more serious expression, but he had the same warm brown eyes and thick head of hair, which made him seem familiar to her in a way. He walked around the table and held out a chair for her.

'It's a pleasure to meet you, Amalie. Please, take a seat.'

She glanced at Oskar, who indicated she should accept his invitation. But as she walked, she could feel his mother's eyes following her.

'Excuse my rudeness, I didn't know we would be seeing you again today, Amalie,' his father said. 'A word before lunch, Oskar?'

Oskar looked to her before nodding and following his father from the room. Their voices were muffled, but it was obvious from the tone that they were arguing.

'Amalie, Oskar tells me that you met at the hotel in Sogne-fjord,' Alexander said, his smile kind. 'Have you come directly from there?'

She returned his smile. 'I've actually been home to see my family since then, but yes, that's where we met.'

Amalie reached for the glass of water in front of her, her mouth suddenly dry, but her hand fell away in fright at his mother's gasp.

'What is that?' his mother cried.

She realised her error then, that his mother had seen the diamond ring on her finger, and Amalie looked to Alexander for help, but his face had drained of colour, too. Thankfully at that moment Oskar's father burst through the door, taking the attention from her. Oskar followed close behind.

'They mean to get married,' his father blustered, marching towards the table before pointing at her. 'Did you put him up to this? Was it your idea to—'

'Father, enough!' Oskar interrupted, coming to stand behind her, his hands on her shoulders. 'I asked Amalie to visit today so that we could share our good news. We're in love, and we're to be married.'

'Love? What do you know of love?' his mother exploded. 'You have your whole life planned, Oskar, and there are many suitable girls from wonderful families who'd—'

'Do not insult my fiancée by talking about *suitable girls*, Mother. We are to be married, with or without your permission,' he said. 'I brought Amalie here as a courtesy, so that you could welcome her into our family and celebrate with us, so please, can we put this behind us and enjoy our lunch together?'

Amalie's heart was pounding, and she was grateful for the weight of Oskar's hands on her shoulders.

'Son, I want you to listen to me very carefully,' his father said, his eyes fixed on Oskar. He never even glanced at Amalie. 'You have been born into a place of privilege due to my hard work and that of your grandfather, and with that comes responsibility. You can think about marriage later, once you've established yourself in the business, once you're older, once—'

'I'm not joining the business,' Oskar said. 'I've done everything you've asked of me until now, but I want to be a chef, not a businessman. I'm not like Alexander, or you. Can't you see that?'

Amalie bit down on her bottom lip as tears started to slip furiously down her cheeks.

'Stop behaving like a child!' his father bellowed. 'For goodness sake, Alexander, talk some sense into your brother. You will not be getting married, Oskar, not to this girl or any other of your choosing. Your mother is right, we'll be—'

'Amalie is pregnant,' Oskar said. His words were only spoken quietly, but they still had the power to make everyone fall silent.

Amalie bravely looked up when his mother threw her napkin onto her plate and rose, pausing only to speak to her husband, her fingers like claws around his arms as she gripped hold of him.

'Fix this,' she muttered, before marching out of the room.

'You're certain the child is my son's?' his father asked.

'Father!' Oskar reprimanded.

'It's a reasonable question.'

'Yes. It can only be your son's,' Amalie replied, keeping her voice even and trying not to cry from the shame of it all. 'There has been no one else.'

Alexander stood then, distracting his brother and father as he went to the drinks cabinet and poured a glass. She watched as he took it to his father, passing it to him before placing a hand on his back.

'This has been a lot to digest,' Alexander said. 'I suggest that we take a moment to gather ourselves and then perhaps I could take Amalie for a walk while you both have a more civilised discussion.'

'There is nothing to discuss,' his father said, after downing the drink. 'Oskar, it's no exaggeration to say that you'll be throwing your life away if you marry this woman. But you're a grown man and the decision is yours to make.'

Amalie's heart began to race again, but she could see from the look on Alexander's face, the way his hand lifted to his head as if he were in pain, that he knew the situation was about to get worse.

'Should you choose to make this decision, though, you must know that it comes with consequences,' his father continued. 'I have raised you to take over my business with your brother, and failure to take up a position at my company after graduation will result in you being disinherited. You will receive no further dividends from our company or be able to draw money from your trust, and you will no longer be welcome in this house.'

'Father,' Alexander cautioned. 'Please.'

But not even his eldest son could stop him, it seemed, and Amalie felt Oskar's pain radiating from him as he stood behind her. She wished to comfort him, but knew that it wouldn't help matters for her to touch him in front of his father.

'And if I agree to join the company after graduation?' Oskar asked. 'After my wedding to Amalie?'

'There will be no wedding. Amalie,' his father said, turning to her, 'I will write you a cheque today so that you can return home to your family. It will be enough for you and the child to live comfortably, on the condition that you are never to contact my son again, and never to divulge his involvement with you.'

Amalie froze. Part of her wondered just how much she was worth, how little the father of the man she loved thought he could pay her to make her walk away.

'If your son doesn't want to marry me,' she said, summoning all her bravery, 'then I will walk away. I don't want your money.'

She saw Alexander from the corner of her eye pouring another drink, but it was he who consumed this one.

'You have a choice to make, Oskar,' his father said, taking his seat at the table again, calm now as if he'd asked his son to fetch him something rather than threatening to disinherit him. 'Now please excuse me while I have my lunch in peace.'

Amalie jumped when Oskar slammed his fist on the table between her place setting and his father's. It was his brother who came round to her and pulled out her seat, offering her his arm and escorting her from the room. It was Alexander who took a handkerchief from his pocket and offered it to her for her tears.

'They're at loggerheads now, but it will all blow over,' he said, his voice low.

'I don't believe you,' she said, dabbing her cheeks and the corners of her eyes. 'I just don't understand why they hate me so much. Oskar and I make each other so happy. All I want is to be his wife.'

Oskar burst through the door then and folded her into his arms. She inhaled the scent of him, holding him tight as his brother stepped away.

'Oskar, I want you to listen to me,' Alexander said. 'If you intend to marry, then do it quietly. Take Amalie away from here and give them time to come to terms with the situation. A grandchild will change everything, once it's born, and they'll eventually soften to the idea.'

Amalie looked between the two brothers, her heart melting as they embraced. She'd been wrong to fear meeting Alexander —despite the parents who'd raised them, or perhaps in spite of it, they were both kind men with big hearts.

'If you need money, anything at all, you let me know,' Alexander said. 'You know I'd never turn my back on you.'

She stood on tiptoe and pressed a kiss to his cheek. 'Thank you,' she whispered.

Oskar and his brother clasped hands, before Oskar put his arm around her and walked her to the door.

Less than an hour later, they sat on a park bench near his family's home, her head to his shoulder as they watched a family picnic, the children running around with a kite that was soaring high in the sky.

'I can't ask you to do this for me,' Amalie said. 'They're your family.'

'You haven't asked me,' Oskar replied, touching his head to hers. 'This is my decision, and one I want to make. You're my family now, Amalie. You and our baby.'

'Then what do we do now?' she asked. 'My father told me not to come home until I was married. He doesn't want a scandal, and—'

'Amalie, I'm not sending you home,' he said. 'We have friends in London, and I want you to go there and wait for me. I'll join you by the end of the month, but I need to get some things in order first.'

'You want me to go ahead without you?' She couldn't disguise the tremble in her voice. 'To another country?'

'I need to know you're safe and settled, and I think it's best if we have a fresh start there. We can get married as soon as I join you, and I can arrange a transfer to a university there. I still want to finish my degree, and after that we can figure out what to do next.'

She breathed deeply. 'If that's what you want, then I'll go. But promise you'll come quickly. I don't like the thought of being alone for long.'

She kept her head on his shoulder as he kissed her hair. 'We're going to have a wonderful life together, whether my parents approve or not,' he murmured. 'And my friends are lovely, I promise you they'll welcome you with open arms. I'll write to them today.'

Amalie had always been reluctant to believe in promises, but Oskar had given her no reason to doubt him. Everything he'd promised so far had come true.

And she knew that in that moment, she'd have agreed to move halfway around the world if Oskar had asked her to, if it meant they could be together.

20

PRESENT DAY

Charlotte had been silent almost the entire last hour of the journey to the hotel at Sognefjord, feigning tiredness from such a big week, but she knew that there was no way she could spend a whole weekend with Harrison and not tell him that she knew. But then she also didn't want to be the one to bring it up, in case it ruined everything. It was a dilemma that was sending her crazy as she tried to figure out when the best time to bring it up would be.

There's no good time to bring up the fact that his wife died. Which, now she thought about it, was probably why he hadn't told her himself. When exactly could he have slipped that into their conversation, even if he'd wanted to?

But by the time they'd checked into their adjoining hotel rooms, it was Harrison knocking on her door, the look on his face telling her that he knew something was wrong. Clearly, she didn't have a very good poker face.

'Hey,' he said, shoving his hands into his pockets. 'I just wanted to check that everything was—'

He stopped talking, clearly having noticed the pained expression on her face as she stared back at him.

'I don't know what to say,' she blurted, hating that tears filled her eyes the moment she said it. She'd been so determined not to get upset or even say anything at all, and they'd barely had time to unpack before she was welling up.

'They told you, didn't they?' Harrison said, running a hand through his hair and looking away as he took a step back. 'I should have recognised that look in your eyes, I've seen it a thousand times before.'

'I'm sorry, I—'

'You know what you said to me, that very first day we went exploring? You refused to let me pity you for what happened with your mum, you even told me off for a look I wasn't even giving you.'

She closed her eyes for a moment. 'I did.'

'You know why I've loved being here?' he asked. 'It's because no one gives me that look here. I ran from it, and now it's caught up with me because someone told you my story before I was ready to share it myself.'

Charlotte forced herself to look at him then. 'You know what, you're right, it should have been you telling me. But I don't pity you, Harrison, I just wish I'd known your pain, that's all.'

'And would you have treated me differently if you'd known I was a widower?' he asked. 'Would you have even wanted to spend time with me?'

Charlotte opened her mouth, but nothing came out. Because he was right; she would have looked at him differently. But she did jump when he slammed his hand into the door before storming the few steps to his own door, not having ever seen him angry before.

'They love you, Harrison,' she called after him. 'They were only trying to protect you.'

'Yeah?' he asked as he turned, his eyes haunted as he shook

his head. 'Well, it was my story to share, and I would have told you when I was good and ready.'

Charlotte stood there until he disappeared, his door slammed behind him, and she quietly closed hers and went to stand at the window. The view was magnificent—their rooms faced the fjord, and it seemed as if nature stretched for miles – —but she couldn't even see it. All she could see was the pained look on Harrison's face, and all she could feel was the pain in his heart. Because he was right; she did know what it was like to receive those looks of pity, knew what it was to run from them, but now she understood that the people who'd looked at her that way weren't judging her.

Now, with hindsight, she could see that it was their way of showing that they cared, just like she did now. She didn't pity Harrison, but her heart was breaking for him.

A thud, followed by two more, echoed out on her door, and Charlotte made her way back across the room. She was just wondering if it was someone from reception, when she swung the door open and found Harrison standing there again.

But this time, he didn't look worried or sad. This time, he looked angry.

'My wife died two years ago,' he said, as she took a step back and let him in. 'Her name was Elly.'

Harrison shut the door behind him, and she stood in front of him as he spoke, his eyes locked on hers.

'When I met you, it was the first time I'd met a woman that I could imagine being with. I'd spent two years refusing to even consider the idea of being with anyone else, but you?' He shook his head. 'You're something else, Charlotte. You're beautiful and talented and funny, and I haven't been able to get you out of my head since that very first time we had coffee. It was like you walked into my life and changed the way I thought about the world.'

She stood still, too afraid to move in case she ruined the

moment, knowing that he needed to get it all out and wanting to hear what he had to say.

'I don't want to be the guy whose wife died with you, Charlotte. I just want to be a guy who likes a girl, as simple as that.'

Charlotte took a tentative step forward, and then another, before slowly lifting her hand until she'd placed it gently against his cheek. When he didn't move away, she took another step, until they were almost touching, parting her lips as she stared up at him, before letting her gaze fall to his mouth.

They stood a second longer, breathing, not moving, until Harrison closed the gap and kissed her. First their lips barely touched, hovering together, and the next thing she knew Harrison was walking her backwards until they were tumbling onto the bed, her legs tangling with his and his kisses consuming her.

Charlotte and Harrison didn't emerge from her bedroom until much later in the afternoon, and although she wasn't convinced their excuse of both being tired and needing a nap was believed, Louisa and Luke were too polite to suggest otherwise. And now she and Harrison were taking a walk along the water, just the two of them again.

Harrison surprised her by reaching for her hand, linking their fingers as they wandered.

'About earlier...' he began.

'If you're going to apologise for storming into my room and kissing me, there's no need. Trust me when I say that it's going down as one of the highlights of my adult life.'

They both laughed, and Harrison lifted her hand in his and kissed her knuckles. 'Just so we're clear, I'm fairly sure *you* kissed *me*.'

Charlotte tried to appear shocked, but it only made them

both laugh all the more—he was kind of right. Although she recalled him being the one who'd taken charge from that moment on.

'In all seriousness, though, I was going to tell you, it just hadn't felt like the right time,' he said. 'I mean, when is the right time to tell someone that your wife died? It wasn't at coffee, and it most certainly wasn't when I was getting to know you on our little day adventure or when we were having dinner.'

'I get it,' she said. 'When I left home and went to London, it was like a fresh start for me. No one knew that I was the girl with the mum who'd run away. Everyone just accepted me for who I was when they met me, and it was like I'd left all that baggage behind.'

'Did she leave your dad for another man?' Harrison asked.

Charlotte decided to tell him all of it, from the very beginning. 'Let's just say that my mum was amazing until she wasn't. When we were young, she was vibrant and fun, she took us on adventures, she was my everything.' Charlotte took a deep breath and stared out at the water, knowing she needed to tell Harrison the whole story—the true story—not the story she usually told anyone else who asked. 'There were little signs that things weren't right, which as a child go unnoticed, but I think, no I *know*, that my dad blamed himself for not doing something. One day, we'd have this mum who'd bake for us and make homemade popcorn, dancing around the living room and singing songs with us, and the next day she'd stay in bed and my brother would look after us while Dad was at work.'

'She suffered from depression?' His words were spoken softly.

'I think so,' Charlotte said. 'We never had a name for it then, and sometimes she'd go weeks without having what we called an episode, but it was after my baby sister was born that things changed.' She inhaled and slowly blew it out. 'She died when she was nine months old, and I don't remember much about her, other than that Mum was in hospital all the time with her. Dad spent longer and longer at work each day. Mum was never there, or if she was, I don't remember it, and Erik, my brother, became almost like a parent to me. But every time I think about those years, I realise how young he was, and how unfair it was that he had no one to look after him.'

They stopped walking and Charlotte stared out at the water, leaning into Harrison when he put his arms around her and scooped her back into his body, his chin resting on her shoulder, their cheeks gently touching.

'Before Mum left, we had this week or maybe even more of her being happy again. The house felt bright, the kitchen smelt of cooking and the bathrooms were scrubbed clean. But then she was just gone. We left for school one morning, and she made our lunches and kissed us goodbye, and when we came home, she'd left. Her clothes were gone, her cosmetics had disappeared from the bathroom, and the only thing left was the scent of her favourite perfume clinging to the air.'

'I'm sorry,' he said. 'That must have been so hard on you. On all of you.'

She sighed. 'It was the beginning of the end for me and my dad, but I guess it's the reason my brother and I are so close. We've been through a lot.'

'Which is why you found coming home so hard,' Harrison said. 'And there I was telling you to go and see your dad, as if you'd just had some petty argument.'

Charlotte turned in his arms, folding herself against him, her cheek to his chest.

'I'm so pleased you did, because you were right. If something had happened to him and I hadn't seen him, I would never have forgiven myself. It's the same reason I went to my mother's funeral.'

'You never saw her again? After she left?'

'I never saw her again,' Charlotte said. 'We found out that

she'd fallen in love with a man, we don't even know where they met, and she just disappeared from our lives. It was as if losing her baby was too much to bear, and maybe it was just easier to walk away from all of us than face loss, day after day. And even now, when I try to tell myself that she must have had mental health problems that were never treated, it doesn't help the little girl who lost her mum. In a way, it would have been easier if she'd died, because at least then I'd have been able to grieve her. We would all have been able to, instead of feeling as if she'd never loved us in the first place.'

Harrison kissed the top of her head and held her in his arms, and she almost felt as if she'd been saving her story to share with him. Because here was a man who understood true loss, who knew what it was like to lose someone he truly loved.

'When I lost Elly, my entire life was turned upside down. I didn't know who I was without her—it had been Harrison and Elly for so long that it had become my whole identity,' Harrison said, his voice low. 'Time does help, but it doesn't heal. Not really. Sometimes I still get so angry that she was taken from me, that she didn't get longer to just walk this earth and see the world.'

Charlotte leaned back in his arms and looked up at him. 'If you change your mind about this, about us being—'

'No,' he said, his voice husky as his hands splayed at her waist, holding her in place. 'You're one of the only things I've been sure about in two years. I don't regret anything that's happened between us.'

She glanced up at his mouth, feeling that pull towards him, that energy that seemed to ignite between them. 'Good,' she said, standing on tiptoe and grazing her lips against his.

This time when they kissed, it was softer, less urgent than before, and Charlotte looped her arms around his neck.

'No secrets,' he whispered, as he broke off their kiss and

gently pulled her down to the ground beside him. 'You can tell me anything.'

'No secrets,' she whispered back, dropping her head to his shoulder.

But as she sat, staring out at the fjord, content in Harrison's company, her mind was suddenly drawn to the secrets Amalie had been keeping, and she reminded herself that she needed to call her grandmother to find out if Amalie had told her any more of her story. Especially as she sat on the banks of the fjord, the water lapping nearby—perhaps in the exact same spot that Amalie had once sat with her beloved Oskar.

21

To say that the trip to Sognefjord had been special was an understatement, and as Charlotte walked through the hotel, she found herself wondering if she was tracing the same steps that Amalie had so many decades before. The last time Charlotte had gone to see her with her grandmother, Amalie had almost seemed hopeful, and Charlotte couldn't imagine what came next in her story and how it all fell apart. Because she'd racked her brain—there had to be heartbreak coming in Amalie's story, and she wasn't sure whether she was ready to hear it. Or if Amalie would even be ready to tell it.

'Hey,' Harrison said when she rounded the corner and almost bumped into him. 'I was just coming to find you.'

'Lucky me,' she said, smiling when he bent to kiss her. And it wasn't a cheek-kiss either; it was a warm brush against the lips kind of kiss that she felt all the way to her toes.

'I've managed to rent us kayaks, and they're even packing us a picnic lunch,' he said, his hand sliding against hers as he led her down the hall.

'What about the others?' she asked. 'They don't want to join us?'

Harrison frowned. 'On our romantic kayak? They can organise their own excursion!'

She laughed, liking the easy manner they'd developed with each other. Somehow, it felt as if she'd known Harrison for so much longer than she had. Even if it was only a summer romance, even if he left and returned to London and she never saw him again, she knew in her heart that she'd never forget him.

'Hey, what's wrong?' he asked. 'You look sad.'

'Oh, sorry, it's nothing. I was just thinking.'

'Thinking about...?'

She grimaced. 'Honestly, I was just thinking about how much I'll miss you when you leave. It's weird how quickly we've fallen into something special.' Charlotte groaned. 'That came out all wrong. It's just, I feel like we've known each other for so much longer than we have.'

He pulled her closer and they walked through to have breakfast, seeing Louisa and Luke waving to them and heading over to join them.

'Morning,' they both said.

'Morning,' Charlotte replied. 'Isn't it just so beautiful here?' The large window in the restaurant was like a frame around a postcard-perfect image, and even though she'd seen the fjord before, her memory hadn't done it justice.

'I'm embarrassed to say I had no idea how picturesque it would be,' Louisa said. 'I've never seen anything like it.'

'Charlotte and I are actually going kayaking this afternoon, so that we can see more of the fjord,' Harrison said.

'We've decided to go with the lazier option of a cruise,' Luke said, before turning to Charlotte. 'I'm not an active relaxer like this one.'

Charlotte grinned. 'Thankfully Harrison and I are on the same wavelength there. I'm so used to being on the go all day, so lying around relaxing is what I'd call impossible.'

'Well, maybe that's why you were drawn to each other,' Louisa said with a wink. 'Luke and I are all about perfecting our sloth routine when we're on holiday.'

Charlotte felt uncomfortable for a split second as she saw the way Louisa quickly glanced at Harrison, as if she might have overstepped in treating them like a couple, but Harrison didn't seem perturbed. And as they all ate breakfast, she was happy to sit back and listen to them talk, liking the way Harrison's face lit up when they teased him, or the way Louisa grinned when he gave it straight back. The rapport they had was special to watch, and it made her wish she'd invested more time in her old friends; the ones she'd been close to when she was younger. Moving away had put more than just a physical distance between her and her old friends—they'd moved on with their lives, some of them already had families of their own—but seeing Harrison with his oldest friends made her even more determined to expand the circle of people she surrounded herself with.

'How's the food, Charlotte?' Luke asked. 'Up to scratch?'

'Any food that's cooked for me is appreciated,' she replied. 'I honestly don't think there's anything about this hotel not to like, the food included.'

'Speaking of food, I think we should finish up here and go and collect our packed lunch,' Harrison said, pulling out her chair when she rose to join him. 'We'll see you two here for dinner tonight.'

Just as he did, Charlotte caught sight of a young chef heading out for a break, and a very pretty maid dashing over to meet him. They kissed before they'd even walked out the door, and she imagined them as Amalie and Oskar; their love forbidden, but still knowing no bounds.

'You're lost in thought again,' Harrison said. 'Are you sure everything's okay? You're very quiet.'

She looped her arm through his, dropping her head to his shoulder as if it was the most natural thing in the world.

'I keep losing myself in thoughts of Amalie and Oskar,' she said. 'Wondering where they were, the places they explored here, the way she felt when she saw him in the hotel. I can't imagine what it must have been like for them.'

'I should have tried to hire a romantic rowing boat,' Harrison said. 'Like the one she talked to you about.' They reached the front desk then and she waited for Harrison to collect the packed lunch he'd ordered.

Charlotte laughed. 'As nice as that would have been for them, I'm loving the kayaking option. It'll be fun.'

'Make sure to wear your running shoes,' he said. 'Apparently, we can go hiking from the place we're heading to. If we still have any energy left after paddling there, that is.'

'Sounds like the perfect way to spend an afternoon.' They'd reached their rooms then, and she took out her keycard to let herself in. 'Meet again in thirty minutes?'

Harrison tousled her hair, his touch light. 'See you soon.'

Charlotte had thought the fjord was beautiful from a distance, but now that she was actually on the water, it was enough to take her breath away. The deep, blue-green water stretched as far as the eye could see, and the mountains on either side of them almost felt as if they were forming a guard of honour, guiding them on their journey out into the wilderness.

'How are you going back there?' Harrison called out, as he slowed and let her catch up.

'I'm distracted by the scenery,' she said. 'But otherwise, it's going great. I'm so pleased you chose this for us to do.'

'Did you ever explore like this with your family when you came here?'

'I remember we did a cruise and I'm sure we hired a little rowing boat, but I was so young that I don't remember any of the scenery, or at least not like this. I guess you don't appreciate the beauty of the water and the mountains as a kid.'

'It's because kids see everything through such a bright lens anyway,' he said. 'Adults are largely disillusioned with the world and appreciate the wonder of natural beauty.'

She'd never heard truer words, and as they continued to paddle, slowly, she realised that she didn't spend anywhere near enough time in nature, especially for a girl who'd grown up surrounded by it.

'May I ask you something?' Charlotte said.

'Of course.'

They were paddling in time with each other, and the fjord was so peaceful they didn't even need to raise their voices. It was almost as if they echoed back to them on the water.

'Is it hard experiencing new things like this, and realising that you don't have your wife to share it with?' she asked, hoping she wasn't overstepping. 'Is it weird to be experiencing it with me?'

He was silent for so long that she began to wish she hadn't asked.

'In the beginning, I'd go to call Elly or send a message all the time, just the little things that I'd usually share with her, and then it would hit me that she was gone,' he said. 'It's taken me a long time to stop doing that. Even meeting you, my first thought was how much she would have liked you, and trust me when I say I know how strange that sounds.'

Charlotte swallowed, a lump forming in her throat as she listened to him.

'It's one of the reasons I took this job and chose to come to Norway. I could have done much of the design work for the hotel in London and just travelled to the site when needed, but moving gave me the chance to start over, in a way. I was able to immerse myself in work rather than face what had happened.'

'And now?' she asked.

'I can't not think about her sometimes, about how much she would have loved something, but it's not the thudding pain it was in the beginning. It's more of a reminder of what we had, if that makes any sense at all.'

'When my mum left us, the hardest part was all the times when I wanted to tell her something. I'd go to call out to her or text her, or even just walk past her bedroom, and it was such a punch to the gut knowing I couldn't share it with her.'

Charlotte had never opened up to anyone properly before about her mother, not even her friends, because at the time she'd been so embarrassed and confused about why it had happened. And she'd also expected her mother to come walking back in the door one day, for it all to have been a big misunderstanding, imagining that maybe she'd just needed a break.

'I remember once, when I had really bad period cramps, and my dad and brother were yelling at me to hurry up. I was too embarrassed to tell them, which seems silly now, but as a teenager those things are so hard to talk about. And I remember just thinking that if only Mum were there, she'd have understood. I wouldn't have had to explain it, because she would have been the one person who got it.'

'I can't imagine what that must have been like for you at that age.'

'My grandmother told me once that one day I'd look back and realise that everything I went through had served to make me the strong woman I'd grown into,' she said. 'At the time, I couldn't understand, but now I get it. I guess I learnt how to be resilient the hard way.'

'No offence to your grandma, because I'm sure she's right, but I hated all the people who'd tell me that I should be grateful for all the good times we had together,' Harrison said. 'I'd be like, and please excuse my language, but *fuck you*. You have no idea the pain I'm going through, and I don't need your pep talk.'

Charlotte burst out laughing, and as she tried to bite her bottom lip to stop, Harrison started to laugh, too.

'I'm sorry, it's just you're so right. Screw the unnecessary pep talks,' she said.

'Hell, yes! Screw the pep talks!'

When their laughter finally subsided, Charlotte went to say something else, but her words caught in her throat.

'Harrison, stop,' she whispered.

He held his paddle when he saw that she'd stopped paddling, and Charlotte pointed ahead to what she was looking at. There, in the near distance, was the unmistakable rise and fall of dorsal fins gliding through the water.

'I don't believe it,' he said, glancing over at her.

And so they sat there, their kayaks bumping together as they watched the small pod of dolphins moving through the water. There was something about seeing nature up close and personal that made a fresh lump form in Charlotte's throat, and when two of the dolphins leapt out of the water in play, she placed a hand over her heart. It was one of the most special things she'd ever witnessed in her life.

They sat quietly and watched them until they disappeared into the distance, and when she looked across at Harrison, she saw everything that she was feeling reflected straight back at her.

'Thank you for today,' she said. 'I would never have thought to book kayaks, but it's been perfect.'

'Well, I can't take credit for the dolphins, but when you see the whales that I organised...'

Charlotte laughed, giving him a push in jest, which she seriously regretted when her boat began to tip side to side, threatening to wobble her straight out into the water.

'Lunch,' Harrison declared once they'd steadied themselves.

'Let's find somewhere to pull the boats in. And if you're game, I think we should swim.'

A short time later, Charlotte and Harrison had found a perfectly secluded spot and had consumed the most thoughtful picnic lunch, full of freshly baked breads, cold meats and cheeses, and they were now spread out, lying in the sun. It was nothing short of perfect, as far as relaxing days went, and she didn't want it to be over.

'You know, maybe I could get the hang of this lying about, relaxing business,' Charlotte said, rolling onto her side to look at Harrison.

He reached out and strummed his fingers across her skin, staring back at her. His gaze made a now familiar heat pool in her belly, and she wriggled closer, intending to kiss him.

'Funny, I was just about to suggest a swim,' he said.

They lay there a while longer, him tracing a pattern on her skin and her lying still as she blinked back at him.

'Are you happy?' she asked. 'Right now?'

'I'm the happiest I've been in a very long time,' he said.

Charlotte leaned forwards and kissed him then, plucking her lips softly against his. 'Me too,' she murmured, when she finally pulled away. 'It's been a long time since I felt like this.'

They made out like teenagers on the banks of the fjord, and when they finally paused for breath, it was Harrison who stood and held out his hand to her.

'Let's go for that swim,' he said, beginning to strip off his clothes.

'What if someone sees us?' she asked.

'Who's going to see us out here? We can just swim in our underwear.'

Charlotte wasn't convinced about swimming, but she wasn't about to say no to Harrison. So she stripped off and they left their clothes on the bank and ran down towards the water. She knew there was nothing in there to be afraid of, but the idea of submerging herself in such deep water was mildly terrifying— she hadn't swum since she was a child.

'Keep hold of my hand,' she said, grabbing Harrison around the wrist. But she'd barely got the words out when she shrieked from the temperature. 'I can't do it, it's freezing!'

'The concierge at the hotel said it was eighteen degrees, it can't be that—' Harrison made a noise that equalled her shriek. 'Holy shit, it's cold!'

They both laughed and shivered their way into the water, step by step, hovering at their knees and then their thighs, before they both cried out with the cold at their torsos.

'Count to three and we go under,' he said, gasping. 'One, two, *three!*'

Charlotte had always been the kid on the sidelines at sports events; she was always the girl on school camp who would put her toe in the water but never quite go for a swim, but today, with Harrison holding her hand, she dropped straight into the water. The cold surrounded her and made her entire body tremble, but she let herself enjoy the moment, and when her face emerged back out of the water and she was gasping for air, there was one thing she knew for certain.

She was truly living again, not just getting by like the hamster on the wheel she'd been for the past eight or so years, and she had Harrison to thank for that.

She also knew that right here, right now, might actually be one of the best days of her life.

***

That night, exhausted from paddling and swimming, not to mention slightly sunburnt from the hours they'd spent outdoors, Charlotte and Harrison lay spread out in his hotel room eating dinner. They decided to order room service, too tired for a proper sit-down dinner with Louisa and Luke, and Charlotte couldn't have been happier. It wasn't that she didn't like Harrison's friends, because she did like them very much; but it was nice to just stay in their little bubble and keep extending what had been a pretty perfect day.

'You know how I said that I love my job and I'd never not want to work?' she asked.

He nodded.

'Well, I think I lied. I could live here in this room forever, eating this food, watching movies and looking at that view. It's perfect.'

She'd almost forgotten how special the long hours of sunlight were after so long being in London, but there was something incredible about still having the curtains open so late at night, and enjoying the light coming through the windows.

'I think you'd be bored within a day,' he said, leaning over and kissing the tip of her nose. 'But I'm glad that you're happy.'

She ate another French fry, feeling as if she might pop but also loving every mouthful. 'Maybe, but I say we try anyway.'

'Honestly, if we didn't have the hotel opening next weekend, I'd be tempted to take you up on it,' Harrison said, ferrying their empty plates and putting them on a tray by the door. 'Actually, speaking of the opening, do you want to go together?'

'As colleagues?' she asked, wishing she hadn't been so quick to ask. 'I mean, we don't need anyone else knowing about—'

'Absolutely, that's what I meant,' he said, interrupting her.

'I'd love to. That will save me from a full-blown panic attack at having to walk in alone.' She was thankful her question hadn't made things awkward between them.

'Good, that's sorted then,' he said, getting back into bed and reaching for her. 'I have one other question for you.'

She smiled against his mouth, kissing him before settling under his arm as he sat back against the huge pillows.

'Yes, I do want to watch a movie,' she said. 'And yes, I would prefer a romcom, thank you for asking.'

He chuckled. 'I was actually going to ask if you want to stay the night in my room, but if you only want to stay for the movie...'

Charlotte closed her eyes and snuggled in even closer to him. It was the perfect end to a perfect day.

'Best idea you've had since deciding to take us kayaking,' she whispered into his ear.

22

LONDON, 1951

Amalie sat and looked out at Hyde Park, a bird in a gilded cage if ever there was one. She shifted in her seat, adjusting her dress for her newly rounded stomach. It was as if one day she'd gone to bed not showing her pregnancy, and the next it was very much on display. Not if she was careful with the way she dressed—to anyone else she would look as if she'd simply indulged in a little more to eat—but when she saw herself before bathing, the evidence was undeniable.

It had been four weeks since she'd seen Oskar, and he'd promised to arrive no later than this week. But the days had passed by and now it was Friday, which was why she was so eagerly sitting with her forehead pressed to the glass, staring out the window and hoping he would appear.

She couldn't keep doing this alone. The family she was staying with were lovely—Rachel and Benjamin had treated her kindly and with all the warmth and respect she'd once hoped to receive from his parents, but she knew that she was starting to overstay her welcome. They had four children of their own, so it was a busy enough household without having a guest to contend with.

Oskar had sent her letters, and even a gift; a delicate watch that she held up to admire now. It was gold and fitted her small wrist as if it had been made for her.

But she didn't want gifts, she wanted Oskar. To hold her hand, to whisper to her that everything would be all right. She wanted a kitchen of her own to cook the types of foods that were familiar to her, and the joy of celebrating her pregnancy rather than having to keep it hidden. She was only thankful that she had her own bathroom in the house, otherwise someone would surely have heard her being unwell in the mornings and through until lunchtime.

Where are you, Oskar? For the first time, she couldn't stop thinking that he might have changed his mind, that his family might have somehow convinced him to stay and turn his back on her.

Amalie reassured herself by taking out his latest letter, holding it to her chest before unfolding it to read again. She'd read it so many times that she should have known it by heart, but she still found comfort in seeing his familiar handwriting, in imagining he was whispering the words in her ear as she read it.

My darling Amalie,

I'm so sorry that so many weeks have passed, but it's taken even more organising than I thought to put all the necessary arrangements in place. I've now secured funds so that we can purchase a home of our own, it will have to be modest, of course, but it will be ours. Alexander has tried to change my father's mind, but alas he is set on forgetting I ever existed, so we shall forge our own path and make our own family without them. For now, anyway.

Please know that everything I'm doing is for us, and I will be in London within the next fortnight, likely the week after you receive this letter. I promise it won't take any longer.

She folded it and tucked it into her dress, leaning into the window once more and staring out.

Please hurry, Oskar, I don't know how much longer I can stand being without you.

Amalie knew something was wrong when there was an urgent knock on her bedroom door late at night. She rose and reached for her dressing gown, covering herself and hurrying across the room to open it.

'Rachel?' Amalie asked, seeing the woman's pale complexion and red eyes. 'What's wrong?'

'Amalie,' Rachel said, taking her hand and guiding her back into the room. 'Please, sit down.'

'Rachel, you're scaring me,' she said, sitting with her, wondering why she still hadn't let go of her hand.

'I'm so sorry, Amalie, there's no easy way to say this, but it's Oskar.'

'Oskar?' she gasped. 'What about Oskar? Is he not coming, has something—'

'He's dead,' Rachel cried, enveloping Amalie in her arms and holding her tight. 'There was a plane crash and we've been told there were no survivors.'

Amalie sat still. She couldn't raise her arms to hug Rachel back. She couldn't cry. She couldn't feel.

'No,' she said, pushing to her feet and pacing across the room and back. 'No, absolutely not. There must be some mistake! Oskar will be here any day now, I've been waiting a month and...' Her voice trailed away as she stumbled over her words.

'He's gone, Amalie,' Rachel said, standing and opening her arms again. 'I'm so sorry, my love, but he's gone.'

This time she fled into Rachel's arms and didn't let go,

crying into her shoulder as the other woman held her tight. Eventually Rachel eased her onto the bed, tucking her under the covers like she might one of her children and whispering to her that everything would be all right. That morning would come and they'd find out more, that answers would help to heal her wounds, that Oskar would want her to be strong.

But it didn't matter what Rachel said; nothing was going to ease Amalie's pain. She had a baby on the way, she was alone in a country that wasn't her own and she couldn't go back to her family, pregnant and unmarried. Oskar's family wouldn't want to hear her name uttered again; they'd probably blame her for their son being on the plane in the first place, which meant that she was alone.

Utterly and completely alone.

'I'm going to get something to help you sleep,' Rachel whispered, stroking her hair before rising. 'Close your eyes, I'll be back soon.'

Amalie started to sob then, her body shaking as she cried until her pillow was wet and her throat dry, until her eyes felt so swollen she knew that come morning, she'd barely be able to open them.

You can't be gone, Oskar. You can't be.

Just come home to me. Please, let this be a horrible dream. Just come home.

Amalie didn't leave her bed for three days. She kept her curtains drawn and her bedcovers pulled over her. Rachel sent up a maid who insisted on spoon-feeding her chicken broth and something to help her sleep, and Amalie obeyed only because she didn't want the child growing inside of her to go without. But she refused to rise or leave the bedchamber.

Until the same maid came back, this time not with broth but with a renewed determination to get Amalie out of bed. She pulled the curtains wide and let in the sunshine, before throwing back the covers.

'It's time to bathe,' she insisted.

Amalie groaned but let her guide her from the bed to the bath that had already been drawn. She raised her arms like a child as the maid stripped her nightgown from her, and obeyed when she told her to get into the tub. She didn't even know the woman's name, but her touch was gentle and she washed her hair for her, and her words became even kinder.

'I can see that you're in the family way,' the maid said.

Amalie had thought she was all out of tears, but more filled her eyes now that someone had said her secret out loud.

'I don't know what to do,' Amalie whispered.

'Rachel will ask you to leave once she finds out. She won't want an unmarried pregnant woman in the house, not with the children here. And there's been a letter.'

Amalie froze. 'A letter?'

'From your Mr Oskar's family. I overheard her and Mr Benjamin talking.'

'Where will I go?' Amalie asked as fear gripped her. 'What am I supposed to do? I only have enough money to tide me over, without Oskar...' She closed her eyes and slipped beneath the warm bathwater, only for the maid to hold her head up by her long hair.

'I know a place. You'll be safe there, and you won't be forced to make any decisions you don't want to.'

Amalie considered her words, realising what kind of place this woman was talking about, the kind of place that women like her ended up in when they were pregnant and alone.

'I know what you're thinking, but it's called Hope's House. I have a friend who's a midwife, she's told me all about the woman there, and I can tell you that she's not like anyone else.'

'You know where this Hope's House is?' Amalie asked.

'I do, and I'll even take you there myself if you need me to. Women like us have to stick together in times of need.'

Amalie reached for her hand. 'I don't know what I've done for you to be so kind to me, but thank you.'

'I can tell you're not like Miss Rachel and her friends, that's why I want to help.'

'I don't even know your name,' Amalie whispered.

'Helen,' she said. 'My name is Helen.'

Amalie cried as Helen rinsed her hair and sponged her body, caring for her in a way that no one had cared for her in a very long time, not since she was a girl.

'Everything will be all right, I promise. You just need to give it a little time.'

Amalie bit down on her lip, trying not to think about Oskar, even though his face was all she could see every time she closed her eyes.

Time was going to do nothing to heal her pain. Not with a child on the way.

23

'I hate doing this to you, Amalie, you know how fond we are of you and how special Oskar was to us,' Rachel said. 'I wish we could have had you to stay for longer.'

Amalie forced a smile as they stood awkwardly by the door, her suitcase at her heel and a bag slung over her shoulder. Rachel had packed a fresh loaf of bread for her as if she was seeing her off on a picnic, and kept talking as if they would be great friends who'd see each other again soon, but Amalie was no fool. This woman wanted her out of her house before there was even a hint of scandal, and she couldn't imagine what Oskar's mother had said in her letter.

'Thank you for having me,' Amalie said politely, biting her tongue when it came to what else she'd like to say.

'You'll be discreet now, won't you?' Rachel said. 'No one else needs to know about your, how should I put it—well, the unfortunate predicament you find yourself in. Helen here tells me that the place you're going to is excellent, and that you'll be back on your feet in no time.'

This time it was harder to fix her smile. She wanted to scream that she was pregnant, not suffering from the plague, and that the baby growing inside her was as wanted as the four children who were galloping around the house behind their mother. But she didn't. If Oskar had been there, she would have given Rachel a piece of her mind, but Amalie knew she couldn't afford to burn any bridges, not now.

'Helen will see you there, and perhaps we could see you after...' Her words lingered, and Amalie spared her the need to continue.

'I understand. Thank you again.'

Rachel gave her a pat on the shoulder and then Amalie left, grateful that they'd at least given her use of their maid and car to transport her there. She was embarrassed enough about where she was going, wondering if people watched this Hope's House to see who arrived. In the night, she'd imagined married women throwing rotten fruit at the young, unwed women who arrived with bulging bellies, even though she'd known it was likely her overactive imagination.

When they finally arrived, Amalie stared out of the window in surprise. They were in a quiet street surrounded by well-kept homes, and the one they were parked outside of was the nicest of them all. A small, discreet sign stating 'Hope's House' was the only indication that it was any different to the other homes on the street, and she found herself staring at the magnolia tree. Despite almost all the other trees on the street losing their leaves at this time of year, it was still covered in lush green leaves.

'This is the place?' Amalie asked.

'This is it,' Helen said. 'Didn't I tell you it would be nice?'

Amalie got out of the car and stared up at the house, admiring the bay windows upstairs. It was the kind of home she'd read about in books, where she might have imagined she and Oskar would end up raising their family if they'd stayed in England, but certainly not what she imagined a house catering for unmarried women might be like.

'Thank you, Helen,' she said, giving her a big, warm hug,

the opposite of the pathetic back pat that she'd given Rachel. 'I'm here because of you, and I'll never forget your kindness when I needed you most.'

Amalie took her luggage from the car and waved Helen goodbye, but she didn't walk straight to the door. Instead, she stood and stared up at the house, before going to sit on the steps. She needed a moment; to accept that this was her fate, that Oskar wasn't coming for her, that it was just her and her baby alone in the world now. A shudder ran down her spine as she imagined the reaction from whoever was behind the door, the way she was going to be looked at and treated, and then she glanced down at the ring on her finger—a promise of what was supposed to come.

Why did you have to leave me, Oskar?

The door opened behind her, and Amalie quickly stood, smoothing the creases from her dress and preparing herself for the worst. But the woman standing there was as unexpected as the house itself.

'Would you like to come in?' the woman said, with the faintest lilt of an accent. She was perhaps twenty years older than Amalie, her hair pulled back into a soft bun and wearing an expression that was more one of kindness than judgement. 'If you'd rather sit a while longer, that's perfectly fine.'

'I—' Amalie started, immediately feeling emotional and having to blink away tears. 'I don't know what to do.'

'Well,' the woman said, coming closer and holding out her hand. 'You could come in for a cup of tea and start by telling me what led you to my door.'

'I don't have to stay?' Amalie asked. 'If I come in—'

'You can stay here for as little or as long as you like,' the woman said. 'Or you don't have to come in at all, we could just sit on the steps here for a bit if you'd prefer. But it's much more comfortable inside.'

Amalie smiled. 'You're Hope, aren't you?'

'I am,' Hope said. 'And it's just me and another young woman here at the moment, so there's nothing to be nervous about.'

'I'm Amalie,' she said, taking the hand that Hope was still holding out to her. Hope's palm was soft, and her clasp was firm yet gentle.

'Well, Amalie, how about I take your luggage for you, and we can go and get that cup of tea on?' she said. 'I have some baking just out of the oven, and if there's one thing I know, it's that most young pregnant women love a little something sweet.'

Amalie smiled through her tears, immediately warming to this woman who was inviting her into her home. She paused before walking through the door, looking up, sensing in the strangest of ways that she was, somehow, exactly where she was supposed to be, and that Oskar was looking down on her.

The house was warm and comfortable, and Amalie found herself seated at a table in the kitchen, watching as Hope moved about and made them tea, with the promised baked goods placed in front of her.

'I can't pick out your accent, Amalie. Where are you from?'

'Norway,' she said.

'And what brings you to England? Have you lived here for long?'

Hope sat down across from her and poured the tea.

'My fiancé was supposed to meet me here,' Amalie said. 'It was to be a fresh start, we were to be married when he arrived but he, well—'

Hope's eyes met hers.

'The plane he was travelling on crashed. There were no survivors.'

Hope's hand covered hers, and she found herself crying into her teacup over this stranger's kindness.

'I can't go home, my father wouldn't allow it, and even if he would, they don't have the means to support me,' she said, trying to keep her voice even. 'And his family never liked me. It's why we were coming here in the first place.'

'I think I read about the crash in the newspaper,' Hope said. 'It was a small plane that left from Oslo.'

Amalie nodded. 'Do you still have the paper, by any chance?' she asked. 'I would like to keep the clipping, just so I...' Her voice trailed off. 'It sounds silly, but reading about it might help me to accept his death.'

Hope rose immediately, disappearing for a few minutes and leaving Amalie to compose herself and take a sip of tea. She'd always preferred coffee, but after the weeks she'd spent in England now, she was starting to get used to it.

'Here it is,' Hope said when she returned. 'Would you like me to cut it out for you?'

'Please,' Amalie said, as goose pimples covered her skin just at the sight of the newsprint.

They sat in silence while Hope took out a pair of scissors and deftly cut the article out, folding it in half and placing it on the table between them.

'You know, every young woman who comes through my door and sits at this table has a story,' Hope said. 'Most have been let down by a man whom they thought loved them. Some have lost the love of their life in circumstances like yours, where they've found themselves pregnant before they were married. But the common theme is that each and every one of them has had their heart broken.'

Amalie listened, not sure whether it made her feel better or worse to know that she wasn't alone.

'But the one thing I can tell you is that everything will be all right. It might not seem that way now, and it certainly doesn't mean that the path ahead will be without pain, but I promise that you will get through this. Not without pain and sadness, but life will be better again one day.'

'What happens if I stay here?' Amalie said, her lower lip trembling as she asked the question.

Hope's smile was kind as she leaned forward. 'It means that you will be safe and cared for. Most of the young women who give birth here ask me to find a family to adopt their baby, but that's your decision. You will never be forced to do anything you don't want to do here, and that's a promise.'

'So, you would let me give birth here and keep my baby?' Amalie asked, barely recognising her own voice, it was so quiet. 'If that's what I wanted?'

'Something I've come to realise is that this world can be so cruel to women,' Hope said. 'We have choices taken away from us, we have decisions made for us, and for the handful or two of women who walk through my door each year, I treat them with the respect and dignity I wish I'd been shown.'

Amalie met her gaze, understanding what this kind, sweet woman was trying to tell her. If she'd been braver, she would have asked her what she meant, but then Amalie had the feeling too that if Hope had wanted to say more, then she would have.

'Do most of the women who give birth choose adoption?' Amalie asked. 'Am I mad for thinking that I might be able to raise this baby on my own?'

'You're not mad,' Hope said, shaking her head. 'Don't ever think that makes you mad. It makes you a mother, and it means that you have a heart.'

Amalie stared out of the window, at the pretty garden that was slightly overgrown but somehow still incredibly charming. 'Why is it that men can make mistakes and be forgiven, but a woman makes one bad decision, and she is shunned or made to relive the consequences over and over?'

'Because,' Hope said, rising and pushing her chair back against the table, 'we live in a man's world. Which is precisely why I'll be helping young women who need me until my very last breath.'

Hope beckoned for her to rise, and when she did, she looked pointedly at the luggage sitting in the doorway to the kitchen. 'Shall we take these things upstairs, or do you need some time to think about whether you'd like to stay or not?'

A sense of calm passed over Amalie, and for the very first time since she'd left home to travel to England, she didn't need to wrestle with her decision.

'Yes, I would like to stay, if you'll have me, that is,' Amalie replied. 'I know I've only just met you, but I feel safe here, and I'm well used to working, so you'll have to let me pay my board in cleaning and such.'

'Amalie, I thought I told you, I don't expect—'

'I insist,' she said. 'Besides, it's the very least I can do. Sitting idle will only remind me of my Oskar. I need to keep my mind occupied.'

'Very well then,' Hope said, carrying the largest piece of luggage up the stairs ahead of her to a room that looked over the garden, with a big bay window and blue gingham curtains that were tied back with a matching bow.

The room was warm and flooded with light, with a bed on one side and a small writing desk and an armchair on the other. And somehow, it immediately felt like home.

It was at that small desk that Amalie sat once Hope had left her to settle in, taking out the newspaper clipping and slowly unfolding it. There was no photo, for which she was thankful, but reading about the crash left her with her fist pressed to her mouth and tears streaming down her cheeks.

Oskar was gone, she finally understood that, but this Hope's House was her second chance, and even though her grief felt like it was ripping straight through her body and threatening to tear her in half, she knew that she had to make the most of it. For her baby, this might be the one and only opportunity they were given to stay together, whether that was for a few days, a week or a month.

I'll do everything I can for our child, Oskar. If there's a way for us to stay together, there's nothing I won't do to make that happen.

I promise.

24

Amalie had spent all night lying awake, thinking about what Hope had said to her, trying to work out what she could do to find another way that didn't involve giving up her baby. And now she was sitting in her nightgown, her hair wild and long around her shoulders, pen in hand as she tried to compose what could be the most important letter she might ever write.

Just write what's in your heart. Beg if you have to.

She exhaled and pressed the pen to the paper, trying to believe that once she started, the right words would come. The more she tried to straighten them out in her head, the more jumbled they became, and so Amalie decided to trust her instincts.

Dear Mrs Johansen,

It was with great sadness that I learnt of the passing of your son, Oskar, on his way to London. Please, if you are thinking of throwing this letter in the fire, I implore you to keep reading.

I understand that I was never the woman you imagined your son marrying, but I want you to know that I fell in love with Oskar the very first day we met. He caught my eye one summer's night, and he saw past my shyness and showed me what it was to fall in love. Your son was full of dreams, full of happiness and light, and the world has lost a beautiful man who would have made a wonderful husband to me, and father to our unborn child.

We discovered I was pregnant at the end of summer, which is why we came to see you that day in Oslo. We were to be married as soon as he arrived in London, a small ceremony, in the hope that by the time we eventually came home to Norway, you would accept not only our union, but also your first grandchild.

So, I write to you, one mother to another, to beg for your mercy. I am due to give birth to your grandchild, to Oskar's baby, next month, and it breaks my heart to think I will have to give the child up soon after the birth. Your son loved me as much as I loved him, and he was so looking forward to being a father, and I have no doubt he would have been a great one.

I will write the address below where you can reach me. I'll be here until two weeks after I give birth, so it will be for at least another two months, if not more. Although I cannot imagine handing my baby over to strangers, I must either choose adoption or poverty if I am to make this decision alone.

If your son had survived, this would have been the happiest time of my life, but instead, the grief of losing my child is matched only by the grief I suffered, am still suffering, over my beloved Oskar's death.

I thank you for taking the time to read my letter.

Yours faithfully, Amalie

She finished the letter and folded it, sliding it inside an envelope and writing the address on the front. Amalie was just brushing away her tears when there was a soft knock at the door.

'Amalie?'

'Come in,' she replied.

Hope had shown her a kindness that she hadn't expected, and when she came in to sit beside her, her arm went around Amalie's shoulders, giving her a small squeeze. 'You wrote the letter?'

'I wrote the letter,' she whispered back. 'I don't know if I've said the right thing or whether she will even answer, but at least I've tried.'

'Grief can change people. I've seen it first hand, so if your Oskar's mother is struggling with his passing, it might make her more inclined to help.'

Amalie sniffed and wiped her eyes. 'Or it could make her hate me all the more.'

Hope sighed and squeezed her again. 'It could. But you won't know until you send that letter and wait for a reply. Would you like me to post it today for you?'

Amalie nodded. 'Please. And if there's anything I can do to repay you, for what you've already done for me—'

'There is nothing,' Hope said firmly. 'I do this because I want to, because life has taught me that women aren't treated with the kindness and love they deserve when faced with the most difficult decision of their lives. So don't you spend a moment trying to think of how to repay me.'

'What will I do if she doesn't reply? If they don't offer to help me?' Amalie asked. *If I'm truly all alone?*

'You have time,' Hope said. 'This baby won't be here for another month at least, and we can work out a plan together. Maybe that plan is adoption, finding a lovely family who're desperate for a child of their own, or maybe it's you keeping the baby somehow. But whatever happens, it will be your decision, Amalie. No one else can make this decision for you.'

'We were supposed to have this beautiful life together,' Amalie said. 'It was supposed to be a new beginning in London.'

'I know,' Hope said, holding her close as she began to cry. 'Unfortunately, life doesn't always work out the way we hoped it would.'

Hope rocked her in her arms until her crying finally stopped, and Amalie had the most overwhelming need to see her mother, to be soothed in her own home, in her own bed, as if she were a girl again. But her father didn't want to know about a pregnant unmarried daughter, and although she'd also received a brief note from her mother that was much kinder, she'd told her there was nothing she could do, other than send her a little money she'd been saving.

'I don't want to give up this baby, Hope,' she whispered. 'With every fibre in my body, I want to be a mother, and I know that Oskar would have wanted me to fight for our child.'

'Then fight,' Hope said. 'This letter is your first step, but it doesn't have to be your last.'

The next day, Hope wrote to her mother again, and to her sister as well. Her sister was already married and Amalie thought there might have been a chance that she would agree to raise the baby as her own, which would have allowed Amalie to at least be her loving aunt as she grew up. But she knew there was nothing more that she could do than ask, and now she just had to wait to see who might respond.

And while she waited, Amalie dedicated herself to helping Hope, knowing that the only way to keep from wallowing in her grief was to stay busy. She aired out the empty upstairs bedrooms and washed and folded laundry. She hung rugs outside and beat the dust out of them, wiped down every inch of the house, and then when there was nothing left inside to clean, she moved on to the garden.

'Amalie,' Hope said, one night as they sat outside and enjoyed a cup of tea. 'I think it's time for you to rest. It's not that I don't enjoy the help, my house has never been so clean, but you might hurry this baby along if you don't sit down.'

'You think the baby might come early?'

'I think,' Hope said, 'that her mama needs to put her feet up and remember that she's with child. But yes, sometimes if a woman does too much, it makes the baby come early.'

Amalie sat with that for a moment, realising what that would mean for her, if she didn't have as much time as she'd thought.

'I still haven't heard back from his mother,' she said.

'I know, but there's still time.'

Her sister had written back telling her she was sorry and wished she could do more, but that she'd found out she was pregnant herself, and she couldn't imagine explaining how she had two babies born less than six months apart. Amalie had tried to understand, but she'd known in her heart that if the situation was reversed, she'd have taken her sister's child in a heartbeat to make sure she stayed within the family.

'We should look for a nice family, just in case,' Amalie said, words she'd never thought she'd utter. 'If I can't find a way to keep her, if—'

'Amalie, I have more than one family who'd adopt your baby tomorrow if they could, but we don't need to talk about that today,' Hope said, reaching over and patting her hand. 'Today, we're just going to sit here and admire how well you trimmed those shrubs.'

They both laughed, and this time it was Amalie placing her hand over Hope's. 'Thank you,' she said.

'You have nothing to thank me for.'

But Hope was wrong. She had everything to thank her for—

for giving her a roof over her head, for her kindness, for her sage words of advice.

'Is it foolish to believe that I might be able to do this alone?'

'Foolish? No. You're already a mother, Amalie—from the moment you feel that child moving in your belly, you're a mother,' Hope said. 'And mothers know best. So, if you think you can do this on your own, then I don't doubt you for a second.'

They sat a while longer, and once they'd finished their tea, she turned to her. 'You know who I didn't think of until now?' she said.

Hope's eyebrows arched in question.

'Alexander. Oskar's brother.' Amalie remembered the kindness he'd shown her, how he was so similar to his brother in all the ways that counted, or at least, that's what she'd seen in their first meeting together.

'Do you think he might help you?' Hope asked.

'I think it's worth asking him. For all I know, he doesn't even know what's happened to me. Perhaps he'd consider helping me financially, just enough to get me on my feet.'

'Well, I'd suggest writing to him then. Like I told you the first time, it's only a letter, and you can but ask.'

'The worst that can happen is that he says no,' she said, repeating what Hope had told her.

'Exactly. But at least you'll know you tried.'

Amalie sat a little longer as Hope cleared their teacups and disappeared inside. She didn't know why she hadn't thought of Alexander sooner.

'Here,' Hope said, placing a fresh sheet of writing paper and a pen on the table beside her. 'You write the letter, I'll post it in the morning.'

Amalie leaned into her as Hope embraced her, and the moment Hope let go, Amalie picked up the pen and began to write. She decided not to hold back, to pour her heart out on the page, knowing that this might be her only chance.

Dear Alexander,

We only met once, but it was enough to leave a lasting impression on me, as you were so like my beloved Oskar. But Oskar is gone now, and I find myself only weeks away from having his baby, alone and scared in London. We'd planned a life together, and now I'm left with few choices about what to do next.

If I'm honest, I don't know what I'm asking of you. All I know is that I need your help. I want to raise my baby and honour Oskar, to never let his memory fade, to keep part of him alive through our child. But I cannot do it alone.

Please, for the love of your brother, can you help me? I will be forever grateful if you can find it in your heart to enable me to keep this baby, and love it with every fibre of my being.

Yours faithfully, Amalie

Now all she had to do was wait.

25

PRESENT DAY

Charlotte sat with her hand in Amalie's, watching her as she slept. Her heart had broken listening to her talk, but it was as if all the pieces of a jigsaw puzzle were coming together. She only wished her grandmother had been there to listen to her today, but Charlotte had made an impromptu call to see Amalie after dropping Harrison back at his apartment.

Amalie's eyes fluttered then, and Charlotte leaned forward, pressing her cheek to Amalie's warm hand.

'I've met someone,' she said. 'And I think he might be as lovely as your Oskar.'

Charlotte closed her eyes then, thinking about the weekend they'd shared and wishing that he had another project in Norway to keep him here; that they'd had longer to be together.

'How did you know he was the one, Amalie?' she whispered. 'How did you know that it was worth sacrificing everything for him?'

'I just knew,' came a shaky whisper in reply.

Charlotte lifted her head and looked into Amalie's kind, tired eyes. But there was still life there, still love shining from them. Charlotte moved so that she was lying on the bed with her as Amalie's eyes fluttered shut again, pressing her body gently against hers and holding her hand again. When she'd been younger, she'd missed her mum so much that she'd sometimes forgotten how fortunate she was for the women who *were* still part of her life, but she certainly cherished it now.

'Thank you for sharing your story with me,' Charlotte whispered. 'You're so brave, Amalie. Braver than I'll ever be.'

On the night of the hotel grand opening, Charlotte had arranged to meet Harrison outside the hotel, and she was so pleased she had so that she didn't have to walk in alone. Huge arches of fresh flowers filled the entrance and there was security checking the tickets of each person arriving, but it was Harrison who caught her eye among all the festivities. He was standing slightly away from the door, dressed in a black tuxedo and white shirt, and she'd never seen any man look so effortlessly handsome. His thick dark hair was brushed to one side, and instead of his usual worn leather boots, he was wearing highly polished black shoes.

'You look great,' she said, looking him up and down. He always looked good, but this was something else, and she couldn't take her eyes off him.

'Well, you look beautiful,' he said, holding his hand so that he could give her a little twirl. 'Absolutely beautiful.'

Charlotte was wearing a mid-calf black slip dress that flared out when she spun round, with an oversized coat slung over her shoulders for warmth. She'd been in the kitchen since first thing that morning and had barely had a chance to catch her breath, so she still felt that it was a miracle she'd managed to get home, change and dress in time for the opening. But it had been nice to have an excuse to dress up for an evening out, and she'd been thankful that her grandmother had forced her to go shopping the day before. Otherwise she'd have found herself woefully underdressed compared to the impeccably well-heeled man in front of her.

'Shall we go in?' he asked, letting go of her so she could slide her hand through the crook of his arm.

Charlotte smiled up at him and pressed a light kiss to his lips, before quickly smudging away the little trace of lipstick she'd left there.

'We shall,' she said. 'But be warned, I'm going to want to head up to your room, curl up in bed and order room service by nine. I'm already feeling dead on my feet.'

'That's absolutely fine by me,' he said with a sigh. 'This is all part and parcel of the job, but it's the part I like the least. I'd much rather be quietly in the wings and let someone else handle the whole public-facing part of my job.'

'You don't like the praise?' she teased. 'What was it that the news article said? London's trendiest young architect takes Oslo by storm. That can't feel half bad, reading something like that.'

He groaned. 'I hate that kind of publicity, but it's being around so many people that I find the hardest. I'm a small group kind of guy, and by the looks of it, half the city has been invited tonight.' Harrison laughed. 'Take me back to the Sognefjord any time.'

'Let's just try to enjoy ourselves,' she said. 'We can whirl around the room, meet everyone and do our duty, and then sneak away without anyone even knowing we're gone. We'll be ensconced in your hotel room before you know it.'

'You really do look beautiful tonight, Charlotte,' he said, his eyes searching her face.

'You're being far too kind, but thank you,' she said, knowing she was blushing.

'You don't believe me?'

'Let's just say that I'm used to praise about my food, not my appearance. The former I'm well versed at accepting, the latter not so much.'

He just shook his head at her before leading her away and through the door, as she looked around in wonder at the enormous wall of balloons that led them through into the foyer of the hotel. It was beyond stunning—someone had put so much effort into making it feel like an incredibly special event.

When they got inside, Charlotte let go of his arm and exchanged it for a glass of champagne, clinking hers against Harrison's as they both took a deep breath. They had a lot on the line tonight; they were both wanting to make the very best impression to everyone in attendance, but that didn't mean they couldn't have a good time. And Charlotte was determined to enjoy herself, no matter how tired she felt.

'Shall we divide and conquer?' Harrison asked. 'I think we might get round everyone quicker that way, and we can meet up later?'

'I agree. How about we work the room in opposite directions? Just promise me you'll come and meet my family when they get here.'

'Agreed,' he said, giving her a conspiratorial smile before draining half his champagne and walking away from her.

Charlotte took a moment to watch him, indulging in the sight of his broad shoulders in his smart black tuxedo, and she vowed to find another event for them to go to together where he could wear it again. But in the meantime, she followed his lead and sipped a healthy amount of champagne before squaring her shoulders and heading towards a group of well-dressed couples who she could already hear were raving about whatever it was the waiter had brought them to sample.

Charlotte had barely spoken to more than a handful of people before she looked up and saw her family standing near the door, and she excused herself to go and see them. She took two champagne flutes from a waiter on her way, giving one to her grandmother and then her father when she reached them. But it was Amalie to whom she spoke first, bending to greet her so that she was close to eye level with her wheelchair. She still couldn't believe that they'd been able to bring her; or convince the respite facility to give her a two-hour pass, for that matter, and Charlotte felt emotional seeing that Amalie was clutching the little wooden box in her hand, wearing the diamond ring. Without that little box, Charlotte knew for a fact that she wouldn't be standing there with her family.

'Amalie, thank you so much for coming tonight,' she said. 'I know it's probably the last thing you felt like doing, but it's wonderful to have you here.'

Amalie's grip on her hand was firm, and Charlotte welled up as she realised that they had four generations of her family in the room, which felt more than special.

'Dad, Grandma, thank you for coming too,' she said as she straightened. 'It means a lot to have you all here.' She only wished her brother had been able to attend, too.

'Of course we're here, we're your family,' her grandmother said.

Charlotte felt a touch to her lower back, and she turned to find Harrison standing there. She beamed at him, so pleased that he'd chosen to come over, especially when they hadn't exactly known each other for long. But she'd talked so much about her family to him, including Amalie, that she imagined he was curious to meet them all.

'Everyone, this is Harrison Reynolds. He's the architect of the building, and he's also one of the first friends I made when I returned to Oslo,' she said. Charlotte was careful to keep things friendly rather than make it obvious they'd been seeing each other romantically, but from the raised eyebrow her grand-mother gave her, she hadn't fooled her.

'It's a stunning building, Harrison,' Charlotte's father said. 'A true work of art, and very fitting for the location.'

'Thank you, sir. The praise means a lot, and everyone tonight has been very generous with their kind words.'

'This is Harrison?' Amalie asked, her eyes cloudy in the light as she looked up at Harrison. Charlotte watched as he crouched down beside her so that it was easier for her to talk to him, her voice fainter than it had been earlier in the week and hard to hear. But she surprised them all when she reached for his hand. 'You're the boy Charlotte keeps talking about.'

Harrison laughed and looked up at her, and Charlotte felt her cheeks burn, but she just smiled. Amalie was only telling the truth—she had talked about him to her. A lot! She just hadn't expected Amalie to remember—or say anything.

'Well, I hope she's only said good things,' Harrison said. 'To say that Charlotte has been the highlight of my time in Oslo would be an understatement.'

Charlotte's cheeks burnt all the more then, but it was a welcome warmth, especially given the way he was looking up at her.

'My husband and I built hotels, you know,' Amalie said, her voice barely audible among the crowd of people. 'I'm pleased I lived long enough to see this one.'

'I think you've managed to impress my mother,' Charlotte's grandmother said, to which Charlotte's father chuckled. 'And take my word for it when I say that's not easy to do.'

They all laughed, but Charlotte noticed Daniel walking towards them then, flanked by a very well-dressed couple, and he was rapidly gesturing for them to join him. Their conversation with her family would have to wait for another time.

'Unfortunately, I think we're needed,' Charlotte said, bending down to tuck Amalie's blanket more tightly around her knees, before giving her grandmother a quick hug and her father a kiss on the cheek as Harrison said goodbye and shook her father's hand. 'Thank you all for coming, though, it means so much to me to have you here.'

'We wouldn't have missed it for the world,' her grandmother said, with the little cough that always managed to give Charlotte a burst of anxiety. 'It's nice to see you in your element and be able to support you.'

'We're both very proud of you, Lotte,' her dad said, and she was almost certain she saw tears shining in his eyes. 'More than I'm sure you could ever realise.'

'I'll see you all soon. Enjoy the champagne, and don't forget to try the nibbles!'

She made her way quickly over to join Harrison and Daniel, or as quickly as she could go in the towering heels she was wearing, pausing only to look at a plate of canapés carried by a waiter dressed all in white. She'd spent hours creating the menu, and then checked in constantly throughout the day on her chefs to oversee everything, and she was very happy with how it had all turned out. She'd wanted to give a teaser to the menu on offer in the restaurant, with subtle flavours and plenty of gorgeous seafood, hoping all of the guests at the opening would be eager to come back for more.

'This is Charlotte, our executive chef,' Daniel said when she joined them. 'Charlotte, this is Max and Chrissy, they're my most important investment partners.'

'It's a pleasure to meet you both,' she said, shaking their hands. 'I hope you're having a wonderful evening.'

'Well, the champagne is excellent, the food is unparalleled, and the hotel is magnificent,' Max said. 'It doesn't get any better than this.'

'It helps when you have one of the best architects on board to design for you,' Daniel said. 'And we were very happy to lure Charlotte back to Norway. She's already proving to be a fantastic asset to our team here, so I really can claim to have the best people in the business working for me.'

'Harrison, are you staying on in Oslo to work on any other projects, or are you heading back to London after this?' Chrissy asked. 'I'm interested in what other work you're generating.'

'I'll be heading back to London eventually, but I'm rather fond of Oslo now, so it's going to be hard to leave,' he said, laughing as he spoke. But the way his eyes darted to Charlotte when he paused made her wonder what he was actually thinking. They hadn't discussed what came next, how they'd make long distance work or whether this was just a light-hearted romance that would last as long as it would last. It wasn't exactly far to travel between the two countries, but Charlotte didn't want to be presumptuous. 'But if you know of anyone needing an architect locally for a commercial space...'

Daniel grinned. 'Perhaps I'll have to propose another project just to keep Harrison here. After all, I am responsible for you two meeting, am I right?'

Charlotte knew her cheeks had turned a deep shade of pink from how much they were burning, and when she glanced at Harrison, he looked as embarrassed as she did. They hadn't talked to anyone about their romantic relationship, other than in front of his friends when they'd been on their little holiday, although clearly they hadn't been discreet enough if Daniel had figured it out.

'You two are a couple?' Chrissy asked. 'What a talented pair you are.'

'We, ah—' Charlotte looked to Harrison for help, but he didn't give her any. 'More champagne!' she said, reaching for the full glasses being passed around on silver trays.

Thankfully her diversion seemed to work, and she quietly excused herself, relieved when Harrison followed so that she didn't have to walk through the crowd alone. Her cheeks were only just starting to go back to a normal temperature.

'Well, that was awkward.'

'Did you tell Daniel about us?' Harrison asked.

'No! Of course I didn't, but I imagine he guessed from the amount of time we've been spending together,' Charlotte replied. She reached out to him, catching his hand. 'I'm sorry if it made you uncomfortable, but I haven't said anything to him or anyone else.'

She tried not to look hurt when he pulled his hand away, sliding it into his pocket instead. They'd spent days in each other's company, not to mention intimately, which made his rebuff all the worse—this wasn't like him keeping a distance when they first met.

'Harrison, we can keep this just between us if you want to,' she said. 'No one else needs to know what's happening with us, but we can't help it if they guess.'

He softened then; she could see it in his face and the way his shoulders dropped from where he'd had them bunched up. It was as if his whole body suddenly relaxed.

'Sorry, it's just...' He sighed and reached for her hand this time, giving it a squeeze. 'I wasn't expecting to be introduced as a couple. It took me by surprise, because I honestly hadn't thought about anyone seeing us like that. I'm sorry.'

'I understand. You have nothing to apologise for.'

Charlotte braved a smile, wishing that she didn't feel so unsure of herself even though she'd just told him that she understood. *He spent his entire adult years being introduced as a couple with his wife, of course this is weird for him.* But even though they'd arrived together, walked together through the room, shoulders brushing, talking to the other guests and swilling champagne, she had the strangest feeling that something had suddenly shifted between them. That the closeness they'd shared as little as fifteen minutes earlier had disappeared, only to be replaced with something that she wasn't quite sure how to describe.

She watched Harrison's face as he spoke to a guest about the design, his expressions bringing his features to life as he talked about his process in creating the hotel, and she knew then why it had hurt so much before when he'd pulled away from her.

I'm in love with him. I barely even know the man, yet somehow I've fallen head over heels in love.

And she had no idea what to do about it, or how to stop her heart from beating double time at the realisation.

———

'Well, that was a night,' Charlotte said, flopping down onto the bed an hour later and kicking off her stilettos. She wasn't used to wearing heels, and certainly not for so many hours straight.

Harrison sat on the edge beside her as she lay back, looking as relieved as she felt that they'd finally been able to escape the crowd. They'd waited until her family had gone, and until Daniel had seemingly introduced them to everyone in the room, and then they'd slid away separately and met at the lifts. Now, they were in Harrison's hotel room for the night, and Charlotte was thinking that it felt as if she was lying on a cloud, the bed was so soft and comfortable. In fact, if she'd just closed her eyes, she imagined that she could have fallen asleep fully dressed and not stirred until morning, she was so tired.

'I've never been so pleased to get back to my hotel room,' Harrison said, taking off his jacket and tie. 'I can't believe how many people were down there, or how many hands I shook in the space of a few hours.'

'Everyone wanted their chance to meet the famous architect,' she teased, reaching out to him. 'Daniel was so proud of you, it was written all over his face whenever he introduced you to someone new. I hope you know what a wonderful success this project has been—everyone loves it.'

He looked back at her and smiled, and she took her chance to stand up so that she could step out of her dress. Harrison's hands were warm against her skin, and she leaned back into him, her back bare, feeling his breath against her. Something had shifted between them tonight, but now that they were alone, they'd slipped straight back into the easy way they'd always been together. And for that she was grateful—she'd had the strangest feeling earlier that Harrison was pulling away from her, that something had changed the way he felt about her. But now, it felt like they'd gone back to their normal, relaxed in each other's company.

Charlotte slowly turned then, dropping her dress and standing only in her underwear in front of him. She stroked her fingers through Harrison's hair as his hands settled on her waist, staring down with eyes that seemed to see straight to her soul.

There were so many things she wanted to say, things she could have said, but she chose to push him backwards instead and lower herself over him. She pressed her lips to his in a kiss that quickly became deeper and more urgent, wanting to show him how she felt instead of having to try to explain it.

I love you. They were the words she most wanted to say, words that had been stuck in her throat ever since she'd realised how she truly felt about him earlier in the night, but by the time she felt brave enough to say them, she suddenly had other things on her mind.

In the morning. I can wait and tell him in the morning. Nothing will change between now and then.

Not to mention that Harrison's hands skimming over her skin soon made her forget everything, and she was even more grateful that they'd chosen to leave the party early.

26

HOPE'S HOUSE, 1951

Amalie sat at the table and held the little box. When Hope had first talked to her about making a keepsake for her child to open one day, she'd balked at the thought, but now that she'd begun to accept that she might have to spend her life without her baby, she'd started to warm to the idea.

'How are you doing?' Hope asked, her hand brushing Amalie's shoulder as she passed. 'Have you decided what to put inside?'

Amalie sighed. 'Yes and no,' she said, staring down at the ring that was still sitting on her finger. 'I want to leave my ring for the baby, it's the only thing I have that is connected to both me and Oskar, but I can't bear the thought of taking it off.' She'd worn the ring from the moment Oskar had slid it onto her finger, and she'd never imagined not wearing it. 'But then sometimes I'm so angry with him for leaving me, even though I know that's completely irrational, that I want to take it off and throw it away.'

'Well, all I'll say is that whatever you choose to put in there, the box will be hidden away safely in my office,' Hope said. 'You can change your mind at any time, and if you'd like, you could even wait until after the baby is born. There's no hurry.'

'I just have this feeling that I want to finish the box today,' Amalie said. 'I've had it beside my bed for so many days now, and I want to know that it's done. That if something happened to me during labour, or if, heaven forbid, I do have to make that decision to part with my baby, that I did this while I was happy, with love in my heart, still believing that a miracle might happen.' Thinking about the box was a constant reminder of the decision she was going to have to make. Being with Hope felt like she was in a little cocoon, feeling safe and protected, but she knew that there was only so long she could stay there; only so long she would have there with her child after the birth.

'Mother knows best,' Hope said. 'I'll give you some privacy.'

'Actually, Hope, could you stay?' Amalie asked.

'Of course I can,' Hope said. 'I could do with a minute off my feet.'

Amalie opened the box and took a deep breath, but she knew what she had to do. She slowly slid the ring from her finger, holding it in her palm and closing her eyes as she remembered the day Oskar had asked her to marry him. She could still feel his warm breath against her skin, still remember the way his lips had felt against hers and the comfort she'd felt with his arms wrapped tightly around her. Tears began to slip down her cheeks as she opened her eyes and placed the ring in the box, knowing in her heart that it was the right thing to do. Oskar was gone now, and if she was going to leave something behind for her baby, she needed it to be a reminder of him. Today she felt strong enough to take it off, but perhaps another day she wouldn't.

'Have you thought of anything else you'd like to put in there?' Hope asked, her voice as reassuring and gentle as always. 'I think two or three things are nice, it makes it a special collection of mementos.'

'I've cut this from a blanket I brought with me,' Amalie said. 'It's an emblem of Norway, so the baby will know where he or she comes from.' She passed it to Hope.

'It's perfect,' she said.

'What have other mothers put in their boxes?' Amalie asked, before realising that what she really wanted to know was how many little boxes just like this Hope had tucked away somewhere for safekeeping. 'How many times have you sat here and helped someone like me make this decision?'

Hope sat back, and for the first time since she'd arrived, Amalie noticed that she looked weary.

'You know, it's the boxes that I find the most emotional of all,' Hope said. 'Once a mother makes one of these, it's as if it contains all her love, all her hopes and dreams for her child, and the belief that one day her child will come looking for her.' Hope gazed out of the window, as if she were lost in thought, but when she looked back, Amalie could see the emotion in her eyes. 'The women who choose to leave these boxes are the ones who truly don't want to be parted from their baby. They're the ones with broken hearts, and that's why I find it so hard.'

Amalie was fighting her own tears again now. 'Not everyone feels the way I feel?' she asked.

'There are some young women who come here and they're only girls. They have their whole lives ahead of them, but a boy convinced them to go all the way and they've paid the ultimate price. They don't want to be mothers, they just want the chance to start their life over again and pretend that it never happened. So they don't leave anything behind because they don't want to be found. They don't even want to remember they ever gave birth.'

Amalie nodded, understanding what she was saying. She could already imagine that type of girl, barely a woman, and certainly not ready to become a mother, because it might have been her perhaps, if she'd made a mistake and ended up pregnant. But nothing about being pregnant with Oskar's child felt like a mistake, which was the reason it felt so hard.

'Then there are the mothers, like you, who have faced great loss. Women like you are making the biggest sacrifice of all to give their child the life they believe they deserve, even though it breaks their heart to do so. They're the ones who will do anything to make sure their child might be able to find them one day.'

'I'm sorry you have to go through this with me,' Amalie whispered. 'I can see how hard it must be for you.'

After another long pause, Hope spoke again. 'Amalie, I was like you once, but I had no one who cared enough to help me. I vowed then and there that if there was ever anything I could do to stop another young mother from feeling the way I was made to feel, that I would do it. And I've ended up dedicating my life to doing just that.'

Amalie's eyes widened. 'You, you were—'

'Pregnant? Yes,' Hope said. 'And these boxes, they're something I wish I could have left for my child, because I truly do understand the sense of helplessness you're feeling.'

Amalie went to ask another question, but Hope shook her head.

'That's more than enough reminiscing for me today. Now, shall we tie this box, or do you have something else to add?'

'I do actually have one more thing,' Amalie said. 'It's in my room. I won't be a minute.'

She stood, stretching her back out before walking down the hall and up the stairs to her bedroom. Her back had been aching by afternoon every day lately, and she'd had some painful contractions only the day before, but today, despite how weary her body was, she felt good.

Amalie went to her bedside table and took out the photograph of her and Oskar, the one that had been taken of the two of them outside the front of the hotel. He'd given it to her as a reminder of their summer, and she'd treasured it ever since. Now, though, she had the most overwhelming feeling that she needed to leave it behind. At least this way, when their child was old enough, they would be able to see what they both looked like, and she preferred that to leaving some mysterious clues in a box that would be almost impossible to solve. Hope had told her that she would endeavour to have the box gifted to her child once he or she reached adulthood, and Amalie wanted to make sure the items inside were worthy of such an occasion.

She turned to go back downstairs just as a sharp pain sliced though her abdomen. Amalie cried out and gripped the doorframe, holding on tightly until the pain subsided. She placed her hand to her side and breathed through it, worried that something was wrong. As soon as it passed, she quickly went back downstairs, holding the handrail tightly for support and shuffling towards the kitchen.

'Hope,' she called out once she was closer. 'Hope!'

Hope appeared, just as another pain sluiced through her. Before she knew it, there was a dampness between her legs that turned into a steady trickle.

'Something's wrong,' she whispered, terrified.

'No, my darling, nothing's wrong. Your baby is on its way.'

'But it's too early!' Amalie cried.

'It's not too early, it'll be just fine. Besides, babies work to their own schedule,' Hope said, patting her shoulder and taking the photo from her hand. 'I'll put this photo in the box for you, and you start to make your way back to your room. Take it nice and slow, don't forget to breathe, and I'll put some water on to boil and get some towels.'

Amalie froze, too scared to move, not wanting to be without Hope for even a second. 'I don't think I can do this,' she whispered. 'I'm not ready.'

'No one's ever ready to birth their first baby,' Hope said. 'Just trust me and trust your body, and everything will be fine. It'll take a while for things to progress, so try to stay calm for now.'

Amalie nodded, knowing that now was not the time to start worrying. She was having this baby whether she wanted to or not. 'That's my Oskar,' she murmured, as a wave of pain made her stomach go taut.

Hope held up the photo and smiled. 'And how handsome he is,' she said. 'Are you sure you don't want to keep the photo a little longer?'

Amalie shook her head, both hands on her stomach now as she braced herself for the next wave of pain.

'Head up those stairs nice and slow, and I'll be up in a minute,' Hope said, her voice so soothing, her experience obvious. 'Just remember you're going to meet your baby soon, Amalie. That's all you need to think about.'

Almost two hours later, and Amalie realised that the pain she'd felt earlier was nothing compared to the deep, rolling pain that kept coming in waves now. She groaned and gripped the sheet beneath her just as a loud knock echoed out from downstairs. Hope brushed her hair from her forehead and held a damp cloth to her skin, ignoring whoever was at the door, soothing Amalie with her words and her touch.

'It doesn't matter if the Pope himself is standing on my doorstep, I'm not leaving you,' she said.

But as the knocking became more and more insistent, Hope eventually wavered, and in between contractions dashed down to see who it was. Amalie hoped it wasn't an emergency, because she was in no state to be moved from the bed.

Another wave of pain clawed at her stomach, and she cried

out just as Hope returned. But she could tell something was wrong the moment she saw her standing in the doorway.

'Amalie, you have a visitor,' Hope said.

'A visitor?' Amalie gasped, barely able to catch her breath. 'Now?'

'Amalie?' A voice she'd never imagined she'd ever hear again reached her, as an impeccably dressed woman with a handbag tucked beneath her arm appeared behind Hope.

Pain clutched her again, the time between contractions so short now that the pain was beginning to feel as if it never stopped.

Hope rushed back to her side and lifted the sheet that was draped across her for modesty, her eyes meeting Amalie's as if to ask if it was all right to have this woman in the room with her.

But as she closed her eyes from the pain, wondering how much longer she could cope, a hand clasped hers. And when she finally opened her eyes, she saw Oskar's mother sitting there beside her, gripping her hand as if her life depended on it.

'You came,' Amalie whispered.

'I'm here, Amalie,' she said. 'After receiving your letter, how could I not?'

Hope's hand touched Amalie's knee then, and Amalie heard the words she'd been waiting for, the words she needed to hear before the pain became too much to bear.

'It's time to push,' Hope said. 'With the next contraction, I want you to grip that hand and push with all your might.'

Amalie gritted her teeth, staring up at Oskar's mother. She'd never noticed before, but his mother had the same beautiful dark eyes as Oskar, and as their eyes met, it was almost as if it was him looking back at her. Telling her she could do it, that he would always be there with her, and it gave her the strength she needed.

Amalie gripped Oskar's mother's hand then, pushing and

pushing until she felt as if her lower half was about to split in two, hearing him in her mind, telling her that she was almost there.

And then a cry that sounded more like a meow rang out through the room.

'Congratulations, Amalie. It's a healthy baby girl.'

27

It was no exaggeration to say that Amalie had spent many hours thinking about Oskar's family, particularly his mother, and resenting the way she'd treated them. She'd lain awake at night imagining what their life could have been if they hadn't had to hide their love, banished by his family. Oskar would never have set foot on that plane, they would never have been parted, and he would likely be sitting beside her right now cradling their baby daughter in his arms.

But now that his mother was here, Amalie had let all those thoughts go. Because she now saw his mother as the person standing between her being able to keep her baby or not, and she intended on doing anything and everything she could to convince her that she and the baby should stay together.

'She's just the loveliest little baby, Amalie,' his mother said, rocking her on the chair beside Amalie's bed. Amalie had been up a lot in the night nursing and holding her, so it was nice to have a little rest. 'My boys were such big babies, but she's perfectly delicate. Our little lady.'

Amalie's ears pricked up at her comment. *Our* little lady. That's what she'd said.

'I, ah—' Amalie began, knowing she would need to be careful with her words. 'I just wanted to thank you for coming. When I wrote to you, I didn't know whether you'd want to hear from me or not, but—'

'Amalie, please,' she said, no longer rocking and instead holding the baby still now that she was asleep. 'We were wrong to treat you so harshly. You must understand that we had different hopes for Oskar. He was our son and we'd imagined a certain life for him, but I can see now that what he needed from us was our support, not our condemnation.'

She listened, hope rising in her chest.

'Oskar loved you, he made that abundantly clear to us before he left that fateful night, and I know that your daughter can't replace him, but she's part of my son. I can't see her turned over to another family, Amalie. She's all I have left of him.'

Her hope was almost immediately replaced with horror. She knew straightaway what was coming; knew that the olive branch she'd hoped for wasn't at all what she'd expected.

'Amalie, you're a mother now, so I know you want what's best for your daughter. Let me take her and raise her. She will want for nothing, and I know it's what my Oskar would have wanted.'

'Wanted?' Amalie cried, her voice so pained that it woke her sleeping daughter. She swung her legs from the bed and plucked her from Oskar's mother's arms before she had a chance to comfort her or scold Amalie for her loud words. 'What Oskar *wanted* was for you to accept us and welcome me into your lives. If it weren't for you, he would still be alive today, so don't you *dare* talk to me about what's best for my child!'

His mother's eyes filled with tears, but the set of her jaw told Amalie that she wasn't backing down. But neither was Amalie. She'd been right: Amalie *was* a mother now, and that meant that there was nothing she wouldn't do to secure a future for her daughter, one that involved either her own mother raising her, or being given to a family who would love and cherish her. Not to this evil woman.

'Amalie, that's not fair.'

'Not fair? Not fair is falling pregnant to a man I adored beyond words, and then having his family make it abundantly clear that I wasn't good enough, that our love meant *nothing*,' she fumed, jiggling her daughter as she cried. 'Not fair is having the man I loved killed in a plane crash! A plane he was only on because he had to flee his family so that we could marry secretly in London!'

Amalie could barely breathe, her chest rising and falling rapidly, her hands shaking. And she'd never been so grateful to see anyone in her life when Hope came running into the room, out of breath likely from having to hurry up the staircase.

'What's happening in here?' she asked, looking between them and seeing how distressed Amalie was. She immediately came to stand beside her, placing a protective hand on Amalie's shoulder before turning to her house guest. 'Perhaps it's time for you to leave?'

Oskar's mother began to cry then, a little hiccup of a tear that turned into chest-heaving sobs, and it only made Amalie more upset. This woman had lost her son, they shared the same grief, and yet they were still worlds apart.

'The way I see it,' Hope said, 'is that you're both grieving. And you have this beautiful baby who has two women in her life who could love her. But Amalie is her *mother*, and I won't see her bullied into anything.'

Oskar's mother's tears were slowly subsiding, and Amalie whispered to her daughter, cradling her close and deciding to nurse her to comfort her.

'Amalie, I'm sorry,' Oskar's mother said, wiping her eyes and her cheeks as she straightened her shoulders and faced her. 'I loved my Oskar so very much, even if you didn't get to see that love first hand, and I only want what's best for the baby.'

'So do I,' Amalie whispered, careful not to scare her daughter again. 'But what's best for my child is to be with her mother, and nothing you say will convince me otherwise.'

Hope looked to her, giving Amalie the strength to continue.

'If you want your granddaughter in your life, then you will have to accept me, too. You either welcome us both into your life, or neither of us.'

'And if I was to do that, what exactly would you propose? This darling girl would still be a bastard in the eyes of—'

'Don't you say that word ever again about my daughter,' Amalie said. 'She is the daughter of your son. We were engaged to be married, and our wedding was to be within days of Oskar's arrival, so I will not stand to hear such a thing said about her, as if she was a mistake or an afterthought.'

She fixed her gaze on Oskar's mother.

'I would ask that you give me a day or two to send a telegram to my husband,' she said. 'May I ask that you don't make any decisions until then?'

'You may,' Amalie said, finding a strength she didn't even know she possessed. 'And until then, I would ask that you give me space to spend time with my daughter.'

It may have sounded cold, but she was starting to realise that the only way for her to receive respect was to act as if she held all the cards.

His mother stood, staring down at the now sleeping baby who was still nestled against Amalie's breast. 'Of course. I'll see you tomorrow or the day after.'

Hope stood as well, to see her out, but when she reached the door, she turned around and gave Amalie a smile that imbued her with all the strength she needed not to burst into tears the moment she was alone in the room.

When Oskar's mother returned two days later, it was as if she'd become a different woman. She came with a bag full of tiny clothes that looked far more expensive than anything Amalie or her family could ever have afforded, and also with a wrapped gift for Amalie. But it wasn't just the things she'd brought, likely as peace offerings. It was almost like a weight had lifted, that there was no longer such a divide between them.

Amalie slid her fingernail beneath the seal of the tissue paper parcel on her lap, surprised to find a beautiful lavender-coloured dress and a jacket to match, with striking gold buttons. The fabric felt almost buttery against her skin; more luxurious than anything she'd ever touched before.

'Thank you,' she said, eyes wide as she glanced up. Amalie had no idea where she might wear something so luxurious, but she was most grateful for the experience.

'Amalie, I know we've had our differences, and I know that it will take a long time for you to trust me, especially after our last conversation,' she said. 'But will you return to Oslo with me? To our home? Will you let me look after you both?'

Tears filled Amalie's eyes as she looked back at the woman who'd once been so cold towards her, and who was now her saviour. She had no idea why the sudden turnaround, but however it had happened, she was going to accept it.

'Yes,' Amalie said, holding her daughter to her chest and nuzzling her little downy head. 'So long as we can stay together, we'll return with you.'

Amalie hadn't dared to hope, hadn't wanted to dream that there might be a chance she wouldn't be parted from her daughter. But she'd been right to stand up for herself, to fight for what she knew was right. It might have been hard at the time, but in the end, she'd received the respect she deserved.

'When do we leave?' Amalie asked. 'Will we travel together?'

'As soon as I can secure passage, we'll return home,' she said, looking as relieved as Amalie felt. 'You don't have to worry about anything, Amalie, we intend to take care of you, just as my Oskar would have done.'

'Your husband, he agreed to this?' Amalie asked, feeling a flicker of worry inside. 'You're certain that he'll welcome me into your home? That he'll accept me? Is that why you're here?'

'I received a telegram just this morning from him,' she said. 'We'll have to discuss arrangements further once we're home, but you have my word that you'll be able to stay with your daughter, and we'll support you so long as she remains a part of our lives.'

Amalie's worries slowly lifted. There were so many reasons not to trust the woman standing before her, but she felt content in the idea of moving back to Norway—to speak her language, to be in a city, a *country* that she knew, where she didn't feel like a fish out of water with no control over her own destiny.

'Your daughter will keep Oskar's memory alive every single day,' his mother said. 'Please accept my heartfelt apologies and know that from this day forward, you will be a member of our family. We will treasure you and our granddaughter, and treat you both with the respect you deserve. And you will help this grieving mother, because I miss my wonderful boy so much, and this will be like having a piece of him still with us.'

'Thank you,' Amalie said, even though she still felt a flicker of doubt as to whether she could trust her. 'I'm grateful for the chance for us to stay together. Adoption would have broken my heart.'

'And mine, too, Amalie. I couldn't have let that happen.'

Amalie saw that Hope was hovering in the hallway, having clearly overheard what was being said but not wanting to intrude.

'Hope,' Amalie called. 'We have wonderful news to share with you.'

Oskar's mother bristled, her coldness not completely gone

as Amalie passed her baby to Hope for a cuddle, now that she was fed and freshly changed. Amalie could see that she was a woman she would always have to be on guard around, not to mention careful about just how much influence she had over her daughter.

'We're to return to Oslo,' Amalie said. 'We won't be parted after all.'

'That *is* wonderful news,' Hope said. 'Congratulations.'

Amalie glanced at her daughter's grandmother, and as elated as she was, she knew better than to think it would be without its challenges. But as Hope passed her baby back to her and she traced her eyes over her perfect little nose and pink mouth, her tiny hands fisted as she gazed back at her mother, Amalie knew that it would all be worth it. She was a mother now, and there was nothing more important to her in the world.

'Oh, and Amalie?'

She looked up.

'I thought you might like to wear that dress to travel home in, since I wasn't sure whether you had any other suitable clothes, and I'll be certain to have some more outfits delivered to our home for you on our return.'

Amalie imagined she might feel like royalty travelling in such an outfit, and she wasn't certain how she would nurse during the journey, but she gave her a polite nod, anyway.

'That was very thoughtful of you, thank you. It will be nice to wear something fashionable now that I have my figure back somewhat.'

She knew it was silly, but Amalie couldn't help wondering why Mrs Johansen wanted her dressed so impeccably for the journey, or who might be seeing them at the other end when they arrived for her to make such an effort. But then again, there was a chance she was overthinking the entire situation and that his mother was simply trying to be kind and show her change of heart with gifts.

Either way, the outfit was stunning, and she didn't intend to let Oskar's family down now. If they wanted her well-heeled, then she certainly wasn't going to complain.

Four days later, Amalie stood on the doorstep with Hope and hugged her goodbye, wondering how she was going to cope without having her by her side, as a constant source of comfort and love. Her own family had turned their backs on her when she'd needed them most, but Hope had been her everything, and she only wished she had the words to express how much she'd come to mean to her.

'I can't believe it's time to go. Thank you, for everything. It goes without saying that I would have been lost without you.' Amalie couldn't imagine what would have happened to her if she hadn't found herself at Hope's House, so she didn't even let her mind take her there. She'd had nightmares and woken up some nights in a sweat, tangled in her sheets as she imagined herself on the streets, begging for money and clutching her bulging belly, or more recently, holding her daughter against her body in a ragged blanket.

'I want you to make me one promise before you go,' Hope said, holding her tight.

'Anything for you.'

'I want you to promise that you'll live a beautiful life full of happiness with your gorgeous daughter,' Hope said. 'You've suffered a great loss, but you've also been given a source of joy, so don't ever forget that. No one can take your daughter away from you unless that's what you want, so you keep fighting to live that beautiful life together.'

Amalie wished they'd had longer, that there had been time for her to ask Hope more. But there could be no more questions, only goodbyes. She realised then why she loved Hope so much

—it was because she wasn't afraid to tell Amalie to dream, to fight for what she wanted, and the only other person in her life who'd ever said those things was Oskar. Which led her to imagine that Hope had suffered just as much as many of the girls who walked through her door, if not more.

'I'll never forget you, Hope,' she murmured as they embraced one last time, ignoring Oskar's mother clearing her throat impatiently on the footpath as she waited for Amalie to join her. 'I only wish we weren't going to be so far apart. I can't imagine my life without you in it.'

'And I will never forget you,' Hope said, kissing first Amalie's left cheek, and then her right. 'Write to me, won't you? Don't let this be goodbye.'

'I will. Of course I will.'

When she finally let go and joined Oskar's mother in the car, Amalie stared after Hope until she couldn't see her any longer, her heart aching. And it wasn't until they were far from Hope's House that Amalie glanced at her finger and realised what was missing, what she'd left behind without even thinking.

She'd forgotten all about the box she'd made; the ring Oskar had given her was still in there, waiting to be discovered by the daughter who was instead safely in her arms. It had been such a whirlwind since her daughter had arrived, and it wasn't until now that she'd even thought about it.

I'll have her send it to me, Amalie thought to herself. But she knew in her heart that as much as she missed the ring, it was nothing compared to the pain she would have felt if she'd been forced to leave her daughter to discover the diamond one day.

That would have been a pain I'd never have survived.

'I think I finally have a name for her,' Amalie said, smiling down at her daughter. She'd been reluctant to name her until she knew they were going to stay together, and then she'd found it almost impossible to think of something that suited her.

'I will call her Aina,' she said. 'I was thinking of naming her

Hope, but I think this suits her, or at least it suits us and the journey we've been through.'

'Aina it will be then.'

Amalie stared down at her daughter, whispering her name over and over as the baby gazed back at her, her fingers clutched tightly to Amalie's finger. Her name meant *forever*, it symbolised eternity, and she knew in her heart that there couldn't be a name more suitable for the daughter she'd almost lost, but who was now going to be by her side for the rest of her life.

28

This time when Amalie walked through the door of the Johansen family home, she was escorted with the kind of importance that made her nervous. On the journey from London, she'd imagined being imprisoned in an upstairs bedroom like Rapunzel, or worried that her baby might be snatched from her, but so far Oskar's mother had kept her word and had been perfectly pleasant.

But she could tell that something was about to happen when they arrived, and she asked her to go through to the sitting room and take a seat.

'What about my luggage?' Amalie asked. 'I'd like to change Aina and...'

'Just wait a moment, Amalie. I know someone has been waiting to see you.'

She nodded and politely did as she was told, imagining it was Oskar's father wanting to welcome her. Amalie rocked the baby and walked around the room, staring out of the window at the grounds and imagining what it had been like for Oskar to grow up somewhere so grand. She didn't know where she'd be living, whether it would be here or perhaps somewhere more modest, but either way she would be happy, so long as her daughter was with her.

A man cleared his throat and she turned, expecting to see Oskar's father, but instead found herself facing his brother.

'Alexander!' She smiled the moment she saw him, seeing such similarities to Oskar as she studied his face that it was impossible not to warm to him. Not to mention how he'd been so kind to her when they'd first met. 'You've come to meet your niece?'

Amalie held her out in her arms, thinking he might like to cradle her, but Alexander clasped his hands behind his back instead, looking unsure of himself.

'You look well, Amalie,' he said. 'I trust your journey was comfortable?'

She frowned, wondering why he was behaving in such a formal manner. 'Alexander, I'm so sorry about Oskar. I loved him so much, but I know the pain of losing a brother must be even greater.'

He nodded, and just as he raised his gaze and looked into her eyes, as if he were about to say something, his mother entered the room. Her perfume filled the air and she touched her son's arm on the way past, giving him a look Amalie couldn't decipher.

'Well, I'd hoped your father would be here for this, Alexander, but Amalie, I want you to know that we have his blessing.'

She glanced between them, not liking the way Alexander looked at the ground, avoiding her gaze. Amalie held her daughter tighter to her chest.

'Have his blessing for what, exactly?'

'Amalie, you must understand that we cannot have you living with us, *in society*, as an unmarried mother with a...' Her voice drifted away, and she gave a tight smile. 'Well, we cannot have a child in the family without a father, can we?'

Amalie stared back at her. 'But you said I was welcome, you said—'

'What my mother is trying to tell you is that we're to be married,' Alexander said. 'I will marry you and raise my brother's daughter as my own, thereby erasing all hint of a scandal.'

'But—' Amalie's heart began to race.

'Oskar would have wanted this,' he said. 'I know it doesn't feel right, but my mother isn't wrong this time. If we want to give his daughter the future she deserves, this is the only way.'

'You'd marry me?' Amalie asked, feeling at once overwhelmingly grateful but also nauseated at the thought of marrying a man, *any* man, so soon after Oskar, not to mention his brother. 'I cannot ask that of you, I—'

'You don't have to,' he said, somewhat drily. 'My mother is the one who asked me, and I could see no good reason not to accept. My brother adored you, Amalie, and I shall care for you in his absence and try to be the very best father I can be to your daughter.'

Alexander moved closer to her then, taking a ring box from his pocket and falling to one knee as Amalie tried to hold back her tears.

'Amalie, will you marry me?' he asked.

She nodded, quickly, not wanting to say yes because it felt like a betrayal of Oskar's memory, but knowing that she had to give her consent for her own sake, and for her daughter's.

'You will accept me as your daughter-in-law?' Amalie said, glancing over at his mother.

'I will.'

'Then yes, Alexander, I will marry you, if you're certain you're not being coerced into this union.'

He looked into her eyes, and she saw both pain and kindness there. He was a man mourning his brother, but he was also a good man, the kind of man who would do whatever he had to do to keep his brother's daughter close.

Alexander took the ring from the box and slid it onto her finger. It was a setting of three diamonds, each one larger than the single one Oskar had given her, on a gold band that fit snugly against her skin. She couldn't take her eyes from it as he rose, feeling the weight of it and imagining that this would be the ring she'd now wear for the rest of her life.

'Thank you,' she said, standing on tiptoe to press a light kiss to his cheek. 'I will never, ever forget your kindness in my moment of need, Alexander.'

His cheeks coloured and she held Aina out to him, gently placing her in his arms.

'This, Alexander, is your nie—' She stopped herself and smiled, forcing the words out. 'Your *daughter*, Aina. Isn't she beautiful?'

As if on cue, Aina woke and stretched one perfect little pink fist from the within the blanket, her mouth twisting as she yawned and opened her eyes. And as Amalie leaned into Alexander, she could almost imagine that it was Oskar whom she was standing beside, both men different yet so similar in many ways. Even the faint scent of his cologne reminded her of him.

'You're to be married this week, in a private ceremony,' his mother said, interrupting the quiet moment between them. 'Alexander will be travelling for work after that and you shall accompany him, and when he returns, we'll tell everyone that you both married privately some time ago. No one will dare ask questions, not if we have our story carefully planned out.'

Alexander passed the baby back to Amalie then as she began to cry. 'I'll do whatever you ask of me,' Amalie said. 'But may I be shown to my room so that I can feed and change my daughter?'

. . .

A short time after settling in, after she'd fed and bathed Aina, there was a knock at the door. She straightened her dress, still wearing what she'd arrived in, and called out. 'Who is it?'

'Alexander.'

She took a deep, shaky breath and opened the door. But the smile he gave her told her that she had nothing to worry about.

'I wanted to speak to you without my mother overhearing,' he said. 'May I come in?'

'Of course.'

She noticed that he left the door open, for which she was grateful. There was a fine line between speaking in private and making it appear as if they might be acting inappropriately, and she certainly didn't want to jeopardise her new relationship with the family.

'Amalie,' Alexander said, pacing to the bed and then taking the chair. 'I want you to know that it wasn't my mother's idea for us to get married.'

Amalie sat down, placing the baby on the bed beside her. 'When you never wrote back to me—'

'Wrote back to you?' he said, looking puzzled. 'When did you write to me?'

'To ask for your help, after Oskar died and before the baby...' Her voice trailed off. 'Your mother must have intercepted the letter.'

Alexander's face hardened. 'Tell me what you wrote.'

She nodded. 'I asked for your assistance. I told you how heartbroken I was and that without your help I would be forced to give up—'

'Enough,' he ground out. 'Oskar was right to send you away, even though it had terrible consequences. He knew that it was best to make a new life far away from here.'

'And you?'

He sighed. 'I'm my father's only heir now, and he's ready to hand over the business in the coming years. If I had to, to protect you and the baby, I would willingly leave it all behind, but...' Alexander looked uncomfortable.

'If you're afraid of telling me something, you needn't be. If we're to be married, I need you to speak your mind.'

'It's not that I don't want to marry you, Amalie, it's just...' He shook his head. 'You were the love of my brother's life, and I don't want to disrespect his memory.'

'You're not,' she said, leaning forwards and touching his knee. 'You're saving me, Alexander, truly you are. And if we're to be partners, then you need to know you can confide in me.'

'I've never hidden my ambitions, and I want to take over the family business, but to do that, I, *we*, need to bide our time. I won't stand for any bad behaviour towards you, but we need to tread carefully.'

Amalie understood what he was saying, or at least she thought she did. 'You keep my daughter safe, and I'll stand by your side and do whatever you ask of me,' she said. 'We might not be in love, but there's no reason this marriage can't be a success.'

Alexander's smile reminded her of Oskar's again, but it was slightly more reserved, and she had a feeling she knew why.

'Did Oskar ever talk to you about his dreams?' she asked.

'When we were boys, yes, but not in recent years. Why do you ask?'

'The first night we met, he talked to me of his dreams, and I think that's what we need to make this marriage a happy one,' she said. 'We need to share our dreams, for us and for Aina, and work together to make those dreams come true.'

'Then dream we shall,' Alexander said, holding out his hand to her.

She placed her palm in his, feeling a sense of calm as an understanding of sorts passed between them. Amalie didn't love Alexander, but she respected him, and she knew that maybe one day that might slowly develop into something more. But for now, she had an ally, someone who acutely understood her grief; and someone whom she knew would grow to love her daughter just as much as she did. For he would see himself in Aina, begin to feel that she was truly his, and although it wasn't the life she had imagined for herself, Amalie was prepared to accept it.

Because in her heart, she knew that Oskar would accept it, too.

'May I ask something of you?' Alexander said. 'And I want you to answer truthfully.'

Amalie met his gaze.

'I don't want anyone to ever know I'm not Aina's father,' he said, his voice low, almost pained. 'If even one person found out our secret, it might change the way people looked at her, and I want more for her. I want more for us. I want to keep the truth a secret, forever.'

'Then we won't ever tell her,' Amalie said, as tears pricked her eyes. 'She will be your daughter, Alexander, and no one but us ever has to know the truth.'

Amalie thought of the little box then, of the photo, and as much as she'd wanted to retrieve the ring Oskar had given her, she wondered if she might not write that letter to Hope in the morning after all. Because even though she was prepared to agree with Alexander now, there was a little part of her that wanted that box to remain hidden with the photo of her and Oskar inside. Just in case there was ever a reason for the truth to be discovered, before all evidence of her daughter's true father was erased for good.

29

PRESENT DAY

'Harrison, what do you say we go out for brunch soon and then come back to...'

Charlotte stopped, her long wet hair wrapped in a towel and her body enveloped in Harrison's thick towelling robe. She'd been in the shower for ten minutes, luxuriating in the hot water that had been almost impossible to step out from under, and in that time, it seemed that everything had changed.

'What are you doing?' she asked, still standing in the same spot as she surveyed the suitcase half packed on the bed and the wardrobe almost bare.

Harrison had been in bed when she'd risen, and now he was throwing clothes and belongings into his suitcase with a methodical-looking urgency that scared her.

'Harrison?' she asked, closing the distance between them and placing her hand on his shoulder.

He spun around, and she had the strangest feeling that she was looking at a stranger. He couldn't look her in the eye, and she could see how upset he was. It was written all over his face.

'I'm sorry,' he said. 'I'm so, so sorry, Charlotte.'

'Sorry for what?' she asked, confused. 'What are you apologising for and why are you packing?'

'I can't do this,' he said, his voice barely a whisper as he ran his fingers through his hair. 'I thought I could, but I just can't.'

'Us?' she asked, incredulously. 'You're trying to tell me that you can't do *us*?'

He turned and threw more things into his case, but she pushed his shoulder, forcing him to turn around; *demanding* that he turn around.

'Why are you doing this? What's changed?' She looked around the room as if she'd missed something, as if there would be something glaringly obvious blinking at her and telling her what had gone wrong in the short time she'd been gone. 'I don't understand.'

This time his eyes slowly met hers. 'I'm sorry, Charlotte. I don't know what to tell you, but I'm not ready for this. I'm going back to London. I just... I can't do this.'

'To *London*?' Her eyes widened. 'Earlier this morning we were in bed, we had an amazing time last night at the opening, I thought we were...'

He shook his head and zipped up his bag as she stood, helpless, in the middle of his room. 'I can't face losing anyone else again, and every time I look at you...'

Charlotte swallowed. 'You see your wife?' she whispered.

'No, it's not that,' he said. 'I mean, it is, but...' He tipped his head back, like he couldn't find the words he needed, or maybe he'd hoped to disappear when she was in the shower so that he didn't even have to face her.

'I thought this was the start of something special, but you know what? You're just like everything else good in my life. Eventually, everyone I love leaves me. I should have seen this coming.'

Harrison reached for her, but Charlotte pulled away and stepped back, shaking her head.

'No, you don't touch me,' she said. 'You don't treat me like you love me and then just up and leave.' *That's what my mother did to me. She made me think that she loved me, and then she disappeared as if I'd meant nothing to her at all.*

Charlotte's skin burnt with the shame and hurt of it all, like someone had set fire to her. She wrapped the robe even tighter around herself, feeling like such a fool, hating that she'd let herself fall for him.

'Just tell me,' she asked, her throat choking up with emotion. 'Would you have left without saying goodbye? Were you trying to pack before I came out of the shower?'

'I would never have left without saying goodbye,' Harrison said. 'But I can't do this, Charlotte. I can't open myself up and risk losing you. I couldn't live through that again. I'm not ready now, and I don't know if I ever will be.'

'But what if it's worth it? I know what it's like to lose someone, to have that person disappear from your life, but don't we have to at least try? Isn't that what life is about, trusting that the next time will be different?'

'I can't,' he said. 'I'm sorry, Charlotte, but I just can't.'

She quickly brushed her eyes, not wanting to cry but finding the tears impossible to stop. They were falling furiously now, and the fact that Harrison had tears in his eyes didn't make her feel any better. Because he was the one choosing to leave. He was the one who was breaking her heart. He was the one doing this to them.

'Just go then,' she said. 'If that's what you want, just go. Please.'

'I didn't mean it to end like this,' he said.

'And yet you're doing it anyway.'

Harrison stood and she turned her back, waiting for him to go. She listened to the thud of his suitcase as he pulled it from the bed, but it was the crack in his voice that really sent a knife through her heart.

'Stay here as long as you want, the room is paid for,' he said. 'And I am sorry, Charlotte. I do wish things could have been different for us.'

Charlotte listened to him leave, waited until the door had opened and shut and she'd heard his footfalls down the hall, before she slid to the floor, crumpling forwards until her forehead touched the carpet. And then she cried so hard that her body trembled and her lungs gasped for air.

All these years she'd protected her heart, not letting anyone close enough to hurt her. Then along came Harrison, and she'd been so quick to let down her guard that she hadn't even seen the end coming.

Charlotte walked into the room to see her great-grandmother, but Amalie was asleep, and so she sat quietly beside her and reached for her hand. She didn't know why she'd come back to see her again, and she knew there was only a short time before the nurses would ask her to leave for the night, but she hadn't known where else to go.

'I think I need your help, Amalie,' she whispered, thankful when her great-grandmother stirred, her eyes fluttering open.

She made a little noise in her throat, and Charlotte stroked her hand, scared of how paper-thin the skin was, of what old age could do to a person. She clutched her fingers and tried not to cry as she spoke to her, as she asked what she'd come here to say. For there seemed no one else in the world who could understand the pain Charlotte was going through more than Amalie.

'How did you survive a broken heart?'

Amalie was silent, her breath even and telling Charlotte that perhaps she'd fallen back to sleep, but a nurse came in then. Her smile was kind as she saw Charlotte's tears, and she passed her a tissue box.

'There's nothing easy about seeing someone you love fade away,' the nurse said. 'Please don't feel as if you have to hide your tears from me.'

Charlotte nodded politely, not about to tell her that her tears were for more than her great-grandmother.

'Oh, and while I'm here, we found a letter among Amalie's things today. We were searching for a photo she wanted, and we found this. I thought you or your grandmother might want it.'

Charlotte thanked her and took it, letting go of Amalie's hand and settling back into the armchair beside the bed. Part of her wondered if she should have let her grandmother read it first, but her curiosity was too great.

To my darling daughter,

I've wrestled with telling you the truth every month, every year, every decade of your life, but something has always stopped me. Your father was everything a father should be to their child—loving, kind, warm, respectful—and my reason for not telling you is because I never wanted to take any of that away from him. I never wanted you to look at him differently or wonder about the decisions we made. But the truth is that he was not your biological father, and that's a secret we kept to protect you, and perhaps to protect him, too. And as easy as it is to look back and wonder why the truth was never told, there is never a right time to reveal such a secret. Once you're a mother, you will understand that mothers will do anything to protect their child and not be parted from them. I suppose I was always afraid that if I told you my secret, everything would fall apart, and I couldn't stand to ever see you or your father with a broken heart, to shatter the wonderful bond that you shared.

Charlotte brushed away fresh tears and folded the letter,

tucking it into her pocket so that she could give it to her grand-mother when she went home.

'Amalie,' she whispered, leaning forwards and taking her hand again, thinking about the difficult decisions she'd been forced to make. 'Amalie?'

The room suddenly felt empty, as if she was the only person there, and when Charlotte placed her palm gently on Amalie's chest, her breath caught in her throat as the most terrifying feeling passed over her.

'Amalie?' she said, giving her a little shake with her hand. 'Amalie!'

But Amalie didn't move, and Charlotte knew then that she was gone. While she'd sat there and read her letter, she'd quietly slipped away.

'Fly high, Amalie,' Charlotte whispered, sitting back in the armchair and drawing her knees up to her chest as she stared at the white-haired little lady who'd shared so many secrets over her final days, tears openly falling now as her lower lip trembled. 'We're all going to miss you so much.'

Thank you, Charlotte thought. *Thank you for telling us before it was too late. We'll never forget the story that you shared with us.*

If she hadn't come home when she had, Charlotte would never have heard Amalie's stories from the past; her secrets would have been lost forever. And although she knew it had been painful for her grandmother to hear the truth about her conception, it was a story that deserved to be told. Of a woman who'd loved two men, and who'd prospered when life had been so heavily stacked against her. Who'd made a *wonderful* life for herself, despite her pain.

Charlotte stood then, knowing she needed to notify some-one, and no longer wanting to sit in the room now that Amalie had gone. But she would forever be grateful for the time they'd spent together, and now she had to try to find the same strength in her own life. To move forward on her own, to not keep yearning for the past, but to enjoy every step into the future instead.

She bent low and whispered a final kiss to Amalie's cheek, grateful for the small miracle that she hadn't been alone when she'd passed. Once she'd found a nurse, Charlotte went to her car and sat a moment, letting herself cry before taking a deep breath and calling her grandmother.

'Charlotte?'

'Amalie's gone,' she said, through her tears. 'I was sitting with her and she just... she just slipped away.' *Someone else has left me. Someone else I loved has gone.*

'Where are you?'

Charlotte blew out another breath. 'In the car park outside.'

'Then come home, dear girl.' Her grandmother's voice caught then, her next words unable to hide the tremble of emotion. 'Come home so that we can open my best bottle of wine and remember the wonderful woman my mother was.'

'Grandma, she told me something today, something I want to tell you now before I forget it,' Charlotte said, her voice still shaky. 'She looked away and stared out of the window as if she was looking for you, and she wanted me to tell you that she was sorry. She said that they thought keeping it a secret would give you the life she deserved, and that Alexander *was* your father. She said he became the most wonderful father she could ever have imagined you to have, and she wanted you to remember that.'

Charlotte closed her eyes and remembered the way Amalie had held her hand, only a few hours before; of the way she'd turned and looked to her, as if to implore Charlotte not to forget her words. She would tell her grandmother about the letter when she got home, because it only reinforced what Amalie had said.

In that moment, it had never been clearer to Charlotte that Amalie had loved both men, very much. One for only a handful of months; the other, for a lifetime.

'Charlotte, I want you to come home. This isn't a time to be alone.'

She found herself nodding and doing as she'd been told, deciding to tell her grandmother that she'd been to see Amalie earlier in the day, too—that she'd only come back to ask her one final question.

And now at last she knew the rest of Amalie's story—she supposed it was hers to share now that she was gone, to make sure everyone knew the love story of Alexander and Amalie.

When Charlotte arrived back at her grandmother's house, she sat outside for a few minutes to gather her thoughts before going in. It had been a long day full of emotions, and even after crying so many times and feeling as if she was completely out of tears, she still found herself on the verge of welling up again as she let herself into the house.

'Is that you, Lotte?'

'Just me,' she called back to her grandmother.

She found her in the kitchen making hot chocolate, and when she turned, Charlotte could see that her eyes were red-rimmed. Charlotte immediately went to her, folding her into her arms and holding her tight.

'I can't believe she's gone,' her grandmother whispered.

Charlotte eventually let go of her and they sat down together at the table, hot chocolates in hand as they blew on them and took tentative sips.

'I'm going to miss her so much,' her grandmother said. 'I'm just so grateful you were with her when she passed, that she wasn't alone. If I'd known, if there had been any warning she was so close to the end...'

Charlotte nodded, taking a deep breath. 'It happened so quietly, so quickly.' She cleared her throat. 'I was reading a letter when she passed, one that I think was written decades ago. I don't think she could ever bring herself to give it to you.' She took it from her pocket and placed it on the table between them.

'Thank you,' she said. 'For everything. For being here while she told her story, for coming home, for—'

'Grandma, you have nothing to thank me for. I'm just so happy that I was able to spend time with her, and with you, too.'

'Why do I feel there's a *but*?' she asked. 'Has something else happened?' The way her grandmother looked at her, the way she patiently waited, made it even harder for Charlotte to tell her.

'Harrison left today.'

Her grandmother's face fell, as if she could acutely feel Charlotte's pain. 'He left Oslo?'

Charlotte only just got the words out before she burst into tears. 'He left Oslo and he, well, he left me. But now isn't the time, after what happened tonight—'

'Oh, sweetheart, I'm so sorry.'

'No, it's fine,' Charlotte said, quickly wiping away her tears. 'You've just lost your mother, I barely even knew Harrison for more than a few weeks. It's nothing, I shouldn't have even told you.'

'Amalie would have understood your broken heart more than anyone else,' her grandmother said.

'It's why I was there,' Charlotte whispered. 'I just needed to tell her that I understood how she could have been so deeply in love with her Oskar after such a short time, because it's exactly how I felt about Harrison.'

She stood up and took the chair beside her grandmother so

they could put their arms around each other, needing to hold her close.

'I know it's stupid, but I had this feeling that he was the one.'

Her grandmother smoothed her hair, stroking it gently back over and over again. 'Perhaps he still is.'

'No,' Charlotte said, reaching for her hot chocolate and realising that her hand was shaking. 'If you could have seen the look on his face, the way he told me he was leaving...'

'All I'm saying is that sometimes people change, circumstances change,' she said. 'If he's half the man you said he was, then maybe this isn't the end.'

Charlotte wished she shared her grandmother's optimism, but every time she thought of Harrison, she knew in her heart that she was never, ever going to see him again. Not after the way he'd left.

'What do you say we curl up and watch a movie?' her grandmother asked. 'Tomorrow is going to bring decisions about things I don't even want to think about, but tonight? Tonight we can enjoy spending time together, just the two of us, and pretend that all is still right in the world. What do you say?'

Charlotte didn't even have to force her smile this time. 'I say that's the best idea I've heard all day.'

Her eyes were sandpaper dry and red, her heart hurt and her body was exhausted; but there was nowhere else she'd rather be than curled up on the sofa with her grandmother.

He might have broken your heart today, but tomorrow is another day. You're too strong to let a boy break you. You're going to survive this just like you always do, she thought, giving herself a little pep talk.

'I'll bring the hot chocolates, you get the blanket from the hall cupboard,' her grandmother said, her eyes still full of her own tears.

And just like that, Charlotte was a little girl again, being comforted by her grandmother, who'd been the one grown-up in her life who'd never, ever let her down when she needed her the most.

30

OSLO, 1954

Amalie sat beside Alexander, her head dropped to his shoulder as they watched their daughter toddle about. She was an endless source of happiness and amusement, and she was also the glue that had held their marriage together as they'd struggled with their loss of Oskar in different ways. Amalie had grieved Oskar when Alexander had tried to touch her, confused about how she was feeling in the wake of his passing; and Alexander had been racked with guilt at times when they were together, feeling as if he'd stepped into his brother's life and somehow taken it from him. But more recently, they'd settled into a new life together, one that kept his mother at bay as much as possible, and allowed them to slowly develop feelings for each other that continued to grow, hour by hour, day by day, week by week. The more time they'd spent alone, just the two of them, the more they'd seen the life they could create.

Now, Amalie realised she'd known Alexander for two years, compared to the two months she'd known his brother, and her grief had slowly turned into a new-found love. Not the passionate, all-consuming first love she'd felt for Oskar, but a slower, more considerate love that had grown steadily between them, fuelled by their desire to give Aina the best life they could. It felt like a more mature love, and one that she hoped would only continue to grow with every passing year.

'Is it strange for me to say that I can see why my brother fell so hard for you?'

Amalie laughed. It was a comment they could never have shared in their first few months of marriage, even the first year, but they certainly could now.

'I often wonder what would have happened to me if I hadn't found my way back to you,' she said. 'To think that I might not have seen my daughter, *our* daughter, grow...'

Alexander held her hand and lifted it to his lips, pressing a kiss to her skin, his lips hovering. It was a thought too painful to imagine, for each of them. She didn't often let her mind wander to the past, not anymore, because she was no longer interested in looking back.

'Are you happy?' he asked, keeping hold of her hand. 'Truly happy?'

'I am,' Amalie whispered, even as she fought against tears. 'I'm grateful every day to be here with you.'

He shook his head. 'That's not what I asked. I want to know if you're happy, Amalie.'

She placed her hands on either side of his face, staring into his eyes. 'I am happy,' she said. 'Truly happy.' Then she kissed him, his warm lips moving beneath hers, a kiss that now filled her with warmth and anticipation.

'Sometimes I worry—'

'Shhh,' she said, as Aina came running towards them with her little arms outstretched. She watched as Alexander caught her and held the little girl high in his arms as she cried with delight. '*We* could not be happier. We love you, Alexander, both of your girls love you with all our hearts.'

They sat together as Aina got down and ran off again,

squealing with excitement as she put out her arms and giggled to herself about whatever game she was playing.

'Mamma!' she called. 'Pappa!'

Amalie glanced at Alexander and saw the smile that stretched his face wide as his daughter called for him. Sometimes now, she forgot entirely that Aina wasn't his natural-born daughter, because it was often Alexander who the little girl would run to, wanting to be lifted onto his shoulders or carried in his strong arms. It was Alexander she wanted curled up to her in bed, reading stories, with space made for Mamma on one side so she could listen, too.

She'd never dared to ask him what he'd given up for her. Whether there was a lover or a girlfriend he'd had to part with, whether he'd even wanted a family of his own or a wife. Because they had found their own way in the world, come to an arrangement that had become a beautiful union in so many ways, and the love she had for him now was deeper and more meaningful than anything she'd ever felt before.

'I think our daughter wants us,' she said, as Aina called their names again.

Alexander took her hand and they walked towards her, laughing as she ran circles around them and then caught Amalie around the legs, holding her tight.

'Come on, little one, it's time for lunch,' Amalie said. 'Let us swing you all the way in.'

Aina giggled with delight and ran between them, her warm little hand in Amalie's on one side, and Alexander's on the other, as they swung her back and forth between them.

Amalie thought of Hope then, as she looked up at the blue sky, and wondered what she was doing, whether she was happy. The one promise she'd made to Alexander was to keep their secret about Aina's conception, and so she'd never written to Hope to ask for her ring back, even though it had almost broken her heart not to. One day she would; one day she would find her way back to London to see the woman who'd made it possible for her to be a mother, but for now, she was content with the life she'd created.

'Mamma, why you crying?' Aina asked, tugging on her hand.

'Because I'm so happy,' she said, blinking away her tears and lifting her to sit on her hip. 'Sometimes I have tears when I'm with you, because you make my heart so full.'

Aina placed her hand on her mother's chest, and Alexander slung his hand around her waist, dropping a kiss to her hair. His eyes asked a question, but she leaned into him, nestling her head to his shoulder.

I am happy, Oskar. I might not have you, but I have a life that brings me joy. But without you, I would never have had our little Aina, and for that alone, I will never, ever forget you.

31

PRESENT DAY

Charlotte stopped outside her grandmother's house and stretched, her body already aching from her run. She'd started to run for longer and longer each day, pushing herself to her limits to clear her head each morning, and so far, it had been working. Between running and work, she was too tired to lie awake each night in bed tossing and turning, and most of the time it kept her mind from pulling her back into the past. She'd wanted a fresh start in Oslo, and she was determined to give herself one, despite the rocky start she'd had. It had been a few months now since Harrison had left, and it was still taking all her willpower not to think about him or google him to see what he was doing.

But now that enough time had passed, she was starting to see that she was absolutely fine on her own, just like she'd always been. Her brother Erik had been to visit, keen to see the new hotel and even more interested in having a little family reunion of sorts now that she'd mended fences with their dad. The sting of pain about the way Harrison had left was still there, but she'd begun to make her peace with it as best she could, moving on with her life and refusing to dwell on what could have been.

'Morning.' Her grandmother called out to her as she let herself back in. Charlotte lifted her head, surprised to smell something sweet in the air.

'Morning,' she called back, following her nose into the kitchen. 'You've made us breakfast?' Her grandmother wasn't usually in the kitchen so early; she was usually tucked up in bed still with a good book.

'Lotte, I think it's time that we had a little talk.'

She groaned. This felt like being a teenager all over again. 'I promise I'm moving out soon, I have an apartment to look at later today and—'

'I don't want you to move out,' her grandmother said. 'Actually, I think you should move out because no one wants to live with their grandmother at your age, but I want to make sure you're okay. I'm worried about you.'

'And you thought waffles and coffee was the way to get me to open up?'

Her grandmother laughed. 'Did it work?'

'It did, actually.' Charlotte sighed and sat down at the table. 'But honestly, if you're worried about me, I'm fine. I have work, I'm fit, I have a shortlist of apartments to look at and—'

'I'm not asking if you have your life together, Charlotte,' her grandmother said as she set a plate in front of her and a steaming mug of black coffee, just how she liked it. 'You left home at eighteen, I know you're perfectly capable of looking after yourself, but I want to know how you're feeling, or if there's anything I can do for you.'

She took a bite of waffle before speaking, wanting to think about how she answered her grandmother's question. 'Right now, I'm feeling like it's impossible to have everything. That what we're told when we're little girls, that we can do anything, is a lie. Because I think it's easier to do one thing well, and for me that's my job. I'm just lucky that I love what I do, and if I get lonely, I can always get a dog.'

Her grandmother's gaze softened and she sat down across from Charlotte. 'You still miss him?'

Charlotte immediately had tears spring to her eyes, and she hated that just one mention of him could have that effect on her. 'Like you wouldn't believe. But I'm trying every day not to think about him. I mean, how can I miss someone I only knew for such a short time? It's ridiculous, and I keep telling myself that.'

Her grandmother patted her hand before rising and going over to the counter. She returned with her own plate of waffles and coffee.

'It's not the length of time we're with someone, it's the connection we have. Amalie's story alone should have taught you that—the great love she had for a man she only spent one summer with, but whom she remembered clear as day all these decades later. You don't have to pretend with me.'

Charlotte nodded. 'I know, but I can't compare what I had with Harrison to what she had with Oskar. It's nothing like it.'

Her grandmother shrugged. 'Maybe not, but maybe he was your Oskar? My point is, just because you've lost him, it doesn't mean you can't find happiness again. If he *was* your Oskar, then maybe it means you have an Alexander waiting for you somewhere in the world. Preferably in Oslo, of course, because I have no intention of letting you leave here again.'

She leaned over and gave her grandmother a hug. 'Well, in the meantime, I'm very happy to eat my feelings, so I'll take waffles any morning they're on offer. I have no intention of letting any man break my heart ever again, or leaving here for the time being, so I'm very happy with being married to my work.'

She could only imagine what her grandmother would have liked to say to that but, bless her, she just sighed and neglected to offer any further opinion on the topic. And so they sat back and talked, eating, and Charlotte sipped her grandmother's strong black coffee, and she couldn't help but feel grateful for the time they were spending together. It was the same with her father—ever since she'd arrived home, it truly felt as if she were catching up on lost time, and she wouldn't have traded that for anything in the world.

Later that morning, having finally decided which apartment to rent, Charlotte signed the papers, meaning to take her grandmother furniture shopping with her the next day to celebrate. But there was something else she wanted to do before it was time to get ready for work, and she knew that if she didn't do it today, it would be one of those things that she might neglect forever.

She drove along the quiet street and parked farther down the road from the cemetery. She'd almost turned around on the drive there, but Charlotte had forced herself to keep going, knowing that it was something she had to do. And she'd wanted to come alone, so that she could sit quietly with her thoughts.

When she reached the gate, she stood for a moment before forcing herself forward, walking down the rows and trying to remember where to find her mother. And then she found it. Only Charlotte had expected the stone to be covered in mud and dust, neglected for all the years she hadn't been there. Instead, she found a gravestone that had been recently wiped clean, with a small posy of flowers left there that had only just begun to wilt. Saying she was surprised would have been an understatement.

Charlotte bent down, placing her hand on the stone and closing her eyes for a moment. Then she moved to her right, touching her fingertips lightly to the smaller stone beside it, the one that belonged to her baby sister.

She sat down on the grass and drew her knees up to her chin as she read their names.

I wish you were here, Mum. I wish we'd had the chance to reconnect like I have with Dad. I wish we'd had time to find our way back to each other. She sighed. *I wish you'd never left us.*

The thing that Charlotte would never know was whether her mother had ever wanted to reconnect. When she'd left them, it had almost felt like a cruel magician's trick. One day she was there, the next she was gone. There had been times when Charlotte's grandmother had suggested that it was because her mother wasn't right in her mind, that it had been losing her baby daughter that had tipped her over the edge and made her want to run away. But Charlotte still didn't know whether that was the reason, and she'd hated her for it all the more. *You still had me, Mum. You still had Erik, and we both needed you. It wasn't fair that you left us and started a new life with someone else.*

She'd overheard her father on the phone one day having a heated conversation, and as a girl she'd often wondered what it was about, but as she'd grown, she'd come to understand that her mother had fought for the money she'd believed was hers. She hadn't fought for her kids, hadn't returned for them and apologised for the pain she'd caused, but she'd fought for the money she needed to live.

That's what had always made Charlotte wonder if losing her child had been an excuse, or the cause. And the hard part was that she'd never know why; all she knew was that as a child she'd gone to school one day, and when she'd returned, she'd no longer had a mother. It had been akin to someone dying.

Whatever the reason, I just wish I'd had the chance to ask you why.

Charlotte hadn't forgiven her mother so much as accepted what had happened so that she could make peace with her life, and she didn't know whether she'd ever come back to visit her grave again, but she was pleased that she'd chosen to come today. As she stood, looking down one last time, Charlotte reached into her pocket to take out her phone and call her father.

'Hey, Dad,' she said, when he answered.

'I'm just heading in to see a patient, so I might have to call you back,' he said. 'Unless something's wrong?'

She smiled into the phone. 'Nothing's wrong, I just...' Charlotte took a breath. 'I'm at the cemetery. I wanted to see Mum's gravestone, and I noticed that someone has been tending the garden around it and keeping it clean.'

Charlotte waited, the silence deafening as she hoped he would say something.

'You said something to me when you first came home, about worrying that you'd never have been able to forgive yourself if you hadn't come back for her funeral, even after everything. It made me realise that no matter how much she hurt us all, she was still your mother, and I wondered if I might not be able to forgive myself for not doing that one thing for you.'

She smiled into the phone. She'd known in her heart it was her dad, but she'd needed to hear him say it.

'Thanks, Dad, it means a lot.'

'I'll see you Sunday for lunch?' he asked.

'You will. See you then.'

Charlotte slid her phone back into her pocket and tilted her face up to the sun, closing her eyes and enjoying the warmth on her skin. The last few months hadn't been easy, but they'd been worth it. Reconnecting with her father, spending time with her grandmother and having the privilege of hearing Amalie's story, and even the time she'd spent with Harrison; she wouldn't have traded it for the world. Because as much as he'd hurt her, and as reluctant as she would be to ever let anyone close like that again, it had shown her that she could. She could fall in love, she could open her heart, and she could mend relationships that she'd thought were well beyond repair.

She began walking back to her car, glancing back once and wishing she had somewhere to go to remember Amalie. But her grandmother hadn't yet decided where they should bury or scatter Amalie's ashes, so for now they were tucked safely away in a cupboard.

With that in mind, she hurried the rest of the way and drove as quickly as she could back to her grandmother's house. She'd spent longer than she'd intended to at the cemetery, and now she would be late for work if she didn't hurry.

Charlotte was in the kitchen working alongside her team later that night, on what had turned out to be a very busy Friday, when her sous chef nudged her with his elbow. She glanced up, thinking he'd bumped her by accident. But she could see from the creases on his forehead that it was intentional. They were already under a lot of pressure with some of the kitchen staff having called in sick, so she knew that it must have been important for him to interrupt her.

'Chef, I think you might know the guest at the table. He hasn't taken his eyes off you since he arrived.'

Charlotte turned to look at the chef's table, not having seen anyone being seated. Usually, she greeted the guests and explained the menu to them, all part of the exclusive experience she'd created by having the table in the kitchen, but with her having to help with service, she simply hadn't had the chance yet. It had been a real night, and it wasn't even eight o'clock yet.

But her heart almost stopped when her eyes landed on the table, and she was thankful she wasn't holding a knife, as she might have sliced her hand. Because there at the table she'd once shared with him, was Harrison; sitting on his own, positioned to face into the kitchen. And her sous chef had been right—he was most definitely staring at her, and it took all her willpower not to stare straight back at him.

'Thank you,' she said, nodding to the younger chef. 'Can you take over here, please?'

'If he's making you feel uncomfortable—'

'It's fine, thank you for being so thoughtful. You were right about us knowing each other. I'll only be a minute.'

Charlotte wiped her hands clean and took a deep breath. She didn't have time to check her appearance and her skin was slick with sweat from the heat in the kitchen, and she hoped she looked presentable. This was certainly not how she'd imagined a reunion between them might go.

The short walk from her station to the table felt unbearable, especially when she could feel Harrison's eyes on her, but she held her head high, trying her best to look far more confident than she felt.

'Chef,' one of the servers said, dashing into her path and leaning close. It was their job to tell her the names of the guests at her table before she introduced herself. 'One guest tonight, his name is—'

'Harrison,' she said for her, their voices low given how close they were to the table. 'We're already acquainted. Did he book the table for one, or is he expecting company?'

'Yes, he booked it for one. He's the architect of the hotel, so maybe he wanted to see what it was like dining here? We should have had him flagged in our booking system as a VIP, I don't know how—'

'Please don't worry, I'm almost certain he wouldn't have said anything when he booked the table,' Charlotte replied. 'I'll take it from here.'

The cost of booking the chef's table was enormous; a hefty price tag befitting the personalised service and carefully curated menu, and certainly too expensive for one person. When she'd seen him sitting there, Charlotte had imagined he might be here with friends, that Louisa and Luke might have convinced him to come back for a holiday with them since she'd known how much they loved Norway. But clearly that wasn't the case—the table was only set for one.

'Harrison,' Charlotte said as she approached the table. 'Welcome to our chef's table.'

She knew she sounded too formal, but what was she supposed to do? Bend down and hug him? Kiss his cheek? None of those options seemed appropriate, either, so she gritted her teeth and continued with the professional approach, hoping that she was able to hold her nerve, especially given her staff were in such close proximity behind her.

'I know I should have just called, but it's been so long, so I thought...' He groaned. 'This seemed like a great idea when I booked it, but now that I'm here, and I'm trying to explain it, I can see it might not have been my best decision.'

'Did you actually book our most expensive table in the restaurant for one just to say hello?'

'Honestly?' His voice was deeper than usual, husky almost. 'It felt like the only guaranteed way to see you.'

Charlotte met his gaze, wanting to know why he was here; why, after so many months of silence, he'd chosen to come into her space and surprise her like this. She crossed her arms and stared at him. She'd wondered what it would be like to see him one day, how she'd react, what they would say, how awkward it would be; but seeing him was harder than she could have imagined. Especially caught off-guard like this.

'Are you in Oslo for work?' she asked.

'No, Lotte,' he said, his eyes never leaving hers. 'I'm here to see you.'

32

Charlotte blinked back at him at the same time as a crisis unfolded behind her. She heard something drop and one of the chefs curse, which usually she would have reprimanded any of the kitchen staff for when they had a guest at the chef's table, but this time she wasn't capable of reprimanding anyone. Her gaze was trained on Harrison, and the only words she wanted to hear were the ones coming out of his mouth.

'You came to the restaurant to see me, or—' She needed to hear him say it, to make sure she understood what he was trying to tell her, that she wasn't imagining a hidden meaning.

'I came to Oslo to see you,' he said, his expression so earnest it threatened to break her heart all over again. 'And then I booked the chef's table because I didn't know whether you'd even take my calls. It seemed like the only way to guarantee that—'

'Chef!' someone called, interrupting him.

'This is my place of work,' Charlotte said, keeping her voice even, not wanting to get emotional or react in anything other than a professional way in front of her staff or Harrison. 'I can't do this here, I can't—'

'After your shift,' Harrison said, his eyes pleading with her. 'Please. Just give me an hour. Half an hour, even. If you don't want to see me ever again after that, then I promise I'll leave you alone and never come back.'

'The hotel bar. Meet me there once the kitchen closes,' she said, hurrying back into the kitchen and wondering how she was going to concentrate throughout the entire service with Harrison sitting there watching her. But he was right; she wouldn't have taken his calls, no matter how much she might have wanted to, because he'd already broken her heart once. She'd opened up to him and he'd left her, and it had been *months* since they'd last seen each other.

Harrison had shattered her trust. All the walls she'd previously built around herself were very much in place again, and she'd had no intention of ever taking them down.

'Chef? Everything okay?'

'Of course,' she said with a smile, not about to let anyone she worked with sense how rattled she was. Charlotte had a reputation for always staying calm in the kitchen and dealing with any crisis that came her way, so she wasn't about to change that tonight. 'Now let me taste that sauce before it goes out.'

'Do you want me on chef's table?' asked her head chef from across the kitchen.

'No,' she said. 'I'll remain in charge of that table tonight. Thank you.'

Harrison might have hurt her beyond words, but she had every intention of impressing him, regardless. He was a guest of the hotel, and an important one at that, and she was determined to show him just how talented she was, and that she'd continued to thrive even after he'd walked away.

And so Charlotte did what she always did when she was nervous or upset—she began to cook as if her very existence depended on it, pouring all her heartache and hope into the most incredible food she could create. If nothing else, she was going to ensure that Harrison never forgot his culinary experience.

Charlotte had often worked under highly stressful conditions. She'd cooked for celebrities and chefs she admired, in the very best kitchens throughout London, but nothing had ever felt as stressful as tonight. With Harrison's eyes on her, she walked over to give him his first plate, placing it in front of him with a curt nod. Then she'd done it again and again, until now she was finally presenting him with dessert. The night was a blur of furiously fast plating and curious glances in his direction.

Each time the server had cleared his table, she'd given Charlotte the highest compliments from him, but this time, now that the kitchen was slowing down for the night, Charlotte told the server that she would take over from there. And so she took two plates of dessert and placed one in front of Harrison, sitting down across from him with her own very large slice of cake. Somehow, it felt like one of the bravest things she'd ever done.

'I remember this, it was called...' His voice trailed away as he seemed to search for the name.

'Kvæfjord cake,' she said. 'It's not usually something we'd serve to the chef's table, but I remembered how much you liked it. I'm sure the other chefs think I've gone mad for serving it to you.'

'It was the best cake I'd ever eaten,' he said, taking a forkful and groaning. 'I'd almost forgotten how good it was.'

Charlotte reached over and took his glass of wine, taking a long sip before passing it back to him. He responded by nudging it back across to her, clearly realising that she needed it more than he did.

'Harrison, why did you come back?' she asked. 'What are you really doing here?'

'I came back because I realised what a fool I'd been,' he said. 'I realised that I had a chance at being happy again, and instead of being open to it, I ran away.'

She took another sip of his wine, then realised that it wasn't wine she wanted. She wanted Harrison—she wanted his arms around her and his words against her skin—and now that he was sitting right in front of her, all she could think about was how much she'd missed him. She'd missed him as if they'd known each other for years, not months, and a huge part of her wished he'd never come back, because it only hurt seeing him again.

'I'm not going to lie, you broke my heart when you left the way you did,' she told him, blinking away the familiar prickle of tears as she stared into his eyes. 'I honestly never thought I'd ever see you again, after the way we left things.'

'If you want me to leave, Charlotte, I'll leave,' he said. 'But if there is even the smallest chance that you'll let me back into your life...'

She stared at him across the table. 'I don't want you to leave.'

'Good, because I don't want to leave, either. I don't think I ever really wanted to, but I didn't know how to stay.'

Charlotte felt a lightness inside of her that had been missing for months. She'd tried to pretend that she was fine, that she had everything she needed in her life, but she'd only been fooling herself. But she couldn't just forgive him, could she? Because what if he did the same thing again to her in a week or a month or a year?

'Let me get changed and I'll meet you at the bar.'

'It's really good to see you again, Charlotte.'

Charlotte stood and looked down at Harrison. 'It's really good to see you again, too,' she said back. Because it was. As much as she'd wanted to hate him when he'd left, it was an impossible task.

Harrison caught her hand, and she held on to him for a long moment, wishing her heart wasn't such a traitor.

By the time Charlotte slid into the seat across from Harrison, her heart was thundering. He'd chosen a table tucked into the corner of the bar, and she shivered despite the fire that was casting heat from nearby.

'So, how's London?' she asked, grateful when the server arrived with two glasses of wine that Harrison must have ordered before she joined him.

'It's...' He shrugged. 'I actually don't know how to answer that, because I haven't exactly been social.'

'Work is good, though?'

'Work seems to be my one consistent, although I'm between projects again at the moment. It felt like the right time to take a short break.' His eyes met hers. 'I figured there were more important things in life than just working all the time.'

She sipped her wine, her eyes widening as he leaned across the table and covered one of her hands with his.

'I want you to know that I'm sorry, Charlotte. I was a coward, and if I could take back that morning, the way I left, I would.'

She caught her lower lip beneath her teeth, her breath catching in her throat. 'What you did, Harrison, it hurt. It hurt more than I want to admit, and I can't open myself up to that kind of pain again.'

She could see tears shining in his eyes, the visible lump in his throat as he swallowed.

'I don't want to lose you,' he said. 'I don't know if I'm ready for this, or if I'll ever be ready, but if you give me a second chance—'

'You don't have to hide your past from me, Harrison, but

you do need to promise that you won't leave me like that again,' she whispered. 'I can't do it again, so if we're going to try this, if we're really going to make this something, you have to promise me.'

'I promise,' he said. 'The way I left, the way things ended, there was nothing about that that was okay. I'm sorry.'

Her breath was shaky when she exhaled. "So if we're going to do this, I need to know what *this* is.'

His fingers looped into hers, and he squeezed. 'I'd very much like to take things slowly and find our way, but what I do know is that I want to be with you. If you'll have me.'

That was all Charlotte needed to hear, because it had been the very worst ending, and one that had haunted her for months. Maybe she should have made him wait, maybe she shouldn't have let him back in, but her heart and her mind were both telling her that she loved him too much not to.

'Will you give me a second chance?'

She sighed as warmth spread through her, as happiness settled over her body at her decision. 'I will.'

Harrison's eyes crinkled at the corners when he smiled, his forehead touching hers as he leaned in across the small table.

'I won't waste this second chance. I promise,' he said. 'Also, Louisa told me that if I came home and hadn't made up with you, she would never speak to me again. It seems that you made quite an impression on her.'

Charlotte kissed him, drawing him closer, smiling against his lips and then laughing when her stomach rumbled loudly.

'Have you eaten tonight?' he murmured.

'Well, to start with, I was too busy cooking for a guest at the chef's table to think about myself, and then there was the other part where this gorgeous man kept staring at me all night and made me forget about almost everything else.'

'Can we still order cake as room service?'

She nodded.

'Then come with me to my room and we can lie in bed and eat it.'

When Harrison stood and held out his hand to her, he didn't have to ask twice.

By the time Charlotte had showered and wrapped herself in the fluffy hotel robe, Harrison was sitting on the bed, waiting with the room service he'd ordered.

'Sit and let me feed you,' he ordered.

Charlotte obeyed, laughing when Harrison held out a forkful of cake. She opened her mouth and willingly took it, swallowing and then opening her mouth for another until every last piece was gone. She couldn't remember anyone caring enough about her to actually feed her, and she certainly wasn't complaining—it was nice to be pampered.

'You have a little piece of cream just there,' he said, reaching towards the corner of her mouth.

She flicked her tongue out and felt nothing. 'Liar,' she whispered, but as she did so she slipped an arm around his neck to keep him from moving away.

Harrison deftly moved the cake box out of the way as she drew him down on top of her, smiling against his lips as he gently kissed her. His mouth was warm, and his hands were soft as he rolled slightly to the side, so they were staring at each other.

'I've missed you so much,' she whispered, as he stroked his thumb across her cheek with so much tenderness it made her want to cry. *I thought I was never going to see you again.*

'I've missed you too,' he murmured back. 'More than I could ever tell you.'

They stared at each other a long moment, until Charlotte wrapped her arms around him, holding him close, needing his body against hers; to listen to his heartbeat, to breathe in the scent of him, still barely able to believe that he'd come back.

Part of her wanted to go slow, to remind herself how much it had hurt the first time he'd left, but another part of her wanted to trust in his promise and surrender to whatever this turned out to be. If Harrison said she could trust him, then she was inclined to give him the benefit of the doubt; she was just hoping he didn't want to go too slow.

'Stay here with me tonight?' he asked.

She smiled against his lips, her arms looped around his neck. 'There's nowhere else I'd rather be.'

33

Charlotte lay in bed with Harrison, her leg thrown over his and the sheets strewn between them. When he'd gone, she'd told herself she was fine and that she didn't need him or any other man in her life. But now that he'd returned, she wondered how she'd ever thought she could live without him.

'I'm sorry it took me so long to come back,' he said, strumming his fingers gently up and down her arm. 'I knew the moment I walked away that I was doing the wrong thing, but I just couldn't bring myself to turn around.'

'Maybe we needed the space to appreciate what was growing between us,' she said, turning on her side so that she was facing him. 'The last few months have been tough, but it forced me to make a life for myself here and to push outside of my comfort zone.'

'It was more than just needing space for me,' Harrison said, trailing his fingers up her arm and across her shoulder. 'I needed time to accept that I was moving on, that my life was changing in ways that I never expected. When Elly was unwell, she made me promise to be open to love again, that she would understand, that she didn't want me to spend the rest of my life alone. It was me who vowed to never be with another woman again, because at the time I couldn't imagine being with anyone other than her.'

Charlotte blinked back at him. She didn't have words—what could she even say to a man who'd lost his wife? She had no comprehension of what it meant to lose the person you loved most in the world. Her mother had ripped her heart out, but it was different to losing a spouse—no one could ever take the place of her mother, so she'd never had to worry about that happening and how to cope with it.

'For the longest time, I'd refused to do anything with her ashes, even though she'd tried to make it easy for me and left specific instructions for what to do after her death,' he said. 'So, when I went home, I did all the things I'd been avoiding. After Elly passed, I barely spent any time at our apartment, it was easier not to face everything, but Louisa helped me to see that it was time.' He took an audibly shaky breath. 'I cleared out her wardrobe and looked over the things she'd kept, memories and photos, all the things that were special to us as a couple. Those things I mostly decided to keep, but there was something thera-peutic about addressing everything I'd been putting off for so long.'

'You have great friends,' Charlotte said. 'I knew when I met them how special they were.'

'They are the best,' he agreed. 'There are times I've tried so hard to push them away, but no matter what I do, they don't budge. They've continued to love me at my absolute worst.'

'Did they tell you to come here?' Charlotte asked.

Harrison's cheeks reddened. 'Well, Louisa may have forced me to buy a one-way ticket from London to Oslo, but booking the chef's table was all my idea.'

She leaned forwards and kissed him, slowly. They were in no hurry; they had the hotel room for the next few days, and as far as Charlotte was concerned, she was staying in the room until she needed to head down to the kitchen to oversee service that night.

'You know, I think the guy who designed this place did a great job,' she said, giggling as he pushed against her and pinned her hands above her head. 'There's something about this room that makes me not want to leave.'

'Really? Why's that?'

'I have no idea, but I think it must be something to do with the design.'

She laughed all the more when he nuzzled her neck, fighting against his hold but not standing a chance. Not that she wanted to—Charlotte would be content spending the entire day confined in his embrace.

'I'm not sure that's what he had in mind when he designed the place, but I think that's a very, very good result. I just hope they do a good room service breakfast. You never know with chefs these days, how good the food might be.'

They rolled around, tangling the sheets farther around them as they became even more entwined in each other's arms. But when Harrison stilled, she cupped both hands to his face and stared into his eyes, committing him to memory all over again.

'I don't ever remember being this happy,' she whispered. 'Being here, with you, like this...'

'I know,' he whispered back, his lips grazing hers again in the sweetest, slowest kiss. 'I think that's what scared me the most, how easy it was to be with you. And then how much I missed you.'

Charlotte wrapped her arms around him, her mouth to his shoulder, closing her eyes and soaking in the feel of him against her. Never in a million years had she imagined that they might be together again, not like this. But it was so natural with him, even though they'd fought against it the first time. She'd never been with anyone in the way she was with Harrison.

'Harrison?' she murmured against his skin.

He pressed up and looked down at her, resting on his elbows.

'I'd like you to meet my family, properly this time,' she said. 'If we're going to do this, if we're going to give this a real go, then I want to do it right.'

'As your…'

'Hmm, as my love interest,' she said, which made them both laugh.

'Charlotte, I'd be honoured,' he said. 'As your *love interest.*'

She laughed and managed to flip him so that she was pinning him down this time. 'We'll work on the terminology, because that sounded much better in my head than it did out loud.'

'Later,' he said, kissing her again. 'We've got far more important things to do right now than worry about what you're going to call me.'

'Is it strange that I'm nervous?' Harrison asked. 'I feel like a teenage boy meeting his girlfriend's parents for the first time.'

'Well, you're the first boy I've brought home to meet my father, so you should feel nervous.' Charlotte laughed at the expression on his face. 'But honestly, it's my brother who'd give you a hard time, and you don't have to meet him until the next time we're in London. Erik is far harder on potential suitors, or at least I've always imagined he would be if I was ever brave enough to introduce someone to him.'

'You're not serious? I'm your first?' Harrison shook his head. 'I'm starting to think this was a very bad idea.'

'Oh, I'm deadly serious. I wasn't allowed to date when I was a teenager, and I moved out at eighteen, so you're definitely the first,' she said. 'But my grandmother already loves you, and that's the most important thing. It's her opinion I value above all others.'

'We never did work on a better term than *love interest*,' he said. 'Perhaps we should just stick with boyfriend. Actually, come to think of it, I'm very happy to just be your friend for the sake of your family.'

She had to keep from laughing. 'I think they'll figure out fairly quickly that we're more than just friends.' Not to mention that she'd already told her grandmother *all* about him. 'Also, how is it that you weren't daunted by the design project for the most incredible new hotel in the country, yet you're scared of meeting my family? And you've already met them before anyway, at the opening.'

'Yes, but that was as the building's architect, not as the *love interest*.'

The look he gave her made her think that he was genuinely nervous, but she didn't get a chance to reply and tease him before the front door swung open.

'Charlotte! Harrison!' Her father beamed at them, and this time when he hugged her, it wasn't awkward, it was just a dad throwing his arms around his daughter. 'It's so nice to have you here.'

'Thanks, Dad, it's nice to be here.' And she meant it. Rekindling her relationship with her father had been one of the benefits of coming home, and now she was slowly starting to realise that she no longer wanted a life without him in it.

Harrison and her father shook hands, and she took off her scarf and coat in the hallway and watched them walk away, immediately falling into conversation. It made her heart happy that after so many years, she could walk into her childhood home and not feel on edge, and Harrison had a lot to do with that. All these years she'd tried to run away from her loss and her feelings, but being with him had taught her that there wasn't anything wrong with her, that her response had been perfectly normal for a young woman grieving her mother and rebelling against her dad. What hadn't been normal was how long she'd gone without seeing her father, but as far as she was concerned, they'd made amends, and she'd already moved a long way towards forgiving him for the past.

'Hi, Grandma.' Charlotte walked up behind her grandma and gave her a hug. 'Something smells delicious.'

'Well, it's only because I ordered something wonderful and decided to heat it up and put it on fancy plates,' she said with a wink. 'That's the best thing an old lady can do when she has a chef coming to dinner.'

'At least now we know where my culinary skills come from. I was starting to think that I might have been the one who was adopted for a while there.'

They both laughed, heads bent together as they shared their little joke. It had been particularly incredible for Charlotte to hear Amalie's story, feeling a kinship with her long-lost Oskar and the way he'd yearned to follow his own path.

'I miss her, Lotte,' her grandmother said. 'I knew she didn't have much longer, but now I feel like we missed out on talking about the past. She could have told me all this years ago, and instead...'

'I know,' Charlotte said with a sigh. 'But at least you know what you know. If we'd been given the box a week, even a month later...' She couldn't even imagine what it would have been like, staring at that little wooden box and trying to make sense of the clues that had been left behind.

They both stood a moment longer, until her grandmother patted her hand. 'Come through to see the men. Your father has something for you.'

Something for me? She gave her grandma a quizzical look but only received a shrug in response. But when they walked through to the living room, she saw that there was a bottle of

French champagne and four glasses waiting, and she hadn't a clue what they were there for.

'What are we celebrating?' she asked, glancing at Harrison. 'Have I forgotten someone's birthday?'

'We're celebrating you,' her father said as he eased the top off the bottle. 'I've missed out on years of celebrations with you, so this is a start for all the birthdays and all the career milestones.'

Charlotte found herself with tears in her eyes then, and a lump in her throat that was almost impossible to swallow past. But she accepted the glass from her father when he passed it, wishing she could tell him how much it meant to her, but unable to get the words out.

'To my Lotte,' he said. 'For taking the culinary world by storm, and for never being afraid to follow her dreams. I'm so, so proud of you.'

'To Lotte,' her grandmother and Harrison chimed in, holding up their glasses in unison.

She laughed and then cried, forcing herself to take a sip even as it all felt almost too much. One thing she'd never liked was being the centre of attention.

'I know I should have said it sooner, but I really am so proud of you,' her father said from across the room, his voice cracking. 'And if your mother was still here, I'm sure she would have been very proud of you, too.'

'Thank you,' she whispered, grateful that he'd mentioned her mother. There had been such a big void in her life when her mother had left, and she only wished they'd had the chance to reconnect before her passing.

'Now,' her grandmother said, as Charlotte joined Harrison on the sofa. His hand fell to her thigh, and she nestled against him. 'I want to know what your plans are. Will you two love-birds be staying here, or will we have to come and visit you in London?'

Charlotte glanced at Harrison. 'Well, I've actually decided to stay on at the hotel for at least another year. I feel like I've found the place I want to be, and I'm grateful to have been offered a permanent position.'

'I was going to wait until tomorrow to share this, but I've actually been offered a new project,' Harrison said.

'What? Why didn't you tell me!' Charlotte swatted at him playfully. 'What is it? Where will you be working? Is it another hotel?'

His smile was smug. 'Actually, it's right here in Oslo, which is why I was going to tell you in private. In case you'd rather I turn it down and find another project in London.'

'Here? You've been offered a job *here*?' she repeated. She'd been wrestling all day with her decision to stay in Oslo, knowing in her heart that she couldn't turn down such an incredible job for Harrison, but hoping desperately that they could find a way around long-distance.

'You don't mind?'

She shook her head, unable to hide her smile. 'Mind? No, Harrison, I most definitely don't mind!'

'That's something else to celebrate then,' her father said. 'Congratulations to you both!'

Harrison looked at her and she bit down on her bottom lip, hardly able to believe how well everything had worked out. She couldn't have planned it better if she'd tried.

'You didn't tell us what the project was,' Charlotte's grandmother said. 'Do we have another new hotel being planned for the city?'

'No, I'll be designing a new art gallery here,' he said. 'It's a refurbishment rather than a new build, but the project sounds fantastic. Not to mention it keeps me closer to Charlotte.'

'When would you start?' she asked.

'That's the thing. I thought for once that I might take a month off, enjoy being a tourist here for a bit before launching into the new job. My only problem is that I'd rather not travel alone.'

'Harrison, if that was a hint it wasn't a very subtle one.'

'I was actually thinking you could take a week off and we could play tourist together,' he said, his hand covering hers. 'What do you say? Do you think Daniel will give you some time off?'

'I think if his favourite architect asked him, he might.'

They clinked champagne glasses again and sat back on the sofa together, as her father talked about his work and her grandmother entertained them with tales of her recent cards evening with friends. But eventually, their conversation led them to Amalie.

'Grandma, there's something I've been meaning to ask you, about Oskar,' Charlotte said. 'Were there never any photos of him in your grandparents' home when you were growing up? No mention of the fact that your father's brother had died?'

Her grandmother sighed. 'I've asked myself the same thing over and over. You know I searched all those boxes we had in storage, but there's nothing. It's almost as if they completely erased him from their memory after he passed, because there's not a birth certificate or a photo or even a diary entry that mentions him.'

'It's hard to fathom what Amalie went through, but until you experience loss, you don't know how you'll react,' her father said. 'Sometimes it changes you in ways that you could never have imagined.'

'I can second that,' Harrison said. 'The grief is all-consuming, and sometimes the only way to cope is to lash out at the ones you love, even though all you really want is to draw them close and never let them go.'

Charlotte looked between the two men, and she didn't know whom her heart ached for more—her father or Harrison.

'I don't blame Amalie, not for a second. I always knew she

was brave, but when I think about how terrified she must have been, and how young she was when she found herself in London...' Charlotte's grandmother sighed. 'She was a very special woman, and she carried a burden that no woman should ever have to carry alone.'

'The night of the hotel opening, when she mentioned being in the hotel business,' Harrison said, 'I did some research about her and Alexander when I got home. But everything I read credited only her husband for the empire they built. She wasn't mentioned once.'

'The one thing I do know about Amalie,' said Charlotte's grandmother, 'was that she was as much the driving force behind my family's business interests as my father was. She worked tirelessly, and one of my earliest memories is of her sitting at our kitchen table, poring over architectural plans, and curling up in her lap at night and listening to her talk to my father about what hotel they would open next.'

'Do you think anyone else knew how involved she was?'

'I think Alexander's family did, and I think that's why things changed between them so much. They finally saw her for the woman she was, and realised what she could do for their son, at his side, as he continued to grow the business. I imagine they spent the rest of their lives regretting the way they'd underestimated her, knowing that their son's death was effectively their fault.'

They sat in silence for a moment, sipping their champagne, as if they all needed a moment to digest what Amalie's life had meant, how successful she'd been behind the scenes. Charlotte couldn't imagine what it would be like working so hard without anyone knowing, couldn't help but imagine if it were her, and she only wished she'd known years earlier, so that she could have talked to Amalie about her work.

'When I left, you still didn't have the whole story pieced together, about what happened after she married Alexander,'

Harrison said. 'Did Amalie share the rest of her story with you, or are you just going from your own memories of them now?' He looked to her grandmother, but it was Charlotte who spoke.

'It just so happens,' Charlotte said, speaking for her grand-mother, 'that she did share the rest of her story, right before she passed. I went to see her that morning, and it was when I went back that afternoon that she left us.' It wasn't lost on Charlotte that if Harrison hadn't finished things between them, she might never have gone to see Amalie that day, which would have meant she'd never have heard the final part of her story.

'She was a remarkable woman, my mother,' Charlotte's grandmother said. 'And at least now we know that she shared everything she could with us, before it was too late. Part of me wonders if she was hanging on until she'd shared every last piece of the story with us.'

Charlotte had imagined that Amalie had spent her entire life mourning Oskar, that the great-grandmother she'd known had hidden her sadness. How wrong she'd been.

Amalie had lived her life to the fullest despite her heartache, and if that wasn't an inspiration, then she didn't know what was.

'Did she ever stop mourning Oskar?' Harrison asked.

Charlotte met his gaze, sensing that he had a very personal reason to ask that question.

'Yes, she did,' Charlotte's grandmother said, smiling. 'Which only made me admire her all the more.'

34

OSLO, 1958

Amalie stood beside her mother-in-law, watching as Alexander took his place in front of the hotel holding a giant pair of scissors, preparing to cut a gold ribbon that would officially signal the opening of their new venture in Oslo. Their daughter, dressed in a cream dress with a matching coat and an enormous bow in her hair, stood beside him—she was his constant shadow.

She and Alexander might have been an unlikely pairing in the beginning, but Amalie knew that anyone who looked at them now would think them fated. They'd had their daughter while expanding his family's business empire, and she knew that he'd be the first to say that this new hotel was as much her success as it was his. They'd spent the past three years working on ambitious plans to open a city hotel, different to the ones on the fjords that his family had always been known for, and now here they were, on opening day. She'd sat up with him every night till late when he'd been poring over the plans, or through dinners with investors and advisers, and she'd found that she was almost as attuned to business as he was now. Alexander had wanted her beside him up there, but it was his moment, and she had no intention of stealing it from him.

Once the ribbon had been cut and the invited guests began to mingle and go inside for a tour, Amalie's mother-in-law touched her elbow and steered her away from the crowd.

'Walk with me?'

Amalie nodded. They only saw each other on birthdays and special occasions these days, but they'd managed to establish a cordial relationship, and Amalie knew that the more well-known she and her husband became, not to mention the more successful the business, the more her mother-in-law warmed to her.

'You must be so very proud of Alexander,' Amalie said. 'He's worked so hard, and the hotel is everything I imagined it would be.'

'I don't think Alexander did this alone, Amalie,' she said. 'I know you had a hand in this development.'

Amalie chose not to answer until she'd carefully considered her words. 'Alexander's success is my success. There's no credit due to me.'

'I was wrong about you, Amalie,' her mother-in-law said. 'I thought you were going to lead my boy astray, that his life would be over if he married you, yet here you are, the guiding light to my only son.'

It was a compliment if ever she'd received one, and although she didn't need her mother-in-law's praise, it didn't mean it wasn't nice to hear.

'Amalie, I know this has been a long time coming, you've been a part of this family for so long now, but I would like to apologise to you.'

'Apologise to me?' she asked.

'You were worthy of my Oskar, and if I'd seen that at the time, he would still be alive today. His death was my fault, Amalie, not yours.'

Amalie stopped walking and turned to her, opening her

arms and choosing to embrace the woman who'd once treated her so poorly, whom she'd once hated. 'For so many years I blamed you, but Oskar's death wasn't your fault any more than it was mine. It was an accident, and it's time we both accepted that.'

Her mother-in-law began to cry, and Amalie held her again. There was a time when she'd hated her; when she'd blamed the way her life had turned out on the woman she now held in her arms, but Amalie knew better than to live in the past.

'Without you,' she said, putting a little distance between them so she could wipe her fingertips across her cheeks, 'I would have been destitute. I would have had to place my gorgeous girl for adoption so she could live the life I dreamed for her, or live in poverty and struggle to provide her with enough food to fill her belly. So I forgive you, for it all.'

Her mother-in-law's eyes cleared, and it was as if they finally saw each other for who they were.

'Alexander has been a wonderful husband to me, and a kind, loving father to our daughter. I wouldn't trade the life we share for anything.'

'Not even a chance to go back?'

Amalie thought for a moment. 'I can't answer that, but I can tell you that I'm content. I love Alexander with all my heart, and I cherish every day we spend together. I no longer look back and wonder *what if*, and I don't want you to, either. We can only look forward and enjoy the life that we have.'

A familiar hand touched her shoulder then, and she turned to find Alexander standing behind them. She could tell from the way his eyes shone that he'd overheard what she'd said to his mother.

'Would you ladies like a tour of the hotel?' he asked.

Amalie linked her arm through her husband's, admiring the hotel rising in front of them. It was magnificent, and even though Oskar had never wanted to enter the family business, even though he'd felt it a noose rather than a gift, *she* had come to love being a part of it, and she hoped that he could see, from wherever he was, that the obstacle that had once kept them apart was the same thing that had finally set her free.

EPILOGUE

PRESENT DAY

SIX MONTHS LATER

Charlotte couldn't believe they were actually there, and the Sognefjord was even more magical than she'd remembered it to be. She and Harrison walked hand in hand along the grass, staring out at the water, before turning back to admire the sprawling hotel behind them.

'This is where the photo was taken,' she said, retrieving Amalie's battered photo from her pocket and holding it up for them to study. 'I can almost imagine them sitting there, waiting for someone to click and take the picture. Perhaps a guest or someone else who worked here?'

Harrison slid his arm around her, and they stood for a long time, just admiring the scenery together in silence. They'd both been so looking forward to the trip, but it was certainly an emotional one for both of them. Charlotte had her great-grandmother Amalie's ashes with her to spread around the fjord before they left, and Harrison was remembering his wife on their anniversary, something Charlotte knew that he always found harder to cope with on the date of her passing than at any other time during the year.

'Are you thinking about her now?' Charlotte asked gently, her head still on his shoulder.

'Yes.' She heard the emotion in his voice and knew that if he hadn't already shed a tear, he would soon. 'Does that make you feel uncomfortable?'

She lifted her head to hug him, her chest to his heart. 'Not at all. If Amalie's story has taught me anything, it's that it's possible to love more than one person in a lifetime. I don't ever want you to think you're being unfaithful to me by still loving Elly.'

'It's hard sometimes to imagine that I'll never see her again, but at the same time the only place I want to be is right here with you,' he said, his voice gravelly. 'It makes no sense when I say it out loud, but both things are somehow true.'

Charlotte continued to hold him, needing the contact as much as he did. But she'd been truthful with him—his love for his wife didn't upset her; if anything, it made her love and respect him all the more. And she'd learnt that no matter how he was feeling about the past, it didn't mean he didn't want her in his future.

'Come on,' Charlotte said, sighing as she grudgingly let go of him. 'I could stand like this all day with you, but I have a surprise for you.'

Coming to the picturesque hotel at Sognefjord where Amalie's story had begun had been Harrison's idea, but Charlotte had known what would make it perfect, and as they walked hand in hand back towards the hotel, two familiar figures ran down the steps towards them.

'You didn't.'

She laughed. 'I did. We couldn't come away on your anniversary trip without your best friends, now could we?'

Harrison grabbed hold of her and gave her a big kiss,

twirling her around in his arms before greeting his friends. Their smiles stretched from ear to ear, and Charlotte knew without a doubt that she'd done the right thing in inviting them.

'Thank you,' he said, just before Louisa threw her arms around him, followed by a handshake and backslap from Luke.

Louisa quickly turned to Charlotte, enveloping her in a long hug. 'You're the best. I honestly don't know if I could have coped not seeing Harrison this weekend.'

'As far as I'm concerned it's a tradition we'll always share together,' Charlotte said. 'I'll never ask him to stop celebrating the life he had with Elly, and I'm just grateful that you've let me be a part of it.'

'Is it just me, or is there nowhere as magnificent as this on earth?' Louisa asked as they all turned and stood together, admiring the sparkling blue water and the endless stretches of wilderness that went as far as the eye could see.

'It is,' Charlotte said. 'When I first saw it as a girl, I knew I'd never see anything like it again, no matter where I travelled in the world.'

'I propose we head inside for drinks and lunch,' Luke said, waving them back towards the hotel.

But when everyone else turned, Charlotte stayed.

'You okay?' Harrison asked.

'I'm great, I just...' She smiled up at him. 'Would you mind if I spent a few minutes out here on my own?'

Harrison didn't need to be asked twice; it was the nice thing about the way they were together, and he dropped a kiss to her forehead before following his friends. She watched them go for a minute before walking closer to the water and staring out at the fjord, remembering Amalie's words as she'd described her time there with Oskar, knowing that it was time to scatter her ashes. Charlotte closed her eyes and inhaled the crisp air, seeing them in her mind, imagining what their life was like the summer they'd shared together. What they'd been through when all they wanted was each other.

When she opened her eyes and blinked, she knew that if there was one thing she wanted to do while she was here, it was to float in the water with Harrison just as Amalie had with Oskar. The thought made her smile, and as she looked out at the water again, watching the way the sun sparkled across it, she had the most serene sense of calm wash over her.

It was time to let go of the past and trust in love and family. She was no longer going to live in fear, or worry about what had come before. Charlotte was ready to live life, and as she turned to walk back to the hotel and saw Harrison standing by the door watching her, she knew that she was, somehow, exactly where she was supposed to be. She had a job she loved, a man who adored her, and an entire lifetime to look forward to with him, not to mention an apartment with both of their names on the lease in Oslo that still felt surreal.

Mia hadn't been lying when she'd said the little box bearing her grandmother's name might just change her life.

It was on the last day of their holiday when Charlotte thought of Mia again. She'd intended on sending her a message months ago to let her know what she'd discovered, and promptly forgotten about it. But earlier that day, she'd decided to send her a quick text to update her on what had happened, and to tell her just how right she'd been about the box having the potential to change her life.

'You look deep in thought,' Harrison said, holding out a glass of wine as he came towards her.

It was just the two of them now—the others had left the day before—and they were enjoying their final day before returning to Oslo.

'Do you remember I told you about Mia? The woman who gave me that little box of clues?'

'Of course. She was the niece, wasn't she? She found a handful of the boxes in her aunt's old house.'

Charlotte nodded and took a sip of her wine, passing her phone to Harrison.

'I just received this message from her. She was replying to something I sent her this morning.'

Harrison took the phone and she stared at the screen, rereading the message with him.

Your message couldn't have come at a better time. So happy it all worked out for you. But I find myself with a favour to ask, and I'm asking it of all seven of you who've received boxes. I need help understanding a clue that Hope left behind, a clue that I think might tell me how she ended up in London all those years ago. Maybe even how she came to open Hope's House. Would you consider helping me figure out what it all means?

Harrison handed her the phone. 'What do you think?'

'I think I need to say yes,' Charlotte said. 'I mean, without her, you and I wouldn't have met, I wouldn't have come back, I—'

Harrison laughed, interrupting her. 'You don't have to convince me. I think you should do it.'

'You do?'

He pulled her close and kissed her. 'I think we both know how much that little box changed your life, and if you can help someone else...'

Charlotte was already sending her a message back.

Of course. Let me know what I can do. I feel like all of us share a connection, so it would be great to meet.

She stared at her phone, waiting for a reply. It came almost immediately.

Great. I'll be in touch soon.

Charlotte set down her phone and reached for Harrison, pulling him close. 'We have about twenty-two hours before we have to leave to go back to reality.'

'You know, I kind of like our reality, so it's not the worst thing to imagine,' he said with a grin. 'Now that we're living together, I get you all to myself all the time. But if you have something special in mind...' His lips hovered over hers.

'I was thinking about swimming in the fjord,' she teased, not expecting Harrison to leap up and grab her, running with her in his arms down to the water as she squealed.

He hovered her over the water, before taking a step back and setting her on her feet, wrapping his arms around her and kissing her again instead.

'I love you, Lotte,' he whispered. 'And I'm going to spend the rest of my life making sure you know it.'

Her lips parted, tilting upwards as his mouth moved on hers, unable to help the smile.

I can see why you loved it here, Amalie. It truly is the most beautiful place in the world.

Dear reader,

Thank you so much for choosing to read *The Hidden Daughter*! If you enjoyed the book and want to keep up to date with all my latest releases (including the next books in the series), just sign up at the following link. Your email address will never be shared, and you can unsubscribe at any time.

www.bookouture.com/soraya-lane

I do hope you loved reading *The Hidden Daughter* as much as I enjoyed writing it, and if you did, I would be very grateful if you could write a review. I can't wait to hear your thoughts on the story, and it makes such a difference in helping new readers to discover one of my books for the very first time.

This was the seventh book in The Lost Daughters series, and I'm looking forward to sharing the final book with you very, very soon. If you haven't already read *The Italian Daughter*, *The Cuban Daughter*, *The Royal Daughter*, *The Sapphire Daughter*, *The Paris Daughter* or *The Spanish Daughter*, you might like to read those books next, and enjoy being swept away to Italy, Cuba, Greece, Switzerland, France and Argentina, and falling in love with some truly unforgettable characters. There will be one more Lost Daughters novel published after this one, and I can't wait to uncover more family secrets and finally share with you the story of Hope before this series comes to an end!

One of my favourite things is hearing from readers—you can get in touch via my Facebook page, by joining Soraya's Reader Group on Facebook or visiting my website.

Thank you so much

Soraya x

www.sorayalane.com

Soraya's Reader Group:
https://www.facebook.com/groups/sorayalanereadergroup

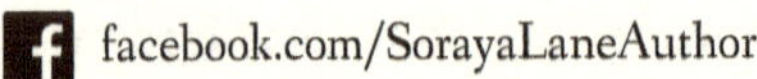 facebook.com/SorayaLaneAuthor

ACKNOWLEDGEMENTS

I honestly can't believe that this is the seventh book in The Lost Daughters series, which of course means there is only one more book left to write until the series is complete. From the very first glimmer of an idea during the pandemic in 2020 to having seven books published—it's been a whirlwind to say the least! But I'm so grateful to have had the chance to publish this series, and I'll always be endlessly thankful to have you, my wonderful readers, on this journey with me.

Bringing this series to life is a real team effort, and I have enormous gratitude and love for everyone at Bookouture—from editorial and design through to sales and rights. One of the highlights of my career was visiting the Bookouture office in London this year and meeting many of the incredible people who've been part of my publishing journey. There are a few people I must thank personally though, who've been instrumental in the success of this series.

First and foremost, I must thank my editor Laura Deacon for sharing my vision for The Lost Daughters series and for being such a talented, encouraging editor to work with. Laura completely understands the type of stories I'm trying to write, and her guidance on this novel, particularly on character development, has been second to none.

Huge thanks (as always!) go to rights director extraordinaire Richard King who, along with the amazing Saidah Graham, is responsible for selling this series in twenty-four languages around the world. Having my book available in so many languages is truly a dream come true, and I thank both Richard and Saidah for their enthusiasm and dedication to selling my foreign rights. I'll never forget that very first email from Richard telling me we'd sold the first translation rights... and the emails just kept coming!

Special thanks also to Peta Nightingale, Jenny Geras, Ruth Jones, Natasha Harding, Ruth Tross, Jess Readett, Melanie Price, copy editor Jenny Page, proofreader Joni Wilson and everyone else at Bookouture who has worked on my series so far —I'm sorry if I've missed thanking you by name, but I appreciate you all!

Thank you to my long-time agent, Laura Bradford, who has been with me since the very beginning of my career, just before my first book sold fifteen years ago. Thank you for your dedication to my work, and for always being there for me and giving me such thoughtful guidance.

My list of people to thank became a lot longer with the publication of The Lost Daughters series, and I'd like to acknowledge the following editors and publishers for their support. Thank you to Hachette; to my UK editor Callum Kenny at Little, Brown (Sphere imprint); my New Zealand Hachette team; Dutch editor Neeltje Smitskamp at Park Uitgevers; German editor Anja Franzen at Droemer-Knaur; Norwegian editor Anja Gustavson at Kagge Forlag; editors Päivi Syrjänen and Iina Tikanoja at Otava (Finland); and French pocketbook publisher Anne Maizeret from J'ai Lu. I would also like to acknowledge the following publishing houses: Hachette Australia, Albatros (Poland), Sextante (Brazil), Planeta (Spain), Planeta (Portugal), City Editions (France), Garzanti (Italy), Lindbak and Lindbak (Denmark), Euromedia (Czech), Modan Publishing House (Hebrew), Vulkan (Serbia), Lettero (Hungary), Sofoklis (Lithuania), Pegasus (Estonia), Hermes (Bulgaria), JP Politikens (Sweden), Grup Media Litera (Romania), Koncept izdavaštvo j.d.o.o. (Croatia), Ucila

International (Slovenia) Kultura (Macedonia) and Dituria (Albania). Knowing that my series is published in so many languages around the world by such well-respected publishing houses is more than I could have ever hoped for, and I still have to pinch myself when I see my name on international bestseller lists!

Then there are the people in my day-to-day life who are so supportive of my writing. I would be remiss not to thank my incredible family, who are always my biggest cheerleaders. Thank you to Hamish, Mack and Hunter for being so understanding of my career and for just making life so much fun—I'm so lucky to have you all! Thanks also to my parents, Maureen and Craig, and to authors Natalie Anderson and Yvonne Lindsay for the daily support. I also have to say a very special thank you to my assistant Lisa Pendle, who is in charge of many things behind the scenes.

But as always, my biggest thanks go to you—my readers. You are the reason I have this incredible job—thank you so much for buying my books! I love hearing from readers, so please don't hesitate to email me—hello@sorayalane.com—and if you want to be connected on a regular basis I encourage you to join my Facebook Reader Group—https://www.facebook.com/groups/sorayalanereadergroup.

Soraya x

PUBLISHING TEAM

Turning a manuscript into a book requires the efforts of many people. The publishing team at Bookouture would like to acknowledge everyone who contributed to this publication.

Audio
Alba Proko
Sinead O'Connor
Melissa Tran

Commercial
Lauren Morrissette
Hannah Richmond
Imogen Allport

Cover design
Debbie Clement

Data and analysis
Mark Alder
Mohamed Bussuri

Editorial
Laura Deacon
Melissa Tran

Copyeditor
Jenny Page

Proofreader
Joni Wilson

Marketing
Alex Crow
Melanie Price
Occy Carr
Cíara Rosney
Martyna Młynarska

Operations and distribution
Marina Valles
Stephanie Straub
Joe Morris

Production
Hannah Snetsinger
Mandy Kullar
Nadia Michael
Charlotte Hegley

Publicity
Kim Nash
Noelle Holten
Jess Readett
Sarah Hardy

Rights and contracts
Peta Nightingale
Richard King
Saidah Graham

RAISING READERS
Books Build Bright Futures

Dear Reader,

We'd love your attention for one more page to tell you about the crisis in children's reading, and what we can all do.

Studies have shown that reading for fun is the **single biggest predictor of a child's future life chances** – more than family circumstance, parents' educational background or income. It improves academic results, mental health, wealth, communication skills, ambition and happiness.

The number of children reading for fun is in rapid decline. Young people have a lot of competition for their time, and a worryingly high number do not have a single book at home.

Hachette works extensively with schools, libraries and literacy charities, but here are some ways we can all raise more readers:

- Reading to children for just 10 minutes a day makes a difference
- Don't give up if children aren't regular readers – there will be books for them!

- Visit bookshops and libraries to get
  recommendations
- Encourage them to listen to audiobooks
- Support school libraries
- Give books as gifts

There's a lot more information about how to encourage children to read on our websites: **www.RaisingReaders.co.uk** and **www.JoinRaisingReaders.com**.

Thank you for reading.